Beginning

STANLEY MIDDLETON

Hutchinson

London Sydney Auckland Johannesburg

The right of Stanley Middleton to be identified as Author of this work
has been asserted by Stanley Middleton in accordance with the Copyright,
Designs and Patents Act, 1988

This edition first published in 1991 by Hutchinson

Random Century Group Ltd
Random Century House, 20 Vauxhall Bridge Road, London SW1V 2SA

Random Century Australia (Pty) Ltd
20 Alfred Street, Milsons Point, Sydney NSW 2061, Australia

Random Century New Zealand Ltd
PO Box 40–086, Glenfield, Auckland 10, New Zealand

Random Century South Africa (Pty) Ltd
PO Box 337, Bergvlei, 2012 South Africa

British Library Cataloguing in Publication Data

Middleton, Stanley *1919-*
    Beginning to end.
    I. Title
    823.914 [F]

    ISBN 0 09 174821 6

Set in Plantin by Deltatype Ltd, Ellesmere Port
Printed and bound in Great Britain by Biddles Ltd, Guildford, Surrey

To John and Julietta Harvey

'In my beginning is my end.'

T. S. Eliot: *East Coker*

I

Midday in late August.

The young man stepped briskly uphill along the road in a dappled shade of large sycamores and limes. As he crossed a side-street he glimpsed a figure against a high stone wall, but he had completed a dozen rapid paces before he stopped, considered, and went back. He rounded the corner to where the person held the same awkward position, head on chest, two white plastic carrier-bags on the pavement in front of him.

'Are you all right?' the young man asked.

The other glanced up. He was elderly, his face putty-coloured; thinning hair straggled: the moustache bristled untidily, and though his suit was well-cut and expensive, he wore no tie.

'Just short of breath.'

Each looked the other over.

'Would you like a hand with your bags? Have you far to go?'

'That's very kind of you.'

The voice sounded gruff if weakly, but the accent was southern standard. The older man breathed in and out noisily in a short, rhythmical pattern: one, two, three, four, as though following a prescribed exercise. Finally he was ready to speak again.

'About a hundred yards or so up the hill. Number 34.'

Again he sucked in air through his mouth, but this time involuntarily, as if breath had been knocked out of him. After a pause he was capable of speech once more. 'I'd be grateful.'

The young man bent to the bags. 'Are you ready, then?'

After a further interval of recuperation, the older man shuffled forward and the pair set off.

The pace was funereal, but there were no stoppages. It took the whole of five minutes and by the time they reached the gates the old man was panting almost violently.

'Take it easy,' the younger advised. 'We're there now.'

Now the older man leaned heavily on the stone wall of No. 34, but this time with his back to the street.

'Old age is not pretty,' he gritted. It seemed foolish to waste breath. The carrier-bags, neither very heavy, stood together again on the pavement as the young man stretched and rubbed his hands, looking about him.

'Would you . . . would you . . . ?'

'Give you a hand along the path? Surely.'

Again the interminable wait. The young man studied the substantial house which rose thirty-odd yards back from the front garden wall. The building was Victorian, its upper two storeys covered in a beige-coloured stucco. Windows stretched large and well-cleaned while paintwork shone unblemished. A flagged path led to the house between laurels on the left while to the right was a narrow flower-bed, free of plants as if it had been just forked over, and a recently cut lawn. Two mature cherry trees and a prunus randomly placed cast squat shadows.

'I'm ready.'

'After you, then.'

The young man held the gate open to allow the other to enter, and turned for the bags. He handled the iron-work carefully, finally readjusting the latch, to allow his companion time to progress along the path. They processed slowly to a door at the back of the house, where the old man searched in his trousers pocket for keys and then held a Yale, pointing upward clear of the bunch. The younger realized that he was expected to deal with the door. Smiling, puzzled at the mute invitation, he put down the bags, performed his duty, returned the keys and waited. His companion seemed in no hurry either to move or to speak.

Once they were inside, in the kitchen, the host made for a Windsor chair at one end of a table. He sat there, but before resting his hands on the arms he signalled by awkward gestures, forefinger straight, that the carrier-bags should be placed in front of him. He did not acknowledge the carrying-out of his order, but with eyes closed recovered his breath.

'Would you,' his hands began to move again as if to make up for the inadequacies of words, 'would you . . . ? Are you in any great hurry? Perhaps you'd be good enough to make us a cup of coffee?' He pointed at mugs on a cup-tree, at a large bottle of instant coffee and with ferocious finality at an electric

2

kettle. The young man, grinning at the pantomime, set about his task.

The two now sat either side of the table with their mugs.

'Thank you,' said the elder. 'Very kind of you. I'm always glad to rest for ten minutes after the drag up that wretched hill, and for once you've allowed me to do it all in comfort.' He lifted his coffee and then returned it to the table: presumably his fingers warned him that it was too hot to drink. 'The name is Stapleton.'

The young man inclined his head.

'Ernest Stapleton.' He rubbed his mouth. 'Aged seventy-five, and feeling every month of it.' He touched the table round the mug. 'Does the name mean anything to you?' The head was cocked.

'I'm afraid not. Should it?'

'No scandalous connotations?'

'I'm afraid not.'

'Good, good, good.' Stapleton put his finger-tips together in satisfaction. 'I'm glad.'

The two waited, touching their mugs. 'Are you local?'

'No. I've only been here for a few days.'

'From where?'

'I've come from Hampshire, from Winchester. I was born in London.'

The young man explained that he had taken a teaching post at the High School, and had just spent the Thursday morning there helping the Head of his Department sort out new books for the term which would begin on Tuesday of next week. This was his second post, after three years in a local authority comprehensive school where he had taught English.

'Do you know this part of the world?'

'Not at all.'

'Never been here before?'

'Except for my interview, no.'

'Why did you come, then?'

'The school has a very good reputation. I think I was lucky to be appointed.'

He made a few remarks about his time in the comprehensive and why he had enjoyed himself there, but added that a year or two in the private sector would do his career no harm. Mr Stapleton was now abstractedly drinking his coffee.

'You're not married?' he enquired.

'No.'

'A possibility?'

'In the future. Yes.' He grinned again.

Stapleton clutched his mug before making circling motions with it, though whether to cool the liquid or to disturb it without spilling it the young man, following the largish gyrations, could not determine.

'You've not told me your name,' Stapleton said. He spoke with a still confidence as if his age excused any impertinence.

'Anthony,' the young man paused, 'Clark.'

Stapleton put down his mug and held out his hand.

'Welcome to the city, Mr Clark. I'll wish you that in the absence of anyone better. It is not such a bad place.'

He waved out of the window towards the brightness of August sunshine, apples and pears on old trees, distant houses, broad blueness of sky.

'I'm a native,' Stapleton continued. 'A citizen of no mean city. Do you know who said that?'

'St Paul.'

'Ah. Even to old men this place is agreeable. I suffer from angina.'

'I'm sorry.'

'Oh, I've my bottles of tablets handy. They've worked the oracle so far. I expect the condition will do for me one of these days. We have to die of something. "I owe God a death."' He looked up in interrogation.

'Prince Hal before Shrewsbury, *Henry IV*, Part I.'

'"Thou art a scholar."'

'Sir Toby to Sir Andrew. *Twelfth Night*.'

Stapleton's beam of pleasure was interrupted by a ring on the front-door bell.

'Go and shoo them away, whoever they are, will you?' He pointed. 'Mormons. Jehovah's Witnesses. Double-glazing.'

The hall struck gloomy, with the front door double-bolted as well as double-locked so that it took Clark some little time to open up.

4

A striking young woman, back to the sun, occupied the porch. He waited for her announcement. None came.

'Good morning,' he said finally, with exactly the right tone of questioning, he thought.

'Who are you, then?' she asked bluntly, obviously about to enter.

Clark held his ground but, nonplussed, did not speak.

'I've come to see my father,' she offered.

'Mr Stapleton?'

'Who else? Is he in?'

Clark stepped back and the girl swept past, leaving him to deal with scent, bolts and keys. He heard no conversational exchanges from the kitchen, towards which he now moved cautiously.

Stapleton sat at the table, his hands still round the empty mug. The young woman had perched on a stool, where the shortness of her dark green skirt matched the elegance of her legs. She examined a bottle taken from one of the shopping-bags.

'Jennifer, this is Mr . . . Mr . . . Damn it, I've forgotten already.'

'Clark, Anthony Clark.'

'Jennifer Hope, my youngest daughter.'

She nodded briefly, and returned to her examination of the bottle, turning it over and over for no good reason.

'Put the kettle on again, Mr er-er. Let's try the everlasting instant.'

Clark obeyed, filling the kettle, swilling out the used mugs, finding one decorated with kilns for the visitor.

'Haven't you a suitable quotation?' Stapleton asked. 'To grace the occasion?'

'"O Jephtha, judge of Israel, what a treasure hadst thou."'

Stapleton shook his head, acknowledging defeat.

'Hamlet,' Clark proffered, 'to Polonius.'

'Who's a pretty boy?' said Jennifer, slipping from the stool to place the bottle on the table. Milk of Magnesia. The woman was older than Clark had thought, perhaps thirty-five, but handsome, with loose blonde hair and a fierce perfume. She

5

walked round the kitchen, stopping here and there, once opening a cupboard door and extracting a jar. She peered into a saucepan, tested a work surface for dust, tried an electric switch, moved a cup and saucer across to the sink with a rattle, tore a leaf from a wall-calendar.

'Satisfied?' her father enquired, sarcastically.

She did not answer but returned to her seat. When Clark placed the three mugs on the table, she picked up hers without thanks, replacing it immediately and staring at her fingers. Her father turned towards her, uncouthly.

'Gave me a hand with my shopping up the hill.'

'Were you walking?'

'Not when he first saw me. I'd come to a standstill.'

'You'll never learn sense.'

The three sat in awkward silence, broken once when Stapleton asked his daughter if she had been to London. She replied that she had, but made no further comment. The old man shrugged his indifference and concentrated on the mug in front of him. Finally Jennifer made an effort.

'Are you local, Mr Clark?'

'I live in Mandalay Grove.'

'Mandalay? Mandalay? Where's that?'

'At the top of the hill. Off Lucknow Avenue.'

'Yes, I think I know.'

'Tommy Turner lived there.'

Jennifer stared across at her father, frowning slightly.

'No, he didn't. 14A fettes Road.'

'Perhaps you're right. This young man teaches at the High School.'

She made the usual polite enquiries, and he answered easily enough, though the girl did not seem very interested. She mentioned that she was friendly with the Head of Modern Languages whom he had not met. Her father sat very still in her presence. She wore, Clark noticed, no wedding ring, no jewellery of any kind, and had a smooth tan as if she had spent the last month in the Balearic Islands or the Canaries. Perhaps it came from a tube.

'Aren't you at work today?' The father asked socially.

'Should I be?'

That seemed unnecessarily curt.

Clark swallowed down his coffee, stood, said he must go. He sensed that he prevented some conversation, some discussion between the other two. Swilling his mug at the sink, he wished them goodbye.

'Show Mr Clark to the door, Jen,' Stapleton ordered. She slipped from the stool, ushered the young man through the hall and front door. To his surprise she came out with him, stood on the path in the sunshine.

'Thank you for your help.'

'Oh, it's nothing.'

'He'd be pleased. These days he seems very unsure of himself. You were swapping quotations, weren't you? He'd like that. His memory's going, but the bits and pieces of learning he picked up at school seem to stay with him. If you visit him again, throw a bit of Latin or Greek in; he'd like that.'

'I'd have to look them up first.'

'He wouldn't mind.'

Out here Jennifer Hope seemed in no hurry, tracing patterns on the ground with her toe, never looking directly at him.

'He has very few friends.'

'Why's that?'

'He makes no effort. I wish he would. He used to be sociable enough. Not now. He's comfortably off. He owns the whole of this house, for instance. But he won't go anywhere where he's likely to meet people he can talk to. He's tiptoeing round the margins of life.' She laughed into Clark's face at her expression. Her teeth were exceptionally even.

'Is there any reason?'

'Age. Ill-health. He has angina, you know.'

'So he told me.'

'Could you drop in on him sometimes?' she asked.

'Would he want me to?'

'Never mind what he'd want. I could see he was pleased with you.' The ends of her eyebrows came sharply together. 'How old are you? Twenty-five, twenty-six?' He nodded. 'There's a big difference between twenty-five and seventy-five, but you seem to know something. He'll like that. He needs young people. I won't do. He sees me still as someone to be wheeled

7

out in the pram or have her nappy changed.' Jennifer laughed again. 'Odd, really. But it means I can tick him off now and then if it's necessary.'

'Will he pay any attention?'

'He affects not to, but there is a basis of sense in him, once a reasonable case is put and he's had sufficient time to consider it. Will you call in on him?'

'I'll 'phone him first.'

She gave him her father's number which he wrote down in his diary.

'Talk to him,' Jennifer said. 'Make him read something. I think he sits half his time asleep in front of the television. He can be lively if he likes. What number on Mandalay Grove do you live at?'

'Nineteen. With a Mrs Mackenzie.'

She nodded, gravely, thanked him again and marched indoors.

Wind swooped into the garden; above, white clouds made speed over broken blue. Whistling, he made his way back to his lodgings.

II

On Friday evening Anthony Clark sat in his room, considering whether or not to waste his leisure in an arm-chair. He had worked for two hours in the morning at school, stamping new textbooks and blowing dust from dog-eared volumes, and the afternoon walking the town. The main meal at Mrs Mackenzie's establishment began sharp at six-thirty. He had done justice to celery soup, meat and potato pie with kidney beans and, refusing ice-cream, had finished with biscuits and blue Stilton. His landlady's portions were generous, her cooking good, so that he now wished he had eaten less. To go out and swill beer hardly seemed attractive. He had offered to help Mrs Mackenzie with the washing-up, but she had repulsed him, quickly putting him in his place. There were no other lodgers in; the other two, schoolmistresses, would return, he learnt, tomorrow.

8

As he lounged, with the *Independent*, not yet having chosen a book, he was interrupted by a tap on the door of his bed-sitter.

'A 'phone call,' Mrs Mackenzie shouted.

She waited for him on the corridor. He had heard nothing, did not know in fact where the 'phone was.

'A Mrs Hope.'

She guided him to a small room, very narrow, formerly a pantry he guessed, next to the kitchen, where the telephone occupied a high plant-stand. He announced himself.

'Jennifer Hope. We met yesterday.'

It appeared that she intended to take her father for a drive in the country tomorrow evening and invited him to join them. 'We shan't be late, but we'll call in at a pub to break the monotony. I take him out about once a month and I hate it, so you'll do me a good turn. Six-thirty start.'

He accepted. The main meals on Saturday and Sunday, Mrs Mac had made clear, were served at one o'clock, so the time was convenient. He thanked her. She advised him not to be too optimistic, but he returned more cheerfully to the arm-chair.

On the next evening, Clark walked jauntily to his tryst.

At Number 34 he decided against the front-door bell, tapped at the back, was called into the kitchen. Stapleton had dressed for the outing in polished brogues, cavalry-twill trousers, a ginger tweed hacking-jacket, open-necked cream shirt with a silk cravat hiding his skinny neck. The thin hairs were oiled down over his pate, but his face looked healthy as if he'd applied rouge. As he moved about the kitchen, doing nothing except flit from point to point, he sang, rather breathily but with clarity:

' "Madam, will you walk? Madam, will you talk?
Madam, will you walk and talk with me?" '

'The chapel concerts of my youth,' he explained, 'were incomplete without it.'

'I don't know it.'

'I've no idea who wrote it. It's a duet. The man promises the lady the keys of heaven and God knows what, but she won't have it. Then he promises her the keys of his heart and she relents and they sing together at last.'

'I see.'

'It recalls the innocent days of my childhood. The girls I

loved, and the streets, and the chance meetings. I once heard
Gwen Catley and Owen Brannigan sing it, beautifully, but it's a
song essentially for the amateurs. Stilted gestures and stiff legs
and dickey-bows.'

'Did the ladies wear bows then?'

'Did they buggery.'

Stapleton's tone twisted suddenly splenetic, as he dashed a
baking-tin noisily to the floor. Swearing, he snatched a stool
from a corner and parked himself on it, his lips working in a
silence of furious anger. He looked older, more raddled, ill,
intemperate. Penitently Clark picked up the baking-tin and
replaced it on a work surface. Stapleton did not look at him, sat
like a dunce in the corner, shamed and dumb, clutching at the
seat between his legs.

In the awkwardness, Clark glanced at the kitchen clock
which showed thirty-seven minutes past six. He compared it
with his wristwatch.

'Is your clock right?' he asked.

Stapleton did not answer. His lips, his face were now still so
that he appeared apprehensive, about to break into tears. Clark
had no idea whether the old man heard the question.

The back door swung providentially open and Jennifer
pushed in.

'Late again,' she called. 'Are you men ready?'

Stapleton staggered down from his stool.

' "The killick of the working-party",' he said cheerfully to
Clark. 'Shall I need my mac?'

'No, it's warm.'

'It rained last night. I think. . . .'

'Oh, please yourself. Keys?'

The father searched in his pockets in vain.

'Other trousers? Wardrobe?'

His voice lacked all power; he sank to the stool.

'Hell's bells,' she laughed, went out but soon returned
rattling the keys.

'Have you checked the front door?'

'Of course.'

'What are we waiting for?'

'You. As usual.'

10

They made their way to Jennifer's car, a Nissan Bluebird, and there Stapleton acted out a lengthy performance of lowering, straining, strapping himself into the front seat.

'Any suggestions?' Jennifer.

'It's no use asking him. He's new to the place.'

'I happen to be asking you.'

'It's all the same to me,' Stapleton answered gloomily.

She drove northwards out of the town. Once or twice she stopped on a side road so that they could admire the view of reaped wheatfields, rolling hills, copses dark blue in evening sunshine. The two young people climbed out of the car, stood together. Stapleton disconsolately refused to unstrap or talk. At the second stop he suggested that Jennifer and Clark should take a short walk together while he sat.

'Path in the woods there.' He pointed, pessimism on his face.

'Are you coming?' Clark enquired.

'Too old, too stiff. I'd trip over.'

'"*Nous n'irons plus au bois; les lauriers sont coupés.*"'

The old man had no inclination for word-games, waved them away.

The track through the wood was narrow so that Clark had to walk behind Jennifer. She moved well, spine straight, buttocks attractively in play. She held back brambles, jumped puddles, once shifted a stone with a neat flick of the foot.

'Does this lead anywhere?' he asked.

'I've no idea.'

'You've not been here before, then?'

'Yes. I think I have.' They were close now to the edge of the wood and the sun flashed with molten light amongst tree-trunks. They stopped by a piece of badly maintained fence and stared down a long, gently sloping, grassy hillside. Over in the distance two fires, of stubble perhaps, were smoking in a bare field.

'Will your father be all right on his own?'

'Why shouldn't he be?'

'It seems hard to bring him out in the country and then leave him.'

'He won't walk. He has the use of his eyes. He can breathe. Why should he complain?'

'Why indeed?'

11

Jennifer meditatively slapped the greening top of the fence with the flat of her hand, which she then examined for stain or damage.

'We'll go a bit further.'

'Is this a private wood?'

'I guess so. I've no idea whether a copse like this is of any use economically these days. When wood was the main fuel it might have been different. Or is it a windbreak, or does it prevent soil slippage? My education is sadly defective.' The advancing, beautiful back arrogantly denied this.

'We could find out.'

'But we shan't. Correction: I shan't.'

She had something of her father's quarrelsome habits, of putting the listener into his reduced place. Clark said nothing, waiting for her to commit herself. Jennifer was striding forward, paying no attention to him. The conversation was finished as far as she was concerned.

'Don't you think we should turn back?' he asked.

'Why?'

'Won't your father be worried?'

'Do him good.'

Though he felt rebuked, she suddenly turned and smiled, then walked on. Jennifer's head now demonstrated jauntiness, as if she enjoyed leading the way, determining the halts and changes of speed. She said very little, but once when they paused at a gap in the hedge she pointed over the harvested fields to the valley below.

'Is there a stream down there?' she asked.

'I don't know. I suppose there must have been one at some time.'

'I wish I understood more about geology.'

'A map would show us whether one existed now.'

'Have you got one?'

'Not here.'

'That's it, then.'

She chuckled, turned away with her sailor's lurch. The next time she stopped she mentioned the brilliancy of the evening sunshine. He answered that the weather often seemed to improve once the school holidays were over.

'Have you started yet?'

'No. Next Tuesday.'

'Are you looking forward to it?'

'I suppose I am. One never knows, of course.'

'Of course.'

She was mocking him. On again amongst the trees and thickets at what seemed increased pace so that he wondered if she were testing him out. If they were moving in anything like a circle, as the sun's position indicated, they must be nearing the road, unless that had veered on some erratic course. A cloud darkened the sun, and their path ran out.

Jennifer peered about her.

'That's it, by the look of it. No exit.'

Whether bushes had overgrown the path, or whether one had never existed here Clark did not know. Without the sun the wood had grown coldly, sombrely dank.

'About turn,' she ordered.

Clark stood back to allow her to pass him.

'You go first this time,' she said, 'and I'll ogle your behind.'

He set off at a good pace, but spoilt the effect by tripping over an exposed tree-root to stagger drunkenly forward. Glad he had not fallen, he kept his eyes to the path. No sound came from the rear. This time they made not a single stop and he, as leader, tried to increase speed.

'Am I going too fast?' he enquired, not pausing.

'No. I'm right on your tail.'

When they were within a hundred yards of the road, though Clark did not recognize the proximity, the sun burst out again and Jennifer began to sing, cheered perhaps by the clean dazzle. Her voice was strong, slightly metallic.

' "Oh, had I Jubal's lyre or Miriam's tuneful voice." '

Handel's chirpy yet dignified air matched the new power of the light. ' "With songs like theirs I would aspire." ' Jennifer was still singing as they emerged on to the grass verge of the road where she stopped abruptly, in the middle of a phrase.

'Was that you singing in the wood?' Stapleton enquired. He had wound his window right down.

'Who else?'

' "And sang within the bloody wood

13

Where Agamemnon cried aloud,"' Clark quoted.

'Who said that?' Jennifer.

'T. S. Eliot.'

'You've been long enough,' Stapleton grumbled.

'Between ten minutes and a quarter of an hour,' his daughter corrected.

'To walk that little wood? At your age I could have been round it three or four times.'

'Fasten your seatbelt.'

They dawdled through a village and into the next where Jennifer stopped outside a pub, the Two Pigeons.

'Will this do?' she asked her father.

'No. I'd sooner go into a town pub on a Saturday night.' The voice snapped.

'As you please.'

Again she drove off, without haste, stopping once to point out her favourite view of hills divided again into fields and copses.

'Isn't it clear-cut?' Clark said.

'In this light, it is. But it never disappoints me.'

'You mean. . . . ?'

'I mean nothing that I need to explain.'

'Children, children,' Stapleton said, rousing himself from a doze. Jennifer laughed.

They found their way into town and the yard of a public house, the Star Inn, perhaps five or ten minutes' drive from home, an uninviting, lopsided place on a corner painted yellow, black and red. The car park was wide; it looked as if a dozen terraced houses had been demolished to make it possible; beyond a children's playground, grassed and with small trees, had been laid out, and further down the hill, back from the road behind trees they saw a new factory in raw, pale brick with a grey roof.

Jennifer pointed.

'They've widened this street, and pulled down rows of little black artisans' cottages.'

'Is that good or bad?'

'This is what's called an industrial estate now, though it's been so for a hundred years and more, with massive factories

14

built in the nineties when the smaller workshops had become inadequate.'

'What did they make?'

'Lace, bleaching and dyeing, textiles, engineering. You name it. Now the really huge factories are coming down and these little modern concerns are being sited. Service industries. And the rows of terraces are disappearing, solid built, decent, two-three up, two-three down, no bathrooms, erected for the factory hands. Now they've gone, in the last five or ten years, one can see the shape of the land again, through the spaces. Not long ago one was shut in between bricks; there were no front gardens, and you couldn't see the backs down narrow entries. Brick walls.'

'You'd be able to see out there, surely, down the hill?'

They looked further out to grey-greenish plain, dotted with tree-tops, houses and workshops, with a feature of dark poplars in the distance, darkening now.

'You could,' she answered, 'but I never did. The houses closed me in, concentrated my attention on the one street. There was always something interesting going on. Now they've opened it all up. Look at that school there; one storey, playing area and trees and hedges all round it. That's an improvement. Before this, the schools would have been two or three tier cross-eyed places, with a tar-macadam playground at the back. They frowned; these are relaxed.'

'I wonder what the children think?'

'They take it all for granted. And surely that's an advantage, to accept the clean and green as your due.'

'Are we going to stand here all night?' Stapleton asked. He had been left to make his own slow, awkward, breathy descent from the car. Now he leaned on the roof, one arm outflung, though his eyes followed Jennifer's finger.

'Here endeth the lesson,' she said.

Street-lamps shone though the expanse of sky in the west, daubed with apricot cloud, was bright still.

Clark looked at a Victorian brick chapel, now bared, the covering houses torn away.

'Inside that,' he queried, 'it will look exactly as it was when it was built?'

15

'I doubt it. They're fond of light paints these days, none of your dark browns and rich greens. All pastel shades and white.'

She took her father's arm almost affectionately.

The saloon bar was not crowded, so that they easily found seats. Clark brought the drinks to their table: pints of bitter for himself and Stapleton, a half of non-alcoholic lager for Jennifer. The place, well-lighted, well-polished, lacked character: a group of men were discussing a football match. Apart from the woman behind the bar, Jennifer was the only female in the room.

She described the district to him, saying it was worth investigation. One or two Georgian houses, small rural affairs for farm labourers, were still standing, surrounded by factories, warehouses, remainders of terraces like rotted teeth, chapels refurbished as Pakistani clubs, the roads blocked to traffic; some of the enormous Victorian warehouses had been razed so that streets which had been dark canyons between great purple-brick walls and black windows were warmed by sunshine for the first time in a hundred years.

'You can trace history,' she said. She spoke with enthusiasm, saying that ten years ago the district had been run down, but now small factories mushroomed and vans banged round the corners.

'Where are the people? Those whose houses are pulled down?'

'Those who have moved away own cars. Quite a few houses remain. Enough, anyway. Employers don't need crowds of hands these days. You look at any large building site.'

Stapleton took no part in this conversation, seemed more interested in the football party. He dipped his moustache into the beer, but drank little. His unsociability made Clark uneasy so that he swigged his drink too quickly, allowed Jennifer to bring him a second.

The footballers were now strident, not ill-behaved but forceful, as if deeply concerned.

'I'm tellin' yo' that you can be booked after th' game's finished right up to t' time you're in the dressing room.'

'I'm not saying you can't.'

'And that's why I ask you what's the sense of that Swinn

16

youth cussin' and carryin' on at the other team while they was walkin' off. Right in front o' the bleddy referee.'

'He always wor a big-mouth.'

'Like his Dad.'

'It don't do nob'dy any good, neither. Not t'club nor 'im.'

Jennifer, who had joined the other two listening to this exchange, now answered the question Clark had posed earlier. Her interest in the area sprang from a WEA class on local history, some six or seven years back.

'Have you any particular connection with the place?'

'I chose it for myself. The tutor made some suggestions in the first instance. But, yes, my grandfather lived hereabouts. My mother's father.'

'Did he work here?'

'Yes. Nearly all his life. In the brewery offices. He lived on the Sherwood Road. Rather a nice semi-detached villa; I'll show you on the way back. There's a big stone wall like a cliff with a garden right up to the top behind it, full of lilacs and buddleia and laburnum. My parents lived there when they first married.'

'I still own it.' Stapleton gloomily behind his glass.

Where were the parents, Clark asked him, but the old man did not answer.

'They moved out to a smaller place out in Wollaton. They're dead now, of course. This is before the War.'

She waited as if expecting her father to take advantage of the opening, but he had returned to lethargy. Brightly she described the house, and an interesting street at the back, full of biggish homes for lower management, chief clerks and the like.

'What date are they?'

'Eighteen-nineties; early nineteen-hundreds. Same time as the big factories and the later terraces.'

Jennifer talked on brightly while her father fiddled with his beer. When the old man had shuffled out to the lavatory, Clark asked, 'Is your father all right?'

'Yes. Why?'

'He doesn't seem very happy.'

'He never is when he's out with me. He thinks I patronize him.'

17

'And do you?'

'Probably. I feel sorry for him. I don't like him.' She laughed, openly, almost brutally. 'I asked you along because I thought it might be easier for me. We don't go out together very often, but I guess he enjoys it in retrospect, even if it's only grumbling about me.'

'Why do you bother?'

'You have me there. A masochist? A puritan with a conscience?' She did not seem serious with these questions dashed off in a bright voice. It was none of his business, he supposed. As she talked on he wondered how she earned her living.

Stapleton returned, was instructed not too quietly to do up the zip on his flies, and they listened again to the footballers. This time the men were discussing a recent outing by bus to a race-meeting in mid-week and the shortcomings of one of their colleagues who had refused to take a day off work to attend.

'Perhaps he needed the money.'

'Not 'im. Both on 'em wo'k, and there's no family.'

'She wouldn't let 'im. That's the long and the short of it.'

''Ad 'e any 'oliday due?'

'Yes, he had. I know for certain he had.'

'Perhaps 'e likes wo'k better than racing.'

They roared approval, revelling in the simplicity of it. The pronunciation of 'work' intrigued Clark who felt the accented, short syllable varied with its place and importance in the sentence. The footballers now revelled in an anecdote about how one of their number, not present, had lost his betting slip for a race where his chosen horse had won.

'Ah thought he go mad.' 'Go mad' was reduced almost to one consonant, 'gmad'.

'Gooin' through his pockets like a lunatic.' Now the vowel lengthened. ''E were frantic.'

'Ah thought he'd strip himself stark bollock-naked there and then. Right in the middle of the course.'

The unfortunate man had, it appeared, handed his ticket over for safekeeping to a friend, who turned up with the winnings to put him out of his fuddled misery.

'Di 'e gi' 'im oat?'

18

'Fifty pee.'

This brought the house down; they thumped the tables. The barmaid laughed as heartily as the men. The chorus of shouts rose rhythmically, almost musically.

Stapleton had finished his beer, shook his head when his daughter suggested another. He paid no attention to the hilarity about him.

'Drink up,' she ordered Clark brusquely. 'We'll be off.'

On the way back she pointed out her grandfather's house, but from the back of the car Clark could see little but a tall section of local stone wall, eight or nine feet high.

Back at Stapleton's Jennifer signalled Clark ruthlessly inside, and asked him to prepare the old man a cup of coffee. He had no sooner filled the kettle than she had wished them goodnight and had run out of the back door like a shot.

'Is your daughter coming back?' he asked at the mug-tree.

'Don't imagine so. No.'

'Is she busy?'

'Is she hell? She's done her bit of duty for September, and that's that.'

'It was kind of her to take us out,' Clark said, mildly provocative, putting their mugs on the table. Stapleton scrubbed at his moustache with a thumbnail by way of answer.

'I enjoyed it,' Clark began again.

'More than I did.'

'It will be worth while walking round that district by the pub.'

Again a blank, as Stapleton seemed deep in his misery.

'What does your daughter do?'

'Suits her own ends. Like most people.'

'I meant what does she do for a living?'

'I know quite well what you meant. She's an accountant and works in her husband's firm, Hope, Burrows and Kirkland. You've heard of them?'

'No.'

'Biggish, thriving concern, on Matlock Drive. Don't suppose schoolteachers need accountants.' Stapleton lifted his head. 'She doesn't live with her husband. Works with him, but they're divorced. Has a flat in the Park. Funny the things people do. In and out of marriage. I shot my wife.'

Clark had no answer to that.

'I've told you before she,' (presumably Jennifer), 'could get round to it. Do you mind switching that immersion heater on for me? I like to clean up for Sunday.'

They finished their drinks. Neither spoke much. Both visited the lavatory, and during Stapleton's absence Clark swilled and dried the mugs.

'I shall have to go,' he said.

The other made no attempt to detain him, but it seemed a long-drawn-out business to extract himself from the kitchen as Stapleton listed his gadgets, opening a cupboard to brandish part of a mixer. The old man did all this grudgingly, without enthusiasm, and yet unwilling to let his visitor free.

Outside it was dark with a pleasant touch of wind. Clark stumbled down the path.

There had been no further mention of the shot wife.

III

Anthony Clark sat in sunshine in a colleague's garden. The Pearsons had invited him over to a barbecue, but had instructed him to arrive early so that he could make himself useful. Hugh Pearson had taken his bottle of wine and had led him round the two lawns, introduced him to his wife and a seventeen-year-old daughter; the women, who looked similar in dress, colouring, even age, had made the correct noises in his direction and had disappeared.

'Let's sit down,' Pearson said.

They occupied two faded, rather dirty deck-chairs.

'There's not a lot to do,' he confided. 'I thought we might have to rebuild the barbecue, but it's perfectly usable. Burnt sausages and gobbets of meat don't need much equipment if you ask me. We'll need to fetch chairs and stools out in due course, but that won't kill us. It's too early to start drinking. If I'm not careful I shall be pissed out of my mind before the night's out. That's why you're here to talk to me, and keep me

20

away from the wine at least until the fire's going. All this is my wife's idea.'

'She doesn't know me. I might be a worse drunkard than you.'

'She knows me. New members of staff, picked for respectable appearance and handsome blue eyes. Credit to us all. And I, mindful of my position as host, mentor, senior colleague, will behave myself. That's the line of reasoning.'

'Is there any truth in it?'

'Yes. I shall talk to you.'

Pearson wore a ragged pullover, but his shoes were excellent if uncleaned. At fifty he still looked boyishly slim, and his hair was copious, wavy and untouched by grey. From five yards one would have thought him the bright student who thirty years earlier had cycled about Cambridge, enjoyed himself in Paris and Vienna, admired and admiring, loving and loved. Now he smiled his way through life, Head of Modern Languages in a good school but without prospect of promotion, comfortable in house and garden, unsure of himself, uncertain why he had failed to live up to expectations.

In this, the first week of term, he had stopped Clark on the corridor.

'Mr Clark? I'm Hugh Pearson. You're a friend of Jen Hope's, I hear. Are you busy next Saturday evening? We're having a small get-together. Half a dozen people of like mind. A *fête champêtre*. We'd be delighted if . . .' And so on, all easy.

Clark had accepted, won over by the modest smile, the diffident grace.

Thompson, a colleague in the English Department, had been impressed, even envious.

'Amongst the upper ten already? They've not invited me yet and I've been here five years. How do you do it?'

Clark mentioned Jennifer Hope: the name meant nothing to Thompson.

'They invite the Head once every two years,' Thompson said. 'But does he go?'

'He'd only be asked the once if he didn't.'

'And is this his year?'

'He hasn't confided in me yet.'

21

Two days later a written note appeared in his pigeon-hole amending first instructions, inviting Clark to show himself at three-thirty if he could manage it.

Now the two sat in bright sunshine.

'It'll be cool this evening,' Pearson said. 'You'll need a pullover.'

'I'll slip back . . .'

'No need. I'll lend you one.'

Pearson pulled at a ragged end on his cuff.

At four-thirty his wife called him back into the house, sent him off in the car. Stranded in his deck-chair, Clark had nothing to read. Miss Pearson appeared to keep him company, flopping down on the grass to display long attractive brown legs and light-blue pants for a second before she wrapped her wide yellow skirt about her knees.

'They've left you here?' she asked. 'Typical. Dad's gone down to the supermarket. You can get bargains at this time on Saturday. They're keen on value for money.'

'Is that good?'

'Two sons at university cost something, and I'm still at school. Not that they're short. It's their way of getting back at the world.'

She giggled almost childishly against the knowing, grown-up sentences.

'You think I shouldn't talk like this, don't you? Especially to a stranger. But you're bound to find out sooner or later. Even if I'm wrong.'

Now she smiled maturely, forgiving his supposed naïvety, treating him to an outline of her plans for the year. Her name, it appeared, was Deirdre.

'Are you in Daddy's department?' When he answered in the negative she did not look surprised. Nothing could come amiss to her. 'You teach at the Boys' High, don't you? How come you're here?'

He explained about his acquaintance with Jennifer Hope.

'A name not to be spoken in this house,' Deirdre informed him.

'Now I'm mystified. Elucidate.' He tried to laugh knowingly.

22

'She and Dad are, were . . . ,' she pulled a wry face, 'no better than they should be.'

Mrs Pearson arrived bearing lemonade. She hoped he could occupy himself, that D. wasn't being a nuisance, and warned that when her husband arrived back from the supermarket she would employ them both in the fetching and carrying of furniture that would be necessary. 'At least the weather looks settled. We shan't have people in and out of doors with muddy shoes.' Mrs Pearson's figure and her long legs were very like her daughter's, but her face from a yard distance looked infinitely older, finely furrowed, lifeless, barren of health. Though she was not made up at the moment, Clark guessed that over-indulgence in cosmetic aids was the cause of the dryness. 'You perhaps wonder why we bother with these functions, but Hugh has some sort of conscience. I tell him that music and dramatic societies, film-clubs, WEA classes all exist for the cultivation of the arts, but no, he must gather his two or three together.'

This seemed second-hand, well-rehearsed to Clark, but he felt vaguely grateful for her attention. The lemonade was home-made, sweet, iced and delicious. Mother and daughter disappeared together, conspiratorially silent.

Anthony Clark, not altogether pleased, set his empty glass on the ground and took a turn round the garden. The dahlia bed dazzled; sedums stood exceptionally large, sunflowers reached up, tall as giraffes; the grass had been cut in neat dark and light swathes; hardly a trace of autumn showed in the leaves. Beyond an escallonia hedge he found, or had not noticed from his deck-chair, a garden hut, pentagonal and newish, with a green felted roof among the apple trees. He stood on the paved patio to peer in at the recently cleaned window. The room was carpeted, had a desk with an electric lamp; book-cases were bright round the walls; a tasteful poster advertising a Degas exhibition was pinned opposite the window. On the surface of the desk were two piles of exercise books, a few letters; near the Degas he made out an old-fashioned filing cabinet. This must be Pearson's work-room; no word-processor, he thought defensively. Did the man sit out here in the winter's cold?

He tried the door, found it locked, examined the York stone patio and path as if he had never touched the knob. Uncertainly he circled the orchard, trying to lengthen the short journey, staring at hedges, grass-tumps, compost heaps, a toolshed; an anthropologist in an alien culture. The place was extraordinarily quiet; neighbours neither mowed their lawns, conversed, nor let their children out. Birds and animals were conspicuous by their absence. No one kept dogs or hens. Cats were not on the prowl. Even the sun made only modest invasions of the bottom of the Pearson garden. Though the toolshed was open, it revealed nothing more than spades, forks, hoes and three bicycles, two with baskets on the front. Hugh Pearson, he remembered, carried about with him at the school a valise, a big folding briefcase in battered leather or pigskin, which could be tucked under the arm however crammed with books.

'There's something sexual in the way he hugs that case,' Thompson had said.

'His old bag?'

'Exactly.'

Clark now retraced his journey the other way about, found his way back to the deck-chair, flopped down to make little of sky and cloud and tree-tops. No sound emerged from indoors. After a time he was relieved to hear a car in the drive. Pearson invisibly hailed him, invited him to help unload.

'It's quiet here.'

'Yes, I suppose it is. Did they come out to you?'

Clark held up his glass in evidence.

'Deirdre. And your wife.'

'Ah, yes. Deirdre of the Sorrows. She baffles me. Sometimes I think she's nearly certifiable, and then the next minute. . . .'

They manhandled cardboard boxes into the kitchen. Neither female appeared.

'Never here when they're wanted.'

Pearson looked troubled, caressing the top of his head as if it were tender.

'Sit down,' he ordered, pointing to a stool. 'We await further orders.' He appeared nervous, muttered to himself, restlessly flitted from object to object, opening cupboard doors, once stood in the middle of the floor chewing abstractedly at a fingernail.

24

Clark heard the front door open.

'There you are. Give me a hand, will you?'

Mrs Pearson led them to the street and instructed them to remove three long wooden benches from a van. These had backs which could be moved through sixty degrees on cast-iron pivoted arms.

'Where the hell are these from?' Pearson asked. 'A Primitive Methodist Sunday School, eighteen eighty-seven?'

'On the lawn.' Mrs Pearson, imperiously.

The men obeyed, were twice commanded to re-site them.

'Bloody ugly,' Pearson said, 'wherever we put them.'

'They're to be sat on, not looked at.' Mrs Pearson parked herself on a bench, awkwardly but with an air of complacent triumph.

Pearson and Clark fetched out, dusted down canvas chairs and set them round together with a long table by the French doors.

'How many are you expecting?' Clark asked.

'God knows.' Pearson seemed hurried, harassed.

They were summoned in for mugs of tea round the kitchen table. That was more comfortable. Mrs Pearson hazarded guesses as to arrival times and worked out the exact moment at which her husband should start his fire. Pearson gave an instructive lecture on fire-lighting and outdoor cooking. Neither partner listened to the other. Both disappeared leisurely for baths. Deirdre was not to be seen, and no comment was made about her absence.

Pearson reappeared in another set of casual clothes just as neat, old and well pressed as those he had discarded. He had shaved, and was discreetly, malely perfumed. He led Clark outside and allowed him to watch the fire-making; he owned a special kit, small coals and all, in a named box. 'All done by numbers,' he instructed.

The first guests arrived at seven and were brought down the garden steps by a resplendent hostess. The first sausages and chops sizzled. By seven twenty-two a dozen or more people were striding and sitting, all declaring that they had been fasting since the early hours. Hot plates, jacket potatoes were produced from the kitchen; cole-slaw, salad, pickles, knives and forks were slapped down on the table. A line of fairy-lights which Clark had not noticed before were switched on. Voices became loud and cheerful; Mrs Pearson dispensed punch, Clark red and white wine.

'You get yourself something now,' the hostess commanded. 'You must be ravenous.'

Clark found himself a seat. Outside in the garden the night chilled, but the food tasted delicious. A woman drew up her chair to sit with him.

'I'm Helena Noakes,' she announced.

'Anthony Clark.'

'And how are you attached to the circus?'

'I teach with Hugh Pearson.'

'Oh, yes. I saw you in Clarissa's kitchen. I thought you might be one of Deirdre's hangers-on. That explains it.'

Mrs Noakes (she wore a wedding-ring) came in from a village about three miles east of the town. Her husband was a barrister, she a solicitor. She had smooth, fair, attractive hair gathered into a bun which she touched with large hands as she cross-examined Clark. She explained that she, her husband and Hugh Pearson had been at Oxford at much the same time, and that her family were 'thankfully' married and living away.

'Are you a grandmother yet?'

'Yes, but I don't boast about it.'

She gave him an account of the cultural scene, advising him not to miss a performance of Blow's *Venus and Adonis* with which she was administratively connected. She bluntly laid it down that the city was a Philistine place, that the University did nothing much to alter this, that she supposed all modern towns were much the same and that their artistic salvation stood or fell with one or two individuals who did what they did, good or bad, merely for their own glorification.

Clark told her she was a pessimist.

'A realist,' she answered. 'And what's your contribution going to be?'

'For this term, nothing. They're piling enough on me at school.'

'If you want something done,' she said, 'give it to somebody who's too busy to do it, and it'll be carried out, and sharpish.'

'But well?' he asked.

'You're a worse pessimist than I am.'

She introduced him to other people. Women talked to him as if he knew the Jills and Sues and Jeremys they mentioned. He felt accepted, but rather cold. He was standing near the dying embers in the grate talking to a tall girl with an astrakhan hat and collar when Hugh Pearson touched his arm, drew him to one side.

'I have to go out. I've just had some bad news.'

'I'm sorry. Is there anything I can do?'

'No, thank you. There's not much I can do either. Thanks for coming, anyway.'

He slid away into the darkness. The tall girl accepted Clark's muttered excuse and continued unconcernedly with her tale of a skiing mishap. The party did not suffer from Hugh's absence.

After eleven-fifteen and a series of barren conversations Clark made his way to the house to announce his departure. Finally he prised Clarissa Pearson away from two elderly and one middle-aged brass-voiced men.

'Thanks for coming,' she said, 'and all your help.'

'Is Hugh back yet?'

'No.' She looked troubled, but vague. 'We hope to see you again.'

In the street Helena Noakes was waiting for her husband to open her car door.

'I've enjoyed that,' she said. 'I'm more and more antisocial as I grow older, but I do like the Pearsons. They're my sort of people.'

'Pity Hugh had to go out.' Information might be forthcoming.

'Did he? I didn't notice. He's quite likely to disappear. He's his own man.'

She ducked down into the car.

IV

Anthony Clark passed Pearson on a corridor at school on Monday. They exchanged complimentary words without actually stopping so that Clark could make no enquiries about bad news. Pearson strode out, head high, rubicund, slim, cheerful, lithe as ever.

On Tuesday evening, while Clark sat alone in the house, Jennifer Hope telephoned, ostensibly to ask if he had seen anything of her father. When he said he had not, she invited him to call in on the old man. He agreed, though he was unsure about his leisure time.

He mentioned, mischievously in view of Deirdre's strictures, the barbecue at the Pearsons' and Hugh's disappearance.

'That would be this Roger Clinton business,' she answered.

'I've not heard anything of it. Who's Roger Clinton?'

'You don't take the local paper?'

'No.'

'Roger was a close friend of Hugh's. Odd, because they were quite unalike. He was in property and property repairs. In quite a big way. My father will tell you all about him. I don't know how he and Hugh became friendly. Perhaps he did some work for the Pearsons, and he had a son at the school. He committed suicide on Saturday.'

'Oh.' Clark waited.

'Walked in front of a train. Miles from home.'

'Do they know why?'

'I don't, anyway. There's nothing wrong with his business concerns as far as anybody reckons.'

'How old was he?'

'Hugh's age. Bit older perhaps. Fifties. I suppose Hugh went to see Roger's wife. Didn't he say?'

'No, just that he had bad news, and had to go out.'

'The stiff upper lip. He'll tell you in time. Or he will if he approves of you, and thinks you won't take advantage of your knowledge.'

'Why should I do that?'

'Why? Because most people do. Must skedaddle now. Don't forget to call in on the old man.'

Jennifer Hope sounded crisp on the telephone, well organized, uninhibited. Mention of Hugh had in no way thrown her; she spoke about her lover, if so he was, in the same tone that she mentioned the suicide, the nuisance of a father,

28

the young man hardly known to her of whom she was asking a favour.

On Thursday evening after dinner Clark walked down to Stapleton's flat. He rang the bell at the front.

The door was opened on its chain after a longish delay, with the random switching on of lights outside and in.

'Who is it?'

'Anthony Clark.'

Again a period of silence. Clark suspected that the old man had forgotten him.

'Your daughter, Jennifer, asked me to call.'

Nothing. Not a word, not a rattle of metal.

'Anthony Clark,' Stapleton said, wheezily, unexpectedly, from behind the door.

'That's right.'

The chain was drawn, the door rapidly clapped shut after the visitor had slipped inside. They made their way to the kitchen.

'We ought to use one of the sitting rooms,' Stapleton began.

'I'm quite comfortable here. In any case, I can't stay long.'

'No. Come on in. She wants me to have some variety, and so I shall.'

He led the way. The room was large, with a high ceiling and a modest, golden chandelier.

The two arm-chairs and settee were of darkish leather, well polished and comparatively new. There was a heavy sideboard, two formidable glass-fronted book-cases and four tables, one tall as if for plants, all in dark oak, matching, almost black and in stark contrast with the white walls. No pictures hung from the oak rail, and above the cornices writhed elaborately. The carpet stretched large, ruby and rich blues, surrounded by a yard-wide frame of floorboards again polished into dazzling darkness. The whole place was dustless, as if it had been cleaned and vacuumed spotless not five minutes before; a faint odour of furniture polish hung pleasantly in the air. Clark had expected neglect: this was as immaculate as the lounge of a city pub at opening time.

Stapleton sat down in an arm-chair and motioned Clark to the other. The old man brooded, blowing out his lips.

'She mentioned Clinton's death,' he began. 'That's why she wanted you here. She thought I'd be upset.' He stared across, almost in hostility. 'Well, I'm not.' He employed a childish emphasis.

Clark waited.

'Shall I draw the curtains?' The old man had stumbled up. 'Not for me.'

'I will. It will do them good. Never pulled.' The curtains, dark red velvet, ran easily although Stapleton handled them clumsily. They covered an entire wall.

'Do that one for me,' he ordered, pointing at the window on the long side of the room. Clark obeyed. Both were now standing. 'Can I get you a drink? Don't say "No", because I could just relish a Scotch.' He fiddled in the sideboard; all his movements were slow, awkward. He fetched out two glasses and handed Clark a jug. 'Water, if you please. In the kitchen. Swill it out first.' The receptacle gleamed, speckless. When the young man returned each glass held an inch of whisky. 'Water? Or do you prefer soda? Water? Pour it out yourself.' They made something of a ceremony of this between them, priest and acolyte, before returning to their pews.

'Let's see. What were we talking about?' Stapleton, having tested his drink.

'Mr Clinton.'

'That's right. Jennifer thought I'd grieve. Don't see why. I've had little to do with the man in the last eight years, and in the last two, since I've settled here, nothing at all. Not even seen him.' He smacked his lips. 'We were close at one time. Put work in one another's way. I liked him well enough. He was nobody's fool. Threw his weight around. Why did he commit suicide? Jen didn't seem to know.'

Clark repeated his story of Hugh Pearson's leaving the party.

'Master at the High School? I know him slightly. Or did. Know nobody these days. Didn't realize he was a close associate of Rodge's. He was into property. In a small way. Like me.' He laughed, as if inviting Clark to deny this disclaimer. 'I thought he was sweet on Jennifer, at one time. Made a bit of a fool of himself there, one way or the other. Married to a real cold arse. Aristocratic connections, hadn't she?' He drained the whisky, stared in amazement at the empty glass. 'So was Roger Clinton, come to that.'

'Married to. . . . ?'

'No.'

'Keen on your daughter?'

'Yes. Not my business. She is quite capable of looking after herself. Always was. Do you mind getting up and giving me the same again? Help yourself while you're about it.'

As Clark was busy at the sideboard Stapleton hummed unmusically, and scratched with horny nails at his trousers' thighs. On the return of his glass he raised it in a mock toast.

'Clinton would be at least twenty years younger than I am. I can't think why he'd do away with himself. Property's not been all that profitable, but one can live. And now it's rocketing again. Don't you think so?'

'It's one topic you can guarantee to hear in the common room; how much your house is worth.'

'So unless he's made a fool of himself? No, he wouldn't kill himself even if he'd gambled every penny away.'

'Is that likely?'

'He'd frequent the clubs. Used to. And they don't go there just for the wine and women. I don't suppose you patronize them.'

'No,' Clark answered. 'I live like a monk. I've a fair amount of reading and marking to do. At the weekend I might try a concert or a play.'

'And does that seem acceptable?'

'How do you mean?'

Stapleton looked up in fear at the question. 'Sitting in a room reading schoolboy essays all night?'

'It has to be done.'

Stapleton shrugged at this compliance.

'You've plenty of time. No, I don't mean hours of the day. Years to come. I'm seventy-five, nearly seventy-six. I can't guarantee myself anything. Now you'd think that would have its advantages. For instance, when I walk out into the garden on a fine morning, you would claim that I ought to make the best of it. The sun's shining; I've only myself to please; I'm feeling fit and sprightly. *Carpe diem*. But it's not so.'

'Why is that, then?'

'I never feel really well; that's the top and bottom of it. Some

31

bit or piece is aching or creaking. It's not so much death as life that's making a fool of me. When I was your age, it would be the time of Munich or just before, we were certain there'd be a war. I'd qualified, done my articles as a solicitor; they didn't bother about universities so much then. I did my Matric at fifteen at your place, and stopped on one term in the Sixth Form doing French and Latin and History. But as soon as I was sixteen and an opening came up, at Lewitt, Drew and Watson's, I was in there.'

He paused, nodding to himself. When he began again, he sat straighter. 'That's one thing the school taught me, to work hard. In the one term in the Sixth Form I beavered away at my Latin as if I were after a university scholarship. Old Fothergill, the classics master, begged my father to let me stay on. It was a waste, he said. You'll know the name, Francis Fothergill, won't you?' Clark did not. 'How are the mighty fallen? A sarcastic old sod he was. None of this making it interesting. "I make it clear; you learn it and that's all there is to it." That was his line. A good teacher, though. "You're only fit to work in a bank," he'd say when you'd done something wrong. Things were different. In school and out.'

'And the War?'

'I went into the Navy. Enjoyed it one way or another. I was fit, young, a rough rug-headed kern. Could put up with any sort of hardship.'

Stapleton lost interest. His voice during this recital had been stronger, harder, more direct, and though his eyes watered the set of his head was firm. Now he drooped, crouched into the back of his chair, shrunken, a mannikin. He finished his whisky, fished for his handkerchief to wipe a dewdrop from the end of his nose and said he was tired.

Clark stood up immediately, commandeered the glasses, and waited for the old man to hobble the way to the kitchen.

'I'll ring your daughter to say I've been.'

'Ye'.' A mere grunt.

'I haven't got her telephone number. I'll find it in the directory.'

Stapleton pointed to a list. Clark went over, searched briefly, took a note. He thanked the host for his hospitality, asked if there was anything he could do. He left by the front door, so that Stapleton could make sure he had locked all up. Clark heard the bolts bang and scrape.

'Good night, Tony.'

The use of the Christian name surprised him, as he made for the street. The air had cooled; under the trees mist hung thinly in the glow of street lights. Clark breathed deeply, glad to be out of that constricting house and company. He began to sing to himself, Lully's '*Bois épais, redouble ton ombre.*' The melancholy lilt of the song lifted his spirits; he felt both happy and ashamed.

V

On Saturday of the same week Anthony Clark had driven down to the school ground to watch the First XV. The afternoon was brilliant, bright harvest-festival weather, and a good turnout of staff and parents bunched colourfully along the touchlines. He enjoyed the determined energy of the boys, their dives into rucks, their ease with the high-flying kick, the skill and dash. Their eyes were narrowed, as cheeks and thighs reddened; orders were issued, gestures rehearsed to perfection. This was, he considered, officer material, young subalterns and captains. Footsteps thudded as the forwards spilt over the touchline, scattering spectators. The school held and heeled, scrum-half to fly-half, who punted toweringly into blue sky. 'On, man, on.' An old grey-head on the line was shouting, hands in pockets, face intent as that of the boys. 'Put them on-side.' The kicker needed no encouragement, arms and whirling legs up the field to tangle with catching full-back and dropping ball.

'Strong team this year,' a voice instructed Clark. Hugh Pearson in blazer and scarf spoke moderately but not to be argued with. 'This is usually the best game of the season; it's a pity it's always first on the fixture list.' The school scored. The sound of clapping seemed both small and civilized in the sunshine. 'I think we shall beat them this year.'

At the half-time whistle Pearson invited his companion to walk round the line with him.

'I never apologized for deserting you last week.'

'I really enjoyed the evening.'

'Did you? Did you? Good.' Pearson's accent was clipped, far-back, almost a parody. 'An old friend of mine had killed himself.'

'I'm sorry.'

'They asked me to go across and see his widow.'

'Yes.'

'Tremendous shock. For his family, and for me. Man in a thousand.' He nodded distantly but affably as they passed the Headmaster disguised in a golfing-cap. 'And there seemed to be no real reason for it.' Clark waited. 'Self-made man, worked his way up in the world without advantages. Hard as nails, one would have said. And yet. . . .'

The pace was sharp, and increasing, but Pearson spoke in the same low whisper, perfectly enunciating, intense, unhesitating.

'He was well-to-do. His ventures flourished. His widow is left amply provided for. I can't understand it.' Pearson tugged suddenly at one end of his scarf as if to throttle truth out of himself. 'He threw himself under a train. Fearful way to die. In Peterborough. It was carefully organized. He left letters in his desk.' Pearson shook his head, not relaxing speed. 'Makes a dreadful mess of the corpse.' He drew in breath.

'And nobody knows why he . . . ?' Clark allowed his voice to trail.

'Nobody knows why. The letters just expressed regret. His affairs had all been carefully arranged. Why should a successful man do such a thing?'

'I've no idea.'

'He must have had a disappointment, wouldn't you say?' Pearson pressed as if his companion held the secret. 'Something had not come up to his demanding standard?'

'In business, or in his private life?'

'We just don't know. His children are off his hands and nicely settled. His wife, his second wife, was perfectly content; she wasn't a demanding woman. He had mistresses from time to time.' Pearson sighed. 'He seemed able to fit them in without undue complication. No. It's a mystery.'

'Old Mr Stapleton said he knew your friend.'

34

'He did? I believe they were in a partnership of some sort or another at one time.' He patted Clark's arm. 'The game's beginning again. Let's wander round to the other side. I don't like staring into the sun.'

Though they stood together for the second half, Pearson addressed most of his remarks to a senior colleague and a parent. At the conclusion of the game, he patted Clark's arm again, leading him towards the line of parked cars. The school had won but with some difficulty, clinging to a small lead over a last desperate ten minutes. Now as the teams trotted away, and the darker-garbed spectators followed more leisurely in the late brightness of the afternoon, Pearson seemed at ease with the world, humming tunelessly to himself, smiling, willing to bestow benignity.

'Doing anything important this evening?' he asked.

'I thought I might try the violin recital at Castle Gate.'

'Who's giving it?'

'Thomas Tring.'

'He's said to be very good. Brother's in the Lower Sixth.'

'Is he a musician?'

'Only incidentally. Well, enjoy it.'

He waved dismissively and made for the pavilion. As Clark strolled towards his car, in the appreciated warmth of the sun, he thought to himself that to someone outside the fence his lot would seem enviable. He belonged to this important little society; the weather was magnificent; the First XV had won; he had spent the afternoon in the company of an influential man; several well-to-do people had nodded agreeably. He had become a member of a paramount educational clique, named on the 'valued file'. It did not feel like this. To these parents, to his pupils even, he'd be a poor bloody usher, unfit to hold down a properly paid job. His car needed cleaning. He wondered if Mrs Mackenzie would consider it infra dig if he went out on to the street in his shirt-sleeves with a bucket, sponge and leather. He'd risk her displeasure.

At twenty-past seven he entered the Castle Gate rooms, looked about him for a place, chose a row where he had empty seats on either hand. Again he felt a stranger; couples entering greeted friends, bared teeth, straightened ties or hair in honour of acquaintanceship. Though the audience was largely middle-aged and elderly, there was a sprinkling of young people with lively faces, bright frocks and open-necked shirts. He himself wore a collar and tie, aligning himself with the wrinklies, he decided. Hardly anyone else of his age graced the concert.

Just after the half-hour one of the chosen grey-suits called them to order, announced an extra programme by a string quartet Clark had not heard of, and said coffee could be bought in the interval down below. He pointed out with a superior embarrassment the exit to be used, and slipped back-stage to hold the door for the artistes.

Thomas Tring, emerging with violin in left hand and bow vertical at the high port in his right, looked about Clark's age, had a long head with thin untidy hair round a clear parting. His accompanist, two yards behind, was ruddy-faced with glasses and black locks held properly in place. They bowed, competently together, and the pianist found and played with his stool. Tring tuned rapidly, pizzicato, adjusted his legs, his fiddle, his head, his bow arm and imperiously set about Tartini's Devil's Trill.

A grave beauty dominated the hall.

Anthony Clark sat upright, transformed by the fluid majesty. That so small an instrument could produce so expansive, so copious a sound, so magisterially decisive, amazed him, worked its miracles as it invariably did. He held himself proudly, lifted from his life, a changed man. Tartini sang, danced, meditated, showed off, instructed, delighted. Clark followed willingly, a servant to this art. For a matter of moments he grew certain that he was greater than himself, a partner of the musician, a soul capable of striking fire from the humdrum flints of his existence. He pressed his back into his chair, his nostrils wide, breathing a larger air. Soon his thoughts would wander, combining the music with the sunlight on the sports field, Pearson's boyish gravitas, the small cloud's speed, the line of poplars. In the interval he would wish for the thousandth time that he had a musicians's mind, concentrated entirely on variations of pitch, volume, rhythm, pattern, but his reaction to the sonata was not such. He listened and the sounds of violin and piano combined to alter his perspective of the world, but in doing so shunted his mind directly away from the music. His reaction was impure, he knew, but the richer for it. Anthony Clark at a recital was a different man from the schoolmaster, the lodger, the transient; he would not forget this performance. This is the day that the Lord hath made. Lord Tartini.

Now the violinist attacked the diabolic trills, nothing dream-like about their strength for all their origin, and Kreisler's ferocious cadenza before he and the pianist conjoined in a chordal beauty both wide, expected and satisfying to the heart's core. Clark clapped loudly, encouraging the rest who needed no encouragement. Ugliness of sound appreciatively succeeded musical art.

The first half ended with three 'sparklers' and the Dvorak Sonatina, a work about which Clark could not make up his mind. Fortunately Tring had no such difficulties so that he and his partner enjoyed themselves to the end.

Queueing for his coffee, looking for a place to stand and drink occupied the first five minutes of the interval.

'Oh, hello.'

A woman's voice, Jennifer Hope's.

He answered. She wore a white blouse and trousers of vivid yellow. Her fair hair was looped up into a bun, rather austerely.

'Enjoying it?' he asked.

'Yes, I suppose I am.'

'Don't you know, then?'

'Music's not altogether my thing. I'm trying to educate myself. I would never put up with piano lessons as a child, and now I wish I had.'

'Just as they said.'

'Just as they said.'

They spoke about music, she without much enthusiasm. Clark reported that he had seen her father, and had intended to report this to her.

'But you didn't?'

'I'm afraid not.'

'I'm glad. You're as efficient as I am. How did he seem?'

'He grumbled, but was lively enough. He praised the school, said they taught him how to work.'

'Yes. He seems to have taken a fancy to you. Thanks,

37

anyway, for calling in. I feel sorry for him; at least when he's not anywhere about.'

As they went back upstairs she invited him to her flat after the concert, issuing directions.

The second half began with show pieces, Tartini's Variations on a Theme of Corelli, more Kreisler, Halffter's Danza de la Gitana, Wieniawski, and ended with the Brahms A Major Sonata. The last movement, the rondo, spoke its broad calm to Clark, as he followed the powerful thrusts of the violinist's elbow and Brahms's long phrases sang. The enthusiastic audience was rewarded by a short piece of unaccompanied Bach and Kreisler's Tambourin Chinois. In no hurry to be outside, Clark saw nothing of Jennifer Hope. He dawdled his way to the car park, and sat for five minutes behind his wheel.

It took him some time to find parking-space in Mrs Hope's street, and at some distance from her flat which formed part of a large square, dark house, a mansion almost, with ten bells outside. He had difficulty in finding Jennifer's card, and in the end rang desperately. No one answered. He peered again at the two banks of names and bells, made sure that he had chosen correctly, and pressed hard. He heard no sign of ringing; waited; tried again. The house stood well away from the street and its lights. After a fifth fruitless attempt, he stepped into the porch towards the front door, a huge affair with three wide panels of stained glass between another four, dimly lighted from behind. To his surprise this opened quietly, easily. Still hesitating, he walked away to poke again at the bell before stepping inside.

Now he found himself in a wide hall, and a broad square institutional staircase. The place was lit from somewhere high above by a bare bulb of low wattage, so that areas of shadow hid its full extent. The newel-post of the stairs, capped with a dark plate of mahogany shaped like the roof of a Chinese temple, seemed a foot square. As far as he could make out there was no furniture, nor were there any coverings on the cold, terrazzo floor. He counted nine doors leading from the hall as he stalked up and down; all but one were carefully numbered, but gave no names, and remained impregnably shut. Clark swore and sat down on the second step, scratching his head.

There was no sound from any part of the building. Either the walls were impenetrably thick, or the inhabitants dumb, motionless, not at home. Time hardly seemed to budge. He hitched his trousers, scrambled up, took another turn, tried to look out of a stained-glass leaded window on the small wall at the bottom of the staircase, but could see nothing.

He consulted his watch, decided he had been here only five minutes, and sat down again with head in his hands. He made himself think of the Brahms sonata, but it did nothing to relieve his irritation. It was half an hour since the concert had ended; she had had plenty of time to walk back, never mind drive. Ten minutes. He stood and swore. Enough was enough.

He let himself out, dashed a heavy, angry finger at the bell, fastened it there, before he tiptoed down the half-dozen steps. No sooner had he reached the gravel of the path than headlights wheeled, flashed along the drive, playing on trees, on the far corner of the house. The car stopped; headlights were switched off; the door slammed and footsteps crunched towards him.

Jennifer.

'Oh,' she said, handling her keys, 'you found it. Good.'

She mounted the steps, bent to the lock.

'This door's open,' she said. 'Anybody could get inside.'

'Yes,' he answered. 'Me.'

'Have you been here long?' He did not answer. 'I'm so sorry.' Jennifer ushered him inside, closed and locked the door, before moving across to the room numbered 1. 'You're angry,' she said, smiling back over her shoulder. 'Come in.'

Room one was enormous, and brilliantly lit. White walls and fresh, matching paintwork shone in contrast to dark Victorian furniture. Jennifer crossed the wide expanse of carpet and drew curtains over the bow-window, large as a cinema screen.

'Find yourself a seat,' she ordered, dealing now with a smaller window. Clark took himself to an arm-chair. 'Are you warm enough? I'm too bad keeping you hanging about in a strange place. I was trying to do good.'

'Is that unusual?' he asked more cheerfully.

'Are you warm enough?' She turned on the gas-fire. 'How do you like this room? It's our old family house. I used to sit in here and read in the school holidays when I was a child. Now, what about a drink?'

She flopped into an arm-chair, slinging her anorak across the back.

'I'm driving.'

'Yes. I'll fetch coffee when I've recovered.' She smiled, snuggling into the dark leather of the chair, cuddling a vast saffron cushion. 'Do you know anything about houses?'

'Not really.'

'I'd parked along Warser Gate, and I was just hurrying along to pick the car up when an old friend stopped me. She'd been at the Tring recital. And she asked me if I'd go to look at a house she's thinking of buying. Or she and her husband. "Why me?" I asked. "One," she said, "your father's into property, so you must know something about it. And, two, you've got a good eye and a lot of common sense." I never felt so flattered.'

Jennifer punched the cushion.

'The be-all and end-all of it was that she gave me a bunch of keys, and like a fool I said I'd go out there tomorrow afternoon and look it over.'

'Will it be interesting?'

'I've no idea. Will you come with me?'

She threw the cushion to the ground, and went out to the kitchen. Anthony Clark, left to stare around, concentrated on a big modern picture over the mantelpiece. Swirling intertwined ribbons of colour curled over a background nearly white at the centre and fading into fog-grey at the edges. The painter's signature was illegible, more logo than name. A plain contemporary, gold square put an end to its energy. Both formal and strenuous, the painting annoyed him. The other pictures were smaller; watercolours of buildings and rivers in wide mounts and old-fashioned, convoluted frames.

He felt warmed through, even sleepy before she returned with a tray. She poured coffee, chattering.

'Do you like this house?' she asked.

'I do. It's spacious, judging by this room.'

'My father still owns it.'

'Your father must be very well-to-do.'

'I suppose so. He's a millionaire, I expect, with today's

property prices. But he doesn't make use of his advantages. He slums about in that kitchen of his all day. What he needs at this time of life is a small, convenient flat.'

'His house is beautifully clean and polished. He took me into his . . .'

'Of course it is. He never uses the place. Just pokes his head in to make sure his cleaner has done her work properly.'

'And if she hasn't?'

'She'll get the length of his tongue, poor woman.'

Clark raised his scalding coffee, lowered it rapidly. Jennifer watched him, amused.

'He said an odd thing,' Clark began hesitantly.

'You surprise me. My father is clever and shrewd, or was at least, but he never struck me as eccentric. But I'm interrupting you. Go on.'

'He said he shot his wife.'

'Yes?'

'Well, did he?'

'Yes.' Jennifer beat the word out.

'You mean he killed her?'

'No. But he probably meant you to think so. He likes to present himself in an interesting light. He's always suggesting that something scandalous attaches itself to him.'

'And doesn't it?'

'No. And especially not nowadays. Perhaps he cut a few commercial corners in his youth, but he's never been in trouble with either the Law Society or the Criminal Courts. He'd like you to think he was an old rip, but he isn't. My brothers, all pillars of conventional society, think he's a stuffed shirt.'

'Brothers?'

'Yes. There are three: a barrister, a solicitor and a medico. All much older than I am.'

'Do they not live near?'

'The nearest in Birmingham. The other two in London. John, the eldest, the barrister, has just been made a judge of some sort. He's fifty.'

'They don't visit your father often?'

'Not very. But don't jump to conclusions. They get on well enough with him, but they're all busy with their own concerns.'

41

'I see.'

Jennifer described her own place in the family, her marriage and her job. She spoke as though she and her husband had parted amicably, but rarely met socially and had little to do with each other.

'We consult each other about problems; we have to. And we can without losing our wool. To tell you the truth, I look on him as an old acquaintance, somebody I knew quite well years ago.' She frowned, chewed on a fingernail. 'The fact we were husband and wife doesn't seem to count. Emotionally. Perhaps that's as well. Do you believe that?'

'I'll take your word for it.'

'Perhaps I've no sense of history. Or a poor memory. We were in love when we first married. At least we thought so.' Her face broke into a smile, mockery of herself perhaps. 'One doesn't know. I was out last Sunday evening and I saw an old friend of my father's and we stopped for a word. He's a nice old chap, clever and dry. He'd just been to church. And I said to him, I shouldn't, I know, "Isn't it boring?" and he said, "Oh, yes, sometimes." And then in a quite different voice, "If you or somebody else, Jennifer, proved to me absolutely conclusively that God doesn't exist, I should be back next Sunday for evensong just the same." And he stroked his moustache and off he went. I've been puzzling myself about it all the week.'

'Why?'

'Why should he want to go if the fundamental ground of belief's removed?'

'Habit. Or the beauty of the liturgy or the building or the singing. My guess is he'd soon find something else to occupy himself with if he's as clever as you say he is.'

'You mean he only thinks he'd do it?' Jennifer.

'Something like that. It's all hypothetical while he's still a believer. His mind is made up for him.'

'Possible.' She looked serious. 'I think it's more subtle than that. It's ingrained in him that that's the only way to think seriously about, well, such questions as why we're here, what's the purpose of life.'

'Doesn't science allow people in the twentieth century to think seriously?'

'It does, I suppose . . . if thinking is the aim. But it doesn't come up with answers as to who lighted the touch paper for the Big Bang or what was there before it.'

They looked each other over. The opening of the Tartini sonata played in Clark's head.

'Did you have a religious upbringing?' he asked.

'No, not at all. I think my mother might have gone to church on social grounds if she'd been encouraged. But my father, to the best of my knowledge, never admitted mystery. That's why he was so good at his job. He'd carefully sort cases out. If it couldn't be explained, then that was because somebody had made an error in the drafting of a law or an agreement. His wasn't the sort of mind to wonder who created the universe.'

'I wonder, but then I'd have never come up with answers about gravity, never mind God.'

Jennifer yawned.

'You're tired,' Clark said. 'I'll go.'

'There's no hurry. Finish your coffee. I kept you hanging about. Do the same for me.' She massaged her face with flat hands. 'I don't sleep very well. It's perhaps better if I go to bed later.'

Now she looked tired, the skin under her eyes bruised. She had lost all impetus in her talk, and lolled in her chair. When he next said he must leave she made no attempt to stop him. He helped her wash the cups, arranged for the meeting next day. She apologized twice for her inhospitality.

Outside small stars pricked the cold sky.

VI

Clark rang Jennifer's bell at two-fifteen, exactly on time.

'Where's your car?' she asked. 'Put it in the drive. We'll go in mine. I don't like to be driven.'

He did as instructed. Her house loomed large in the daylight, square, a black brick wedding-cake, with white windows and doors, all in excellent order. The gravel paths had been raked that morning; the beds were bright with flowers. She had left the front door ajar; he edged into the hall.

'Come in,' she called from her room.

Jennifer had spread a map on her table and invited him to advise her about a route. A minute's exchange showed that she had already made up her mind.

'Where it is in the village, I just don't know.'

'We've tongues in our heads.'

'Gill mentioned a beech hedge. It's called Beech House.'

'I'll look for it.'

'Thank you.'

She darted him a sharp, satiric grin, and shooed him from the room.

The amount of traffic on this Sunday afternoon surprised them as they took to the Fosse Road. They turned off towards the village by a dull lane, hedged with hawthorn and infrequent trees. A square tower, undistinguished, was all they could see of the church from their car. Cottages straggled the main street, which spread remarkably wide. A young woman with three children in tow gave them directions how to find Beech House. They had, it appeared, passed it a hundred yards back.

'So much for your look-out,' Jennifer said, turning the car.

The hedge was dominated by three lime trees; neither the name of the house nor a board announcing its sale could be seen. A large lawn, unevenly overgrown, lay in front of a high building which was grey with stucco. Summer dust dulled bushes, the bricks of the drive, the gate-posts, a garden bench with three clay plant-pots, a metal wheelbarrow.

'What do you think?' Jennifer asked.

'On a bright afternoon like this, pretty well anything ought to look attractive. This doesn't.'

'Exactly.'

She sounded as if she had solved some conundrum.

'What do you mean?' he asked.

'Well, Gill Wycliffe's no fool. She wouldn't be chasing a place with no possibilities. So? There must be something about this which we have yet to see.'

They faced about, and above the hedge and lime trees they could just make out the spacious modern residence opposite, in brick, while to their right the church tower now seemed close. The houses on either side were small but superficially attractive, estate labourers' cottages with extensions and creeper-covered walls.

'We'll try round the back,' Jennifer ordered, leading the way.

The garden, at least a hundred yards in length, and T-shaped, was more disorderly than the front lawn, but a small orchard was cropping heavily.

'Look like Bramleys,' he said. 'Good cookers.'

Beyond the furthest margin, a low-cut hedge, with a squat, irregular oak tree, they saw a spacious, cut cornfield and in the far distance a straggle of wood in the misty sunlight.

'What age do you think the house is?' she asked. He looked back.

'Hard to say. This stucco hides the features. And the windows look Victorian or Edwardian, ordinary sash-type. The sort of thing you find on ten thousand small terraced houses. But it is big, three storeys, so it can't be a labourer's cottage enlarged. That does seem to be overdoing it. I can't tell. I'll guess eighteenth century, harassed out of all shape or reason about 1900.'

'That last bit's right, but Gill says this end is seventeenth century.'

'How do they know that? Deeds?'

'No. I don't think so. It's by the brickwork, I think. But there was considerable rebuilding about 1825, and then another, and this updating about 1905.'

'Is it in good order?'

'That I don't know. We can't pronounce on that, anyway. She will have had a surveyor in, I guess, and he'll have given a favourable report, otherwise she'd have gone no further. We have to squint about for aesthetic possibilities. Gill has a lot of money to play with, and she won't waste it.'

'Who is she?'

'A friend. More an acquaintance. She's a cousin of Clarissa Pearson.'

'Well connected?'

'A cut above you and me. Yes. She married a parson, divorced him, and took on an architect.'

'Why doesn't she ask him?'

'She has, and he's presumably given her an answer she doesn't like. So we're called in.'

'You are.'

'I trust your immaculate taste. Let's go inside.'

The entered by the front way, into a hall that was bare and cramped. Biggish rooms lay on either flank, all unfurnished except for a dull stretch of worn carpet. The walls were marked by dust-lines from picture frames.

'It doesn't smell,' he said, 'of damp.'

'The people have only just left. Last week.' She turned on her heel. 'What do you think?'

'Good, big, convenient spaces. Windows not wide enough. Fireplaces ugly.'

'The whole damned house is ugly.'

'We've not seen it yet.'

The rooms at the back were smaller, a study with bookshelves, a cloakroom and lavatory, two pantries, a farmhouse-sized kitchen with a tiled floor, a scullery, a washhouse and a further storeroom. All the woodwork appeared in good order. Upstairs they found five bedrooms, two bathrooms, a dressing room and small closets. From the upper storey they could see the whole of the church; nave and chancel were dull as the tower.

At the top of the house Jennifer sat on a window ledge and demanded his verdict. 'It's a decent-sized family house. There are no attractive features, and it's rather too dark for my liking. The rooms are large enough to make something of them. You've a very big garden; they've taken over pieces from both neighbouring houses.'

'But?' she said, laughing, not looking at him.

'The village for a start. It's unattractive. I drove round the district the other Sunday and there are two at least that are infinitely preferable to this. The buildings are poor; the river's out of sight.'

'What's good?'

'It's not too far from town. And quiet. Not judging by today's standards. Does she work? Or have children to take to schools? The rooms are a fair size. It's a nice family house. But it's ugly. I won't say ill-proportioned because that's so obvious; it has all the attractions of a barracks or a bus depot.'

'You wouldn't take it?'

'I'm a bachelor. Anyway, it depends on the price. But I'd have a good look round everywhere else in the market before I settled on this, even given that it's structurally sound.'

Jennifer nodded.

'I agree. Gill wouldn't give me any details. "I want your naked opinion," she said. She talks like that. But she has no children by the second marriage, and those of the first are grown up.'

'Where does she live now?'

'In a beautiful Georgian place in the Park. It's big for two people, but they're not short of money. I just don't know. . . .' A car drew up alongside hers in the drive. 'The woman herself. Oh, well. Doesn't trust me.'

Jennifer settled back to the sill and to silence. They heard keys in the front door and a mannish voice shouted, 'Are you there, Jen?'

'Up here,' Jennifer called back. 'Come on.' She and Clark went out on to the landing. 'Face the music.' Footsteps clapped on the bare stairs and Gillian Wycliffe appeared wearing jodhpurs, a misshapen windcheater and a felt hat of a military cut. Red-cheeked, perhaps fifty, she showed surprise at Clark's presence by scrutinizing him from toe to crown, and raising her eyebrows, comically larger than life, in a dumb question to Jennifer, who made brief introductions.

'Have you looked round?' Gill asked.

'Yes.'

'And what's the verdict?'

Jennifer turned back into the bedroom, resuming her seat on the window-sill. The other two followed her.

'What's the idea?' Jennifer asked. 'It's ugly outside and in. You could make it comfortable and attractive, I'm sure, but against the run of the place. It's roomy, but all your spaces are ill-shaped. And look at the hall. It's narrow as the grave. Just compare it with your present house; it's hopeless.'

'That's blunt.' Mrs Wycliffe grinned at Clark.

'Why did you bring me out, Gill? You didn't need me to tell you that.'

'Yes. I see. Why did I?'

47

Gillian marched across bare floorboards to park on the other window-sill.

'Yes,' she said. 'Yes. Mr Clark, what do you think?'

'Much as Jennifer does.'

'You do as she tells you, do you?'

'Don't be a bloody fool, Gill,' Jennifer interrupted. 'What's the attraction of this place?'

'You won't believe this,' Gillian began, clasping her hands. 'I'm very uncertain in my own mind.' She sniffed very loudly. 'We have family connections. Some great-great aunts lived here with a brother-in-law, a retired clergyman, in the eighteen-eighties. My mother used to mention it because it had a ghost. She made stories up for us about Beech House, Welford. And I saw the name in the paper. I thought it poor in possibilities when I saw it, and as to Ambrose, he was scathing. But it's an old house somewhere underneath.'

'Gill, you own a perfectly beautiful house on which you've spent a fortune. Why come out here to this, this barn? You and Ambrose are . . . ?' Jennifer broke off.

'The menopause,' the other answered. 'I fancied doing something up, giving myself an occupation.'

'But did you intend to live here?'

'It never came to such precise questions. The owners or the agents have slapped a ridiculous price on this, that's why it's not been sold even in the present boom, and I wondered in a vague way if I couldn't do something with the place.'

'Why drag me out here, Gill? You knew damn' well what I'd say.'

'I don't know. I honestly don't. It sounds so feeble now. Perhaps it's my time of life and I'm losing my marbles. But I just hoped, I suppose, that you might see something here that I didn't.'

'But Ambrose had come down against it?'

'Ambrose is conventional. You know what architects are. . . . I wanted somebody with flair, a bit of imagination, to look at it, to see something I couldn't.'

'You're disappointed, then.'

Gillian Wycliffe considered this with bowed head.

'No, I'm not. You've told me the truth. And I'm glad.' She

lifted her head. 'I'm sorry I've dragged you out on a wild-goose chase. I trust your judgement.'

There was silence in the room, and outside.

Jennifer held up the keys, rattled them and passed them over to Gillian, who took them into a capacious but delicately shaped hand.

'My apologies, again,' Gill said. 'And to you, Mr Clark.'

'It's interesting,' he muttered.

Jen led them out and after another brief bout of apology and inconsequential conversation on the drive they parted. Gillian stayed behind, legs wide, staring up at the house.

'That was a waste of time,' Jennifer pronounced.

'She was soon convinced, didn't argue much.'

'She knew quite well, she's no fool. And her husband's shrewd. He'd say exactly what the place was worth. And yet she drags us out here.'

'Only you.'

'Me, then. But why?'

'You're about to tell me, I presume,' Clark said.

Jennifer had now turned off the main road again and was making towards the river.

'It can't be the power of words, can it?' she began. 'Beech House and ghosts?'

' "Heaven in ordinary, man well dressed,
    The Milky Way, the bird of Paradise." '

'Come again.'

'George Herbert on prayer. The magic of words.'

Jennifer slapped her wheel, petulantly, but without altering course.

'There must be something wrong with her. That's my opinion.'

'There's something wrong with most of us,' he answered, amused.

'She's a strong-minded, bossy woman, so it would please her to order me out here. On the other hand, she knows what I'd say about a pile of rubbish like that.'

'She perhaps hoped you'd see something in it which she couldn't.'

'Not she; that's just her excuse. She's not gone completely off her head, whatever else is wrong.' Jennifer had drawn up at the side of the lane for no reason. On either side were flat meadows. 'No, I'm baffled.'

'Is she a sensible woman?'

'By and large. She has her off days. She brought up a family of four and acted as a vicar's wife, mothers' union and all that, and then packed it in and married Ambrose, one of nature's bachelors. No children now, few duties, beautiful house, money.'

'You mean she's bored?'

'I don't think so. She'll always find something to do. Home, garden, friends, good causes. And bad. She's an energetic woman. Forceful. I don't understand it.'

Clark shook his head, said nothing.

'It's like this Roger Clinton business. Nobody ever got to the bottom of that. They couldn't find out why he walked in front of a train. His money affairs were in good order; his wife hadn't noticed any signs of depression out of the ordinary; even the letters of apology seemed flat, dull as ditchwater. And yet he was thoroughly determined about it, had it all planned out.'

'Was he a sensible sort of man?'

'I'd have said so, but how can you say that about a man who deliberately plans to walk in front of a train, and picks his right time and place. No, it doesn't add up, does it?'

'Perhaps somebody's keeping quiet about something,' Clark ventured.

'They'll be doing that all right.' She gripped the wheel, then released it. 'Did you see that aquatint I have at home, a church by a river? No? Never mind. It has plain glass on it, and sometimes . . . well, often, reflects the light from the windows. I ought to hang it somewhere else. The picture is very beautiful, but these clean shapes of white light blot it out and yet in a way are just as attractive. Their lives are like that, quite different from what they ought to be. Not what they're meant to show.' She jerked her head upwards. 'You'll think I'm as odd as Gill is.'

'No.'

'Have you ever felt like suicide?'

'No,' Clark answered. 'I've felt very down, deeply disappointed, you know, but never suicidal.'

She took his right hand from his knee and held it in her left, without pressure, almost absent-mindedly. Flattered he squeezed but without response from her, though she retained her grasp. Jennifer seemed caught up elsewhere.

'Don't know why I went on about that aquatint,' she said, returning to earth. 'I suppose I noticed it and was slightly impressed by myself and thought it too good to waste, so I tried it on you. Not as good as George Herbert, though, is it?'

Clark sat still. Interested, he decided silence best suited the moment.

'Do you like women?' she asked suddenly.

'Very much.'

'You're not homosexual?'

'Not at all. Do I show signs, then?'

She did not answer that, but seemed in no way embarrassed by her questions.

'My husband used to drive me spare.'

'You work with him still, don't you? Your father said so.'

'For the same firm. We meet, and consult. But not as often as you'd think. I'm away four days starting tomorrow on a tricky audit. May run to the whole week.' She turned the ignition key, drove gently down to the river where she parked again on a stretch of grass. Four cars already stood there. She had explained the nature of her next week's work, and why it needed an experienced eye rather than that of a young trainee. She became scathing about the masculine ethos of accountancy, but claimed it had advantages, that some men were afraid, on their guard when they saw a woman looking their books over.

'They'll soon get used to it,' he murmured, 'especially if you're efficient.'

'I suppose they do. Sometimes their language is really filthy, and I don't know whether that's because they're scared or because they've accepted me.'

'You don't mind?'

'I can cuss and blind as well as they can. Do you have women teaching at your school?'

'There are one or two. I'd guess they enjoy it.'

'Haven't you found yourself a steady girl-friend yet?'

'I had one at my last place. We still write. It seems less serious. I don't know why.'

'You weren't living together?'

'No. No, we weren't.'

Clark did not resent these questions which she delivered without emphasis, staring out through the windscreen.

'You're not thinking of marriage yet?'

'No. I've only just started here. I'm uncertain what I shall do. About my future career.'

'Was she keen on marriage?'

'That's difficult.'

'Were you in love? Either or both.'

'We thought so. We said so from time to time. It seems different now.'

'You had sex?'

'Yes.'

Now she stopped the quickfire of questions and considered them. Again she tapped the rim of the wheel but this time with the butt of her hand in a steady rhythm, four in a bar, lifting the wrist high for the first beat.

'You must think I'm an oddity cross-examining you like this.' Her hands now lay one on the other in her lap. 'I like to know about people. And the best way to find out is to ask bluntly. It causes trouble sometimes. I've been told to mind my own bloody business more than once, and now and then my questions have been interpreted as a sexual invitation. But on the whole people like to talk about themselves, don't you find? You were remarkably cool about it all.'

'And did that please you?'

'Ah, now we're in trouble. Why should I be pleased or not? I'm curious, and a bit incautious, perhaps, in my methods. Yes, I was pleased, I suppose.'

'If the boot had been on the other foot? If I'd have been interrogating you?'

'Interrogate? That's too strong. I wouldn't have minded, either your questions or my having to answer. If you'd intruded on the one or two corners I want to keep out of sight or mind, I should have warned you off.'

They paused.

'Did I answer satisfactorily?' he asked.

'I'm very, very slow. It takes me months to make my mind up about anything.'

'Not about that house.'

'Oh, that. No, I mean anything serious, or tricky, or complicated. Anybody could see that Beech House was a washout.'

'Except Gillian.'

'Except her. Exactly.'

An elderly clergyman in a flapping cassock wandered into view surrounded by six or eight children and a middle-aged woman with a piece of card in her hand. The children danced round, shouting; about twenty yards short of the car the party stopped and the woman read some instruction. This was greeted with silence, then with argument, then with a word of agreement or warning and the children streamed off, almost running. The parson and the woman, grinning with satisfaction, followed at a good pace.

'Looks like a treasure hunt,' Clark said.

'The modern equivalent of Sunday School. Find Jesus in the hedge-bottom.'

' "And Jesus from the ground suspires." '

The quotation was wasted on her as she sat frowning.

'It seems such a coincidence,' Jennifer began, 'it really does, but I think that's Gillian's first husband.'

'Does he live hereabouts?'

'Yes, he does.'

'He looked old. Seventy.'

'He was a good deal older than she was.'

A motor-boat and water-skier roared past them, the skier zig-zagging across the wake.

'Have you ever tried that?' she asked.

'No.'

'Real ski-ing?'

'I once went on a school party to Austria. I quite enjoyed it, but I've never bothered since.'

'The story of your life?'

VII

Not until a few weeks later did Anthony Clark call in to see Stapleton. Time rushed past; half-term was not far away. Three weeks before he had made a provisional arrangement to visit Daniella and her parents at the break, but had now received a surprising letter from her confessing that she had fallen in love with another man and did not intend to write again. Anthony had been both affronted and relieved. Clearly the visit to her parents' home was meant to clinch and solidify their relationship, to finalize; he had spent some little time on his visits to the town centre comparing and contrasting engagement rings in the jewellers' windows. Now she had put a stop to all that.

Her previous letter had been normal, with an interesting account of a night out with her headmistress, an argument on a sports club committee, a visit of inspection from the county advisor, an evening at the theatre to see a catastrophic performance of Noel Coward's *Private Lives* and a failure to impress anybody at the auditions for *Orpheus in the Underworld* at the operatic society. All this was dashed down in the best of humours, failures and successes treated with a kind of lolloping, easy irony that kept him amused. Eight days later came her glum announcement that this was her last letter. The handwriting was the same, without signs of exaggerated care; the epistolary habits, the month in Roman figures or the small double squiggle under the final 'a' in her name were as usual. She apologized, said she knew how he would feel, gave him the name of the new beloved, Jonathan Saxton (it meant nothing) and wished him well. She would write no more.

He did not reply.

His pride was wounded; he remembered their times of pleasure. Leaden sorrow blocked his throat for two days before he recovered. He looked at the dozen photographs he had of her, thrust them into an envelope and doing so noticed on the back of one: 'To darling Tony with all my love from your Daniella': he had not seen this before. It made him wonder if he had been serious. None of the photos did her justice; when she sat still, she simpered. She showed her best when she demonstrated energy, at tennis, or rushing him along to an event, dragooning somebody, her hair slightly out of true and a bright blush on her cheek. Now she concentrated on her Jonathan. And in no time. He told himself that she had quite probably watched *Private Lives* in company with the man, eating his chocolates, and had been in such a pother of new love that she had not bothered to practise for her audition. He read her letter perhaps twenty times over three days and then burnt it.

Outside rain was dripping morosely from the leaves. He caught a cold, felt sorry for himself a second time.

He telephoned Ernest Stapleton offering to call. The man's acceptance was decidedly grudging.

'Are you busy with something?' Clark pressed.

'What the hell would that be?'

'I'll come then.'

'Please yourself.'

They raced to put the 'phone down first.

This time Clark rattled at the back door.

'Is it still raining?' Stapleton asked, peering.

'Not now. Would you like a run out in my car. I brought it down.'

'Where to?'

'You're the local expert.'

'No, thanks. It's getting dark. And I'm not ready.' Certainly he had not shaved. 'Come inside. Kitchen or lounge? Kitchen, then.' They seated themselves at the table. 'Has Jennifer sent you?'

'Not at all.'

'Your own goodness of heart?' With malice.

'If you're busy. . . .'

'At what?'

'Some programme on television?'

'Watching the telly. Yes, all I'm fit for. No, I shall hang about here until I'm ready for bed. Then it takes me damned near an hour to get myself settled down. The whole of my life consists now of wasting time.'

'Whose fault is that?'

'Fault? Fault?' Stapleton's voice cracked angrily. 'I'm slow

55

for a start. It takes me half an hour to do a five-minute job. And it's painful. Arthritis, bronchitis and angina do not make a good combination. I was energetic, and hardworking and enterprising. I was a decent solicitor, and I made a lot of money in property.'

'But you've lost interest?'

'Not altogether, but it's in the hands of other people. A very good firm. A man I trained. A man I liked.'

'After your own heart?'

'I've not heard that expression for years. But that's it exactly. We meet at least once a month and discuss how things stand.'

'So he's not likely to blue your fortune.'

'No. It would be hard to do that nowadays . . . given the area where my wealth is invested. No. He's good. But he's taken the responsibility out of my hands. It doesn't cost me much to live here. I don't go out very often. I exist like a pauper. I don't support charities or churches. I don't sponsor concerts or sporting contests. I sit in here, in some pain, and waste my time.'

'But you wish it were otherwise?'

'I wish I was young again. Yes. But that's impossible.'

'What about friends?'

'What friends? I don't have any. My own children don't come to see me. You'd think they would in view of my money, but I suppose they think they'd annoy me more by parking themselves on me than by staying away. You don't really like coming, do you?'

'You make it rather difficult.'

The old man laughed, and the sound was hearty, healthy. His last sentences had been delivered with unusual energy.

'Why do you come, then?'

'Your daughter asked me to. I'm a stranger in this town. You represent a part of life I don't know much about. And I hope it might bring you some small pleasure.'

Stapleton cackled, then coughed.

'When I was your age, you wouldn't have caught me on many philanthropic errands, that I can tell you. How old are you?'

'Twenty-six in December.'

'At that age I had a son, John. And a wife, of course.' He

56

laughed, phlegmily. 'I worked long hours. My principal saw to that. And we all expected a war. I wonder now why I had started a family, but we had our second child two years later when the War really had begun. A year after that I was called up for the Navy. My principal hung on to me as long as he could. I was away, abroad, a good part of my service. I enjoyed it, I can't deny that. But you don't want all this rigmarole.'

'Just finish the rest of your family for me. You had another son, didn't you?'

'Julian. After the War. And then last Jennifer, eight years later. Our little mistake.' He laughed wiping the back of his hand across his mouth like a navvy. 'Get the kettle on, young man.'

This brief family history cheered Stapleton to such an extent that he insisted on drinking his coffee in the lounge.

'The best room,' he said, when Clark appeared with the tray. By the time he was half-way down the first cup his spirits had dropped. 'Has Jennifer said anything about Clinton?'

'Roger Clinton? No.'

'He committed suicide. We worked together. Once I'd settled in the office again after the War, I had started looking into property in a cautious way. Years later he came to do some work on a new house we had. We talked. I could see he wasn't prepared to spend the rest of his life as a small-time builder, though he was good at it. I advised him about money and property sales. Then he expanded his firm, did some export stuff, really well, believe it or not. By this time I was principal; two of the old boys had retired, and then Archie Wright popped off. Heart attack. Just on time. I knew the ropes, could appoint my own young men. My younger children were still costing money, so I wasn't averse to making a pound or two. And the Clinton partnership was a little gold mine. Or so it proved. A risk, mark you, but you never make it big without risk. You can't get people to understand that. They want all the advantages and no drawback. Not possible. I might have ended up in prison with the Law Society on my back if things had gone wrong.'

'But they didn't.'

'No. I worked day and night. Neglected my Jules and Jen,

but my wife more than made up for that. She saw to it that they toed the line, did well at school, university. All four have good careers, thoroughly respectable, a credit to her.'

'You don't sound too happy about it?'

'They're stuffed shirts, all of 'em. Jennifer was the only one with a spark, and she married a man just like her brothers.'

'Mr Hope?'

'Mr Hope. Our Edwin. I wonder if they weren't all reacting against me. I cut a few legal corners. My wife must have been terrified. But I was lucky. I lived at a time when the swashbucklers like me and Clinton could make money. He was the age, within a year or two, of my eldest. He was my sort of son as John never was.'

'What does John do?'

'A barrister. Makes a decent living. George is a solicitor, lord high administrator of Northwich. And Julian's a surgeon. None of 'em poor. None very rich, either.'

He sucked at his coffee, and signalled for Clark to pour a second cup. 'And here I sit. I knew how to make money, but not how to spend it. If I made a profit, I sent it chasing off to coin more. People will be surprised when my will is published, I'll tell you. But I might just as well die. In fact it would be better all round. For me. For my children. Like Clinton.' Quite cheerful.

'Had he a family?'

'I think so. Not that he was anything like my age. That's the bastard. Creeping about with your arms and legs creaking. Pain in your back. Can't see anything properly. No energy. But when I was his age, twenty years ago, I was at a peak of achievement, couldn't go wrong. Everything I touched turned to gold.'

'It's a difficult question, but if you knew then what you know now, would you have done anything differently?'

Stapleton considered, narrowing his eyes. His skin looked unhealthy, dirty even.

'No, I wouldn't. Why should I?'

'But if you had learnt how to spend your money, to enjoy yourself, wouldn't that have stood you in good stead now?'

'It wouldn't have cured my aches and pains. Don't think I had no pleasure, I did, but it was minor, marginal.' He stroked his rough face. 'I had to struggle for a start, and five years in the Navy did my career no good. Still, there it is.'

The pair talked. Stapleton seemed friendly, almost animated, glad of company. He described something of his partnership with Clinton, and then their break-up.

'He wanted to go in for a project I considered slightly, er, tricky.'

'Was it?'

'I believe it worked out satisfactorily. It entailed buying Harlaxton Manor, and there were real snags. Legal, as well as anything else. But Clinton took it on, and made something of it. He'd plenty about him. We didn't quarrel. I'd other irons in the fire. He knew I'd a scheme on hand that took up any capital I had spare.'

'Did he succeed?'

'Oh, yes. And I suppose you want to know which came off better? I can't answer. Not much in it, I'd say. But you'll take that as a tacit admission that he had the sounder judgement.' Stapleton grinned. 'I honestly don't know. I think I had the edge. We didn't quarrel about it. My firm, one of my junior partners, did the legal work on Harlaxton for him, but from that time on, ten years ago, I began to take it more easily. Only just for a start. Now, I do very little.'

'This is very interesting to me,' Clark said.

'Well, it's different from drawing a steady wage, as you do.'

'More like a bet on horses?'

'Not at all, though there's an element of gambling; luck must play a part. Just look at these Stock Exchange boys, and the money they drew after the Big Bang. And they were salary earners, like you. If they'd gone into some other career, they wouldn't have done as well. There you are. John, my eldest, is a barrister in Town. He's a QC, but he'll never be amongst the top earners.'

'Why is that?' Clark, gently.

'Temperament, I guess. He's clever. And conscientious. But he always does whatever it is he's doing within his capabilities. That won't do.' Stapleton shook his head, rolled in his chair. 'I sometimes think that you make your own luck, but I suppose that's not altogether right.'

By the time the old man had illustrated this with two long complicated anecdotes, lucidly narrated, one about Roger Clinton, he showed signs of fatigue. Clark took the coffee-pot and cups out to the sink where he washed them. Stapleton pottered about. On his feet he showed his age, staggering, groaning, once cursing himself.

'I'll be on my way,' Clark said. 'Will you be all right?' The host nodded. 'I've really enjoyed talking to you. It's another world.'

'Better?' Stapleton was leaning forward, supporting himself on straight arms above the sink.

'I'm the sort of man who finds pretty well anything more interesting than what I'm doing.'

'Uh.'

Clark let himself out, drove back the few hundred yards to his digs, parked the car, and stood in the mild night on the pavement. He considered a stroll, decided against it and went indoors where Mrs Mackenzie, on the watch, greeted him in the hall.

'Ah, Mr Clark, I'm glad I caught you. There's been a telephone call for you.'

'From?'

He suspected that she was testing the air for alcohol.

'Mrs Hope. Jennifer Hope.'

'I've been to see her father just now.'

'Is that the solicitor? Lewitt, Drew and Hope?'

'Yes, the man.'

'I've written her telephone number on the pad. She wants you to call her.'

'Tonight?'

'At your convenience.'

She led him to the 'phone, leaving the door slightly open so that she could follow the conversation. He told Jennifer that he had visited her father; she showed no interest, not even asking how the old man was. In a rather brusque manner she asked if he was free on Wednesday evening to accompany her to Gillian Wycliffe's house.

'She has Roger Clinton's widow there, and needs company. "Bring that nice young man," she said. I'll pick you up at seven-fifteen.'

Jennifer replaced the 'phone in the middle of his politenesses. Her father's daughter, she had better things to do than talk to him.

VIII

Anthony Clark quietened his class before dismissing them.

He had been reading *A Midsummer Night's Dream* with the 'A' stream of eleven-year-olds, and enjoying their buzzing delight. Teaching Shakespeare to small boys was new to him; at his comprehensive school nobody read the Bard until the Sixth Form. Here, Maddison, his Head of Department, had laid it down plainly: 'They'll do Shakespeare for GCSE and so they'll read one Shakespeare play at least each year until they get there. Even the humblest scientist will know five Shakespeare works by the time he leaves this school.' Clark's colleague, Thompson, had his doubts about this, as about everything else, but Maddison gave him his short answer. 'You think they'll be put off Shakespeare for life. Well, just make sure that they know exactly what it is that they're never going to read or see again.'

'Antedebloodyluvian,' Thompson groused.

'Why don't you tell him, then?'

'All he'd say is, "The figure of speech you're using is called 'tmesis'. Don't forget it."'

'So?'

'Time he retired.'

'How old is he then?'

'Forty-two.'

They both laughed. They both approved of Maddison.

The boys closed books, sat with their hands flat on the desks. A few minutes before they had been rolling in their seats at the antics of the rude mechanicals. A fat boy called Wiseman had swaggered as Bully Bottom, showing off to perfection, combining a strong local accent with a caricature of the walk of 'Bull' Finch, the woodwork master. This lesson was not considered work by the young gentlemen. Some of them would be sorry to stop so soon.

The bell rang.

Clark ordered them to stand in the aisles, and chivvied a slow-coach. He opened the door, ordered them to march out, line by line. They obeyed in silence, but as soon as they reached the corridor the rank broke, splintered into chattering twos or threes. He noticed with pleasure that they did not run, maintained their quick walk until they reached the door out into the yard where boyhood reasserted itself, arms and legs whirled, shouts prevailed. Clark returned to sit at his table, tidying papers and books. The pile of Fifth-Form essays he stacked and loaded into his briefcase. Though he did not look forward to the chore, he would finish the task before he went to bed. Now he could lounge for five minutes, find his friend Thompson in the common room, read a newspaper, perhaps brew instant coffee, listen to the end-of-day arguments or tittle-tattle of the small group who gathered there for half an hour before they left for home.

He had enjoyed the lesson, but was tired.

'Oh, hello there. Are you busy?'

Hugh Pearson came in, crossed the room, sat pupil-like at the table immediately in front of Clark, who said a word or two about the pleasure of teaching clever small boys. Pearson encouraged him to talk, recalled one or two of his own ex-pupils with warmth. The older man sat legs sideways, crossed in the gangway, a length of white calf revealed between sock and trouser-bottom. After a time he stood, asked, 'Have you been seeing anything of Jennifer Hope recently?'

'I shall see her on Wednesday.' He explained the circumstances, the first meeting with Gill Wycliffe in Lowton-on-Trent, the invitation.

'You see Jen quite often?'

'Not really.'

Again an explanation, and this time, deliberately, he included a mention of the Sunday visit to Stapleton, the talk of Roger Clinton. Pearson did not turn a hair.

'I'm fond of Jennifer,' Pearson said. 'She's a real person.'

Clark waited for elucidation, in vain.

'Give her my regards, will you? Tell her I was asking after her.'

62

'Have you known her for a long time?'

'Twenty-odd years. When I first came here, she was a schoolgirl.'

He rose languidly, bent to brush the crease of his trousers.

'Good to talk to you. My wife will be waiting for me. Still, she's never in any hurry, thank goodness.'

Pearson raised his hand, passed from the room, closing the door with speed yet in utter quietness, leaving the young man to ponder the reason for the visit. Perhaps, he decided, it was kindness on his senior's part; Pearson seemed a man of moods.

On Wednesday Jennifer Hope called to pick him up for the trip to Gill Wycliffe's house. She arrived so late that he was wondering whether he'd misunderstood instructions and should telephone. Two minutes before their expected time of arrival she drew up, set Mrs Mackenzie's bell pealing through the whole house, fetched the landlady from her sink and one of the schoolma'ams out on to the corridor.

'It isn't the fire brigade,' Clark said, passing her.

The girl giggled and withdrew.

'Here's the man,' Mrs Mackenzie pronounced. 'He heard you, and saved my legs.'

Jennifer, outside, seemed in no sort of hurry. She was smartly dressed in a trouser suit of a shiny material and wore a turquoise scarf at her neck. No apologies were offered for the lateness of her arrival, and they sat for some minutes in the car while he described his visit to her father.

'And he was pleased to see you?'

'I thought so. At least until he became weary.'

The Park, a residential estate near the Castle for Victorian lace magnates, rich barristers, bankers, moneylenders, landed gentry who needed a house in town, retained something of its former magnificence. The roads were wide, tree-lined with forest giants, so that even at this time in autumn one had the impression of sylvan shade and greenness. Though some of the great mansions had sold off their gardens to speculative builders and the erection of executive town houses, and hardly a single place was now undivided, something of Victorian enterprise or even fantasy still dominated. He noticed a huge Norman doorway in brick, big enough for a cathedral entrance, a pillared Georgian canopy, a glass-roofed walk from street to front porch. Some houses were built to stand on their own, to demonstrate the owner's independence or nonconformity, a hundred or two yards back from the humdrum mortals in the road, while others towered right over the pavements as if to remind these captains of industry of the poor streets where they started or where the work-people lived still. Even now, after a hundred and more years of industrial pollution these edifices (and one needed some such word) kept their original solidity and swagger. Clark said as much.

'They're too big to heat properly, and too inconvenient. You need an army of servants.'

'Do you know anybody who keeps one of the really big houses?'

'Very few. The only people I know are the Misses Meates. Three sisters, all over eighty, and they keep their father's house on.'

'Do they have servants?'

'Help. Though they used to have some old dear living in with them. And it's some years since I went there. I haven't heard they'd died. I must look them up in the 'phone book.'

The Wycliffe house stood on a short, steeply inclined side-road. Its triple-front was early Victorian with a Georgian elegance and formality.

'This is a really nice house,' Jennifer said, parking in the deserted street. 'Too big for most people, but not ridiculously so.'

They rang at the front door of Regency blue and were welcomed by Mrs Wycliffe into a wide hall with a stone floor, two grey-marbled pillars and a stained glass tasteful window dominating the stairs. Three gold-framed oil paintings of red-coated, be-wigged eighteenth-century gentlemen hung on white walls. The floor's area was warmed by carpets of complicated but unfussy design. Gill Wycliffe kissed Jennifer, took Clark's raincoat, and then showed them into a drawing room. Here windows occupied almost a whole wall; three arm-chairs and a settee in matching brocade still left considerable space; tables were antique and the sideboard immense. Everywhere plants flourished and the fireplace was hidden by a bunch of blanched dried honesty, garlic, eryngium. The pictures (there were four, landscapes in oil with ponds and trees) all shone freshly green in wide gold frames.

Gill invited them to sit. The chairs seemed comfortable, supporting the back. Clark's impression was of money very well spent, but though the room was harmoniously light it gave the appearance of a well-kept museum. One must be careful not to spill ash or drink, not to move a piece of furniture by an inch from the advantageous position chosen for it. He knew his judgement to be unfair, but the room seemed unlived in, unsmirched by a child's or careless hand.

Gillian Wycliffe wore a two-piece of green tweed and a white blouse. Her brogues gleamed and these, like her white hands, were small.

'Where's Ambrose tonight?' Jennifer began.

'Some committee or other.'

'An excuse for drinking?'

'I doubt it. Ambrose has little time for social gatherings outside this house.'

'What about his friends?'

'He has acquaintances. That's about it.' Breath indrawn. 'Now I wanted to see you two because I feel I owe you an apology, dragging you out to view that awful place at Lowton. You must have thought I was mad.' She sounded sane, brisk, officerly, superior.

'Hardly,' Jennifer answered into a far corner.

'In a way I was. Desperate. I felt depressed, oppressed, forced into a corner. I know it's a matter of hormones, but. . . . I had been acting imprudently, and I had paid the price. All this sounds mysterious, and I don't want to go into detail. I'm sure I can trust you both, but in matters of confidentiality one has to be, oh, careful. Now this is very silly.' She slapped her ample thigh with the delicate hand. The visitors sat uncomfortably in silence. 'To tell you the truth, it was a love affair, if anything so unimportant and sordid could be called that, but it ended and I was desperate. I had no idea I could feel so strongly. At my age, my middle age, one ought to be unruffled. But I was like a child, cut to the bone. Shrieking. It surprised me.'

The far-back contralto voice spoke slowly, distinctly, as if

Gillian were reading a lesson in church. All controlled, without breaks, the sentences were handsomely delivered, and the face was untroubled, observing the proprieties, immobile. She might, Clark thought, be reciting a speech from a play, at an early rehearsal, when her main preoccupation was to remember the words.

'I shall say no more than that, but that was the reason for my temporary aberration over Beech House.'

'Forget it,' Jennifer said; rudely, Clark considered.

'That's kind of you, but I didn't want you to think I'd lost all taste.' She sat amongst the choice furniture, under the delicate plaster-work of her ceiling, in the brightness of a chandelier, the lustre of wall lamps. 'Or that you have nothing to do in your spare time.'

'Does Ambrose know about this?' Jennifer asked. Gillian narrowed her eyes. 'The affair?'

'I'm never sure what he does know. He has this vague air, but he's observant and can put two and two together when it pleases him. He must have seen that I was acting strangely, but that's what he'd expect, I guess. Women act irrationally from time to time. As I was doing, I admit it.'

'How long have you been married now?'

'Eight years. And nearly twenty to John before that. I shall be fifty this year. That seems very old to you, Mr Clark, doesn't it?'

'Not really?'

'Twice his age,' Jennifer said cruelly. 'How old's Ambrose?'

'Fifty. Two months older than I am. But he's always seemed the same. He must have been in his twenties when I first met him, but he's hardly changed. I take it you're not married, Mr Clark?'

'No.'

'Have you considered it?'

'Yes. I suppose so. But it came to nothing.'

'I didn't know anything about this,' Jennifer said, brightly. 'I didn't realize you had a murky past.'

Clark waved her facetiousness aside with a hand, like an umpire signalling four.

'We're embarrassing you now,' Gillian whispered. He wondered why she had dropped her voice.

66

'It won't do him any harm,' Jennifer answered. 'I take it you've dropped this Beech House business?' Gillian nodded, gulped. 'Anthony here works with Hugh Pearson.' Jennifer spoke as though that was a shared joke, but neither laughed.

'Are you enjoying it?' Gillian asked.

Clark began to describe his work, the advantages and drawbacks. His account of the acting of 'Bully' Bottom and friends amused both women. They, mainly Jennifer, pressed him with questions which he answered with real pleasure. He and Jennifer laughed a good deal. Gillian listened, head cocked, but with features set.

'What's the best thing about the place?' Jennifer.

'They have very high standards, academically.'

'And the worst?'

'I don't know how to put this, exactly, but some of my colleagues don't seem to have grown up. Many of the boys, even the little ones, seem more mature than they are.'

Jennifer cross-questioned him closely about this, asked him to redefine his accusation.

'I don't know really.' He hesitated. 'Perhaps it's the environment. At home they might be quite different. But they seem to concentrate on house-matches or half-termly lists as if the fate of the world depended on them.'

'Doesn't it do to take your job seriously?'

'Of course. As long as you see there are other, more important things happening elsewhere, even to the boys.'

Jennifer laughed, shortly, with implied sarcasm, though whether directed at him or schoolmasters in general he could not tell.

Both women cited from their own school-days examples to support his case. Jennifer was especially fluent in her condemnation.

'Not the happiest days of your life, then?' he asked.

'Certainly not, though I enjoyed school. They asked me to do things I was capable of. That was the beauty. I was their idea of success. I could pass exams, and run, and whack a hockey-ball and look decorative in a play or sing in tune. I didn't get quite such an easy ride at home.'

'Weren't you spoilt?' Gillian asked. 'With all those big brothers?'

67

'Not really. They ignored me. And my father was too busy to pay much attention.'

'And your mother?'

'I don't think she liked children. Not really.'

Jennifer spoke ruefully, seriously, killing trivial questions.

'Did you enjoy school?' Clark asked Gillian.

'Yes, I think so.'

Mrs Wycliffe answered as if from elsewhere. From her appearance Clark would have guessed that she had difficulty in remembering whether she had been to school or not. She rose and drew the great curtains against the dark of evening.

'You both know the Pearsons?' Clark asked.

Again Jennifer took the lead. She lacked embarrassment, talked freely, and described an occasion when she and Gillian had accompanied Clarissa and Hugh to a local race-meeting, and the quite furious debates between husband and wife about the placing of bets.

'Clarissa studied form,' said Gillian. 'She was brought up with horses.'

'I think they just enjoyed arguing, getting at each other.'

'Did they win?' Clark asked.

'I can't remember,' Jennifer answered. 'They must have done well enough. No catastrophe, at least.'

'Hugh was always tight about money.' Gillian.

'Was. Is. But I think they enjoyed niggling at each other. There was enough real feeling involved to make it an interesting risk. Like gambling. And they could keep the argument inside bounds, at least while we were there. What it's like at home I don't know.'

Jennifer went on to discuss the place of quarrels in married life and claimed that Edwin, her ex-husband, had no idea of a furious exchange of views. If one opposed him he immediately began to sulk. 'I enjoy a dust-up,' she claimed, belligerently.

'But do you bear ill-feeling once it's over?' Clark asked.

'No. Why should I? We, whoever we are, have rowed, and it's done.'

'And you don't remember the insults you've traded?'

'No.'

'Not even if they hit home?'

'I'm not saying I enjoy every minute, but, no. I recover pretty quickly. I'm thick-skinned or optimistic or arrogant. I've had some real ding-dong battles with my colleagues and my friends, I can tell you, but it's not made much difference in the long run.'

'I bear ill-will.'

'I hate people,' Gillian said.

'Men, you mean.' Jennifer, chirpily.

Gillian was suddenly crying, silently, the big tears slopping down her face. Clark looked in amazement; Jen seemed not to notice.

Here in the warm, elegant, rich room a middle-aged woman wept as noiselessly as a doll. Her back was straight, her mouth trembling as she stared forward. She made no attempt to cover her grief, to scrabble for a handkerchief, to hide her face. She looked towards the noble fireplace, the great bunch of dried plants, the bland landscape in its shining frame, as tears rolled.

Jennifer playing with her glass, at ease, noticed her friend only after an interval. Clark had dropped his head; two women sat with him, one weeping, the other inattentive, and he had not known what to do or say. When Jennifer finally observed her friend, she did not immediately move but considered her course of action. Her eyes met Clark's wide and puzzled; they were intensely blue, icily light.

She stood up and walked the necessary three steps and sat on the arm of Gillian's chair to grasp her shoulder. Gillian turned towards her, rested her head on her friend's side and reached up blindly with her right hand.

They sat in silence.

'Well, there, then.' Jennifer's words came slow, as to a small child. She nodded towards Clark, startling him. 'Hand Gill her drink, Tony,' she ordered. He scrambled to his feet, clumsily, he thought, in danger of stumbling, but managed to stand with the proffered glass in front of the two. 'There, there. Take a sip.' She eased the other away from her, took the orange juice from Clark's hand, waved it firmly in front of her friend's face. Gillian heaved herself up, sipped uncomfortably, her eyes glassily large with tears.

'Sit down, Tony,' Jennifer ordered. 'You're in everybody's light.'

He was not, but he obeyed, and toyed with his own gin, not drinking.

'That's better,' Jennifer said after a time. 'Tony, do you have a big clean handkerchief?'

He had and fetched it out, ironed square by Mrs Mackenzie, handed it across.

'Blow, darling,' Jen encouraged. 'Mop up.'

Gill obeyed, sitting straight now.

'I'm sorry,' she said at last.

'Don't you bother yourself,' Jen said gruffly. 'Better out than in.'

'I don't know what came over me.' The voice trembled, comparatively small, uncertain. She now wiped her face vigorously with the large handkerchief. Her make-up, if she wore any, seemed intact. 'I am stupid. I do apologize.' To Clark. 'I don't seem able to control myself.'

'Take another sip,' Jen encouraged.

'I'm sorry, Mr Clark. You'll think I'm cracked.'

He did not answer, kept out of the way. Jennifer had now stood, straightened her crease, looked about.

'Is there anything I can get you, Gill?'

'Nothing, thanks.'

'Are you sure?' With that she resumed her seat.

Clark described the school games on Saturday afternoons, and the way some quite elderly men became furious, rushing around, shouting till they were scarlet in the face.

'Objurgations?' Jennifer laughed.

'I suppose so. And encouragement. Of sorts.'

'You're a very competitive place, aren't you?'

'Yes. In every way.'

'Is that good or not?'

He began to explain the advantages of setting one scholar against another or against some national, high standard. He talked without enthusiasm, and Jennifer nodded gloomily with a wiseacre's face. They were both, he considered, giving Gillian time to recover, if that were possible. Certainly she made no attempt to intervene, and sat too stiffly for safety.

'I think we ought to be off,' Jennifer said. They had been in the house less than an hour. Gillian offered no objection, but led

70

them out of the room. In the hall Clark had to ask for his coat. Gillian fetched it, but was very subdued. She and Clark shook hands; she kissed Jennifer. Everything, movement or word, seemed awkward.

Outside in the warm half-dark Jennifer thrust an arm through his.

'God,' she said. 'My God.'

She jerked her hand violently away, unlocked his side of the car, hurried round, threw herself into her seat and drove off jerkily, unspeaking. Three hundred yards up the main avenue she stopped opposite a long, blank brick wall, and sat wordlessly.

'Are you all right?' Clark asked, in the end. The avenue was not well-lit.

'As ever I shall be.' She sucked breath in. 'Just give me a minute or two.'

He watched a couple approaching with arms round each other. They stopped under a lamp to kiss, then broke up to run hand in hand along the street. They passed the car, skipping now like children.

'They look happy enough,' he said.

She did not answer, or move, but looked out through the windscreen into the shadowed spaces. When she finally relaxed, she raised then dropped her hands.

'That was pretty awful,' she said, in her ordinary voice.

'Not good, no.'

'I wonder what it all was in aid of?'

'Is she not usually like that, then?'

'She's a funniosity, I can tell you, but I've never known her go off at the deep end. She's bi-sexual, if that's anything to do with it, so I can't even tell when the lover's male or female. In my eyes, she's lucky now. Her husband's well-to-do, successful and compliant. She has an interesting job, something to do with the Psychology Department at the University. I suppose she regrets that twenty years as a parson's wife bringing up children and stirring tea, feels that she threw away the best years of her life, but she's more than made up for it.'

'Perhaps it's hormonal,' he said.

'What isn't? But she's plenty of support. They entertain a fair

71

amount, never mind what she says about her husband's anti-social attitudes. She has a great number of friends and acquaintances. She has the money for concerts and theatres. And presumably she has, from what she said, lovers.'

'Without scandal?'

'Eh?'

'I said, "Without scandal?" She doesn't advertise her affairs?'

'Why the hell should she?'

'Some people do, if only to make themselves more interesting.'

'Your experience must be greater than mine,' she said sarcastically. 'I never noticed it.'

He smiled to himself, aware of her vulnerability.

'Listen.' She spoke as if this was important. 'What do you make of this town? City?'

'I've hardly been here long enough. And certainly *my* social life is limited.'

'Will you stay here?'

'For a year or two, at least. Then I shall look round. For headships of department, that sort of thing.'

'Are you ambitious?' She chipped in sharply with her question.

'Not very. Not at present. I'm just learning my way about.'

'Ignorance has never hindered ambitious people yet.'

Jennifer fidgeted about in her seat, uncomfortably.

'Let's go back to my place. This has . . . has upset me. Are you busy?'

'Not altogether. There are some books I could mark. They'll have to be done some time.'

'If you prefer . . .'

'No.'

She drove off, efficiently, pointing out places of interest: a Victorian pub, an almshouse, a group of factories, a medieval church tucked away on the edge of a housing estate. She must be taking a wide detour, he decided. Once home, she almost ran for the front door, marched him smartly inside. She drew the curtains, fetched out glasses, tonic water, gin.

'Our two best generals,' he said. 'Booth and Gordon.'

72

Her telephone rang.

'Help yourself,' she ordered. 'That will be Gilly with apologies.' Though there was a 'phone in the room she took the call elsewhere. She returned after two or three minutes. '*My* lover,' she said brazenly. Clark could not answer. 'Your friend, Hugh Pearson. Look, you've not done as you were told.' She slopped generous slugs of gin and went out for ice-cubes. She drank thirstily. 'Not that I see him very often.'

'Hugh?'

'Um. Yes. The bastard. He's an unsatisfactory man if ever there was one.'

'Why are you fond of him then?'

'I'm not. There's nothing between us now. It was nothing to write home about while it was going on. You like him, don't you? He's handsome, I suppose, but that bloody wife of his has sucked all the juice out of him. She's a harpy. He daren't do anything without her permission.'

'He's quite a power in the land at school.'

'Doesn't that tie up? Ordering little boys around? And he's no ambition, even there. He won prizes at the University, and look where it's got him!'

'A senior master at one of the most respected schools in England.'

Jennifer looked him over, not concealing her distaste.

'Somebody has to do it,' she said. 'The trouble with you schoolteachers is that you don't take risks. You find yourself a cosy little corner and stick there.'

'Is accountancy so dangerous then?'

'You give value for money, otherwise you're out on your ear. When industry was running down a few years back we felt the draught, I can tell you.' She continued in this vein, sourly, as if he were to blame for the world's ills.

'Why did you take up with Hugh if he was such a wimp?' Clark retaliated.

'Why does one take up with any man? I'm not saying he's without all attractions. It passed an hour or two, but we were never going to get anywhere.'

'What did you want from him?'

'Some interest, for a start. What was I? A pretty lady he made love to. An adjunct. That's the sort of damnfool word he'd choose.'

' "No adjunct to the Muses' diadem".'

'What's that?'

'Ezra Pound. "Hugh Selwyn Mauberley".'

'You're as bad as he was.'

'Was? Don't you see him now?' Clark asked.

'Not if I can help it. And he'll be pleased about that. He was terrified that I'd shake him until his trousers fell off in some public place, and the blessed Clarissa would find out. You think I'm getting my own back on him, don't you?'

'It had crossed my mind.' Clark, ruefully. 'He's not connected with this Wycliffe business?'

'Not that I know. Why should he be?' She shook her head as one who'd been violently struck. 'That has me worried. It's like the Clinton affair. What will she do next?'

'Is she a close friend?'

'Yes. I'm fond of her. And I thought I could depend on her. She's always presented a good, strong shoulder to cry on if anything goes wrong.'

'And is that often?'

'More than I want. Or bargain for.'

That acted as a password so that she became immediately cheerful, and described how she had spent her last two days trying to sort out the finances of a small industrial concern, something to do with the manufacture of plastic goods, heels amongst other things. The owners, one an inventor, both workaholics, had been instructed by her how to present their accounts. Her ex-husband had hurried her in at the last minute, because he thought the money side of the factory was 'unstable', and he wanted the whole thing made plain to the owners.

'Why didn't he do it himself?'

'Good question. It wasn't difficult, only tedious. I think he also wanted to see if these two would try it on with me, as I was a woman.'

'In what way?'

'Fail to come up with the relevant information. Bluster. Tell me that this, that and the other couldn't possibly be done.'

74

'And did they?'

'No more than anybody else. They didn't see all the ways of saving or making money. Not that I expected it, but intelligent people think they know, and the short answer is that they don't. That's why they need an accountant.' Jennifer spoke without emphasis. 'My own view is that this is a thriving concern, and Edwin will invest in it himself.'

'Why didn't he do the investigation then?'

'He would have satisfied himself that the firm wasn't likely to go bankrupt, and then let me cross the i's. He trusts me in these matters, does our Edwin. And besides, the actual work was, as I've told you, tedious.'

Anthony Clark sat, watching, concentrating on, the appearance of the woman opposite. She spoke as one having authority, and the smartness of her casual clothes, the posture, the careful modulations of the voice impressed him. She could do what she claimed.

'This town's a mystery to me,' he said. 'Your world, especially.'

'All towns are the same, I guess. This one's about the right size. At present there's industrial expansion and so a chance for Dobson and Lang to make a mark. They're small, and are likely to remain so. Even when Edwin joins their board. But they're doing well.'

'And will continue to do so?'

'In the foreseeable future. One doesn't know. They trade at present mostly in the home market. And they can sell everything they make. In fact they're installing new machinery, to Dennis Dobson's designs. And now they're trying for European and overseas contacts . . . which might well come off.'

'If there's a recession?'

'Theirs are marginal commodities. People need heels, but can only wear one pair of shoes at a time. If money's tight, the firm will find orders dropping.'

'And?'

'Redundancies. Economies. And a hope that there's enough to hang on to until better times. That's where Dennis is so good. He's full of ideas, and flexible. A good firm to invest in at present. Edwin won't throw money away.'

'Has he told you he's going to invest?'

'Oh, yes. He'd know I'd not allow him to waste his money.'

'Why should he?'

'That's what accountants are for. And he'd trust me to make a disinterested and thorough scrutiny. Accountants have had a bad press. We're blamed for stagnation by some. We are only capable of drawing up balance sheets, and don't see that a line which loses money for a year or two now will be a real money-spinner in three years time, say. But that's the nature of the beast. We say what we see. We don't prophesy. How can we? I know no more about plastics than you do. Less probably. That's not quite true. I've been round their factories more than once.'

She laughed. They talked in this relaxed way until eleven-thirty, drinking black coffee. Jennifer seemed pleased with his company, but gave no reason for her pleasure. She talked, fluently, instructively as in a radio interview, with no sexual slant.

He walked to his digs from her home steadily and much puzzled. Neither woman had mentioned, nor had he seen, Mrs Clinton.

IX

Clark received a short note of apology from Gillian Wycliffe and a telephone call inviting him to visit her.

He arrived at the appointed time in best suit, with a bunch of ragged yellow chrysanthemums. The day had been mild and he had used it walking two of the local parks, for it was half-term holiday. He had spent the weekend with his parents in London, where he'd eaten well, sat about with them at table or television set, talked a great deal, slept the three nights at length and had driven back, in rain, after lunch on Monday, saying he wanted to explore his new city. He had rather shamefacedly informed them about the breaking off of his engagement to Daniella, and had been shocked at the abrupt way his mother had tried to comfort him by running down the character of the girl.

76

'She was a flibbertigibbet, Tony.'

'She made me laugh, certainly.'

'You know what I mean. There's more to marriage than a few laughs and a good time.'

'You only met her once.'

'That was quite long enough.'

Mrs Clark had, in fact, gone out of her way to make herself pleasant to Daniella, and to some lengths to impress on him how much she and her husband approved of the girl. But once the engagement was off, the mother had no compunction about blackguarding the woman who had refused her son. Not that he was perfect in his parent's eyes; he had his faults, but not such as to encourage an unthinking slip of a miss to decide to throw him over. Mrs Clark spoke with tight lips. The father said nothing; many years of domestic argument had taught him caution. He had liked the look of Daniella; she was pretty, lively, well-spoken, up-to-date. He had approved Anthony's choice, anticipated his pleasure from the company of this bright young woman. They'd chosen to break it up; they knew their own minds, he hoped, and if they didn't there was nothing he could do about it. Besides, Anthony did not seem exactly heart-broken. Mr Clark hemmed, lit a small cigar and was silent. His wife would take him inch by inch through this in the next week or two; he did not mind. It would give Sheila something on which to exercise her mind or her tongue.

On Monday over lunch Mrs Clark offered her final advice. Her husband was at work and she had her boy to herself. His washing was ironed and packed. There were tins of home-baked tarts ready for the back seat. She had consulted and praised the school prospectus he had brought for her, as well as last term's magazine and the bound elaborate history of the establishment. Anthony had made a good move. He easily guessed what her last words on his love-life would be. 'At a time like this, you have to be careful not to do anything foolish on the rebound.' He nodded and hugged her. His mother was not yet fifty, yet she talked like some aged village wise-woman. He had enjoyed the fuss and the food, but was glad to escape. As he drove towards the M1 he wondered vaguely how his parents had met, and what they had been like. They had married in the first year of the swinging sixties. His mother dressed smartly, was good-looking still, used make-up but seemed a throwback to some simpler age.

Now on Tuesday he stood in Gillian Wycliffe's elegant hall, listening to the strong, far-back voice over-thanking him for the chrysanthemums.

She showed him into the drawing room where a young woman hunched in one of the arm-chairs. She wore black which suited her modern air.

'Anthony, this is Elizabeth Clinton.'

The woman made no attempt to turn her body, but wiggled the fingers of her left hand. Her face was pretty, podgy, heavily made up.

'Glad to see you. Gill's been telling me about you.'

'Since I realized you were coming. Liz's staying with me while Ambrose is addressing some conference in Torquay. We're awash with gin and comforting each other.'

Clark noticed, certainly, that Mrs Wycliffe slurred her words. She poured him a large gin and tonic with ice but steadily enough.

'Liz's husband died a few weeks back and she's been preparing to clear out ever since.' Gill sighed. 'They lived in the Old Vicarage at Wellow, an enormous place. It was ridiculous for two, never mind one.'

'Roger had an office there.'

'Are you living there on your own now?'

'Yes. My solicitor has advised me to hang on until the estate is properly settled, or wound up or whatever you call it. And he says the house is appreciating in value from day to day so I'd be advised to sit about.'

Mrs Clinton's voice was quietly attractive, slightly North Country; she seemed amused at this lawyer's concern for her welfare. Gill sighed again, very uncomfortable.

'My husband committed suicide. I might as well make that plain.'

'I'm very sorry.'

'It surprised everybody.' She was aggressive. 'It came out of the blue. Nobody expected it. I hadn't seen him for a day or two, but that wasn't unusual. He'd go off on business trips, and often fail to come back when he'd arranged.'

'I'd have had something to say about that,' Gill stormed.

'I was used to it. I knew him. I'd been his secretary.' She laughed, to herself, and pulled out a handkerchief to dab her lips. 'He'd stay if he saw any advantage to himself. Or even if he was just enjoying it.'

'He could always have rung you.'

'But he didn't.'

To Clark, who swigged at his gin, both women spoke as if Clinton was still alive.

'He was his own man,' Liz said. 'In death as in life. He deliberately walked under a train.'

'That's a damned silly way to kill yourself these days.' Gill.

'Not to him. No sitting down in a chair with whisky and tablets. He'd walk straight on to the line. End. Finis. That would be more suitable.' Though Mrs Clinton looked away all the time from the other two, her voice was without tremor. She might have been speaking about some unsuccessful gamble her husband could easily afford or which even demonstrated his wealth.

'There was no bloody need.' Gill again, angrily.

'I was with the Pearsons when they heard. Hugh went straight out to see you, I think,' Clark muttered.

Mrs Clinton swivelled round to face him, breathing deeply.

'Yes, he did. He thought I'd be on my own. A little woman. In trouble. Shaking.' She laughed nervously. 'I was. But he wasn't much use. How could he be? I'll not have a word against Hugh. He would hate having to come to see me in those circumstances, but he came. He's very feminine in many ways. Don't you think so, Gill?'

'He wouldn't thank you for that.'

'He's like some back-street grandma nipping round to lay the corpse out or say the word of comfort. It's his duty. It's expected.'

'Those crones enjoy every minute. When I was a rector's wife, by God, they were lining up by the dozen to poke their bloody noses in.'

'Did it do any good?' Clark asked abashed.

'That's the criterion, I suppose,' Gill answered. 'Yes. It did. Sometimes. People at those times even want to see keening old hags. That's why Liz is here.'

79

'Excuse me,' Mrs Clinton said, and walked from the room.

'Waterworks,' Mrs Wycliffe explained as the door closed. 'She's a marvellous girl, she really is. Brave. And insists on coming out plain John Bull with her husband's death.'

'Yes. She spoke out about the suicide.' Unsure of himself.

'I suppose there's sense in it. I don't know. But it's her way. We've both had rather too much to drink this evening. To tell you the truth I'd forgotten I'd invited you round. Then somebody rang up, and I had to look in my diary and there you were large as life. A quarter of an hour later you were ringing the door-bell. But we'd started on the gin. I'm hopeless.'

'You should have 'phoned and put me off.'

'No fear. A pleasant young man will do as much good as the bottle. She has to learn that the world goes on. She lived for that man.'

'Was he, well . . . unusual, outstanding? In any way at all?'

'Good at making money. And he had what you'd call a personality. Big, physically. Energetic. Not very well educated, but quick, clever. He'd taken over his father's building concern, and really made something of it. But he worked hard. When he went out he enjoyed himself, but it wasn't too often for all she says.'

'Nobody seems to know why he killed himself?'

'No, I don't. It wasn't business failure. That I do know.'

'People talk about some private sense of not coming up to the mark?'

'Who's that? Hugh? Or Jennifer? I suppose that they like to make out that they know more than they do. Jen's father had a lot to do with Roger at one time.'

'That's ten years or more ago.'

'Yes. It is. You're not in love with Jennifer, are you?'

'Not that I know.'

'She's a very attractive woman, and as clever as they come. I used to feel sorry for Edwin. He was nowhere in the same class.'

Gillian dissected Jennifer's character, but charitably, saying how much she admired her friend. She then described her first husband, and how shocked she had been at this comparatively old widower-clergyman's sexual drives. He was an expert, an athlete, though God knows where he picked it all up. 'Of course,

I was an innocent, really.' She slapped the arm of her chair, stood as if she had made her mind up, sat again. 'He'd ask me to do all sorts of odd things. "I don't want you to wear knickers at matins this morning." I was aghast. It never occurred to me that religious people, no, a parson, should consider such a perversion, never mind saying it. I'd argue with him, I can tell you. I was young, but I knew my mind. "You should be thinking about God, not my sex," I said. "So I am." "How can you be so hypocritical? When you're praying or preaching or dealing in holy things you shouldn't be thinking about my naked genitals." He didn't turn a hair; he'd explain in his dry way, "You wouldn't mind if I asked you to wear a particular dress because you looked so well in it. It would be a small, earthly, innocent pleasure for me amongst the holy immensities I'm touching on. As this request is." "What does God think?" I'd ask him. "He'll judge me, I don't doubt. But this is venial." "You'll be asking me to dance down the aisle stark naked next," I told him, but he just said mildly, "You know that's not so, Gillian. You know you're exaggerating. And you wouldn't do it." I was shell-shocked, I can tell you.'

They heard Elizabeth crossing the hall outside.

'It's the gin loosening my tongue,' Gillian said flatly. 'Does what I've said surprise you?'

'Yes.'

'So it should.'

They waited for Elizabeth to open the door, but this did not happen immediately. She entered smilingly, graciously resumed her seat to ask, 'Well, have the pair of you sorted me out, then?'

'No, it's Gillian's first husband we're going over.'

'And what's interesting about him?'

'He had his little ways,' Gill simpered, acting up.

'Haven't they all?'

'Was he a good parish priest?' Clark asked, solemnly.

'Yes. Given that now I don't altogether agree with what it is he was doing or believed. He looked after people, acted as a social worker, visited, advised, dipped into his own pocket. And he was serious about the religious side, as far as I could tell. I wasn't exactly interested in that even then. I went along with

81

him. But he thought it important that we should consider our destinies, why we're on earth, where we're going and the rest. Again in my view he had it wrong. I couldn't see the need of a God, especially one who was said to have intervened as a human being. It's incredible.'

'That's what the theologians say, isn't it, that it's hardly believable?'

'But what were his funny ways?' Liz asked.

'Sex.'

'Oh, bloody sex. Are parsons interested in that?'

'They're human beings.'

'Well, I know, but . . . I think I'd be, well. . . . Did you ever have it on Sundays?'

'Yes, we did.'

'That's what I like about this house,' Elizabeth told Clark. 'You learn a great deal here. I knew John Stathern when I was a girl and I thought he was a bald-headed, wizened, dry old stick. Bald men are sexy, aren't they? Roger, he had a good head of hair. It was as well, if it's right about bald men. He needed his oats.' She looked up and about as if she'd just heard some interesting noise. 'I shan't ever get over . . .' Voice and eyes dropped.

'One doesn't.' Gillian. She might have been the rector's wife.

'Do what?'

'Properly recover from bereavements, disasters.'

'Some seem to. They even . . . I knew one woman who found out she was pleased when her husband died. And I honestly don't think she knew she would be. What do you say, Tony?' The voice had picked up again, rattled interestedly on.

'I think I agree with Gill. There's always something there. Some scar. Some embarrassment. Some inability to cope with a situation that reminds you of your tragedy.'

'You're Jen Hope's boy-friend, aren't you?'

'No.'

'I thought that's what Gill told me.'

'I'd be very flattered, but it's not true.' He tried to sound amused.

'We'll wait and see.' Mrs Wycliffe, lightly.

'Gilly'll fix you up, don't you bother.'

Gillian came round with the gin, the tonic and ice, all straight-faced but pleased with her role of rescuer. She made Clark give some account of his early life, his time at university, his first job. Elizabeth confessed to being born in Skipton, though she had grown up in Leeds.

'Would you like to go back there?' Clark asked.

'I've never thought of it, so presumably the answer is no. We've lived in big houses since I married Roger eight years ago. This is our fourth, a beautiful eighteenth-century house in a little park. But he was talking about moving again. He had some share or interest in Blythbridge Manor. . . .'

'Where's that?'

'Up in the north of the county.'

'And you were prepared to go?' Clark.

'When you live with somebody like my husband you live on a knife-edge. I'm as ordinary as they come. My dad's neat little detached would have sufficed for me. I like comfort, and money, within reason. But with Roger your feet didn't touch.'

'Why did he choose you, Liz?' Gill asked, impertinently, the question that Clark had not dared.

'I was there at the right time. His marriage to Sally was breaking up, and there I was in his office, all smiles, curves and efficiency.'

'There must have been dozens of secretaries about,' Gill answered. 'His own and other people's. Why did he come down on you?'

'Come down,' Liz giggled.

'There'd be plenty who'd give him sex in return for a good time, but he had something more permanent in mind for you. Now I want to know why.'

'You mean it surprises.'

'What I mean or don't mean doesn't matter. What did he see in you, Liz?'

'Don't know. I was young. Well, twenty-three. He'd been married fifteen or sixteen years to Sally. They'd had enough of each other. I honestly don't know. He made passes at women. Still does, did. But why he wanted to marry me, I honestly can't tell.'

'Now, Tony. Let's have the schoolmaster's view.' Gill, magisterially.

'I'm as ignorant as the rest.' Clark tried to laugh. 'Proximity, as Liz suggests, would play a big part, being in the right place at the right time. But I agree that there'd be something over and above that.'

'What sort of thing?'

'Something he needed. It might have been pure imagination for all I know. But he considered it necessary. Aren't there some people who consider marriage an imperative, who feel they're not complete without a legal partner?'

'Not so much nowadays,' Gill answered him. 'Was Roger an old-fashioned sort?'

'In some ways. Not always.'

'Did he treat his wife as a chattel? Is that how he saw you?'

'I doubt it. His first wife was a great cook, and really looked after him. But now he was coming round to something more sophisticated. His parties were quite something.'

'And were you responsible for organizing them?' Clark.

'I was. And yet. . . . I was a plain Yorkshire girl. He liked that. Under all the Italian froth and Continental fancy-work I was full of common sense. That's what he said sometimes when he'd had a few. Incidentally it's not anywhere near the truth.'

'Why not?'

'It's ballet, travel and wines that appeal to me. I spent all my holidays abroad once I'd started to work. And I loved books on exotic food. I went to courses on French civilization and another on Continental cookery.'

'And you talked to him about these,' Clark asked, 'before you were married?'

'Not particularly. Not that I noticed, anyway. I suppose I must, as I was interested, but it wasn't deliberate.'

'Not a ploy or a bait?' Gill, stroking her chin. She'd be in trouble one day, Clark decided.

'No.' Angelically. 'I never fathomed Roger. I never fathomed anybody, really, but I worked for him for two years, and then lived with him and slept with him for nearly eight, and yet I've no idea what made him tick. I've just a bundle of certainties, and uncertainties, and changes. Odd, because he'd say, "You know me, Liz, better than anybody." But that's when he wanted me to comfort or fuss him. He was driven by this desire to get on, to be the owner of things, and I guess that was the result of success. He was competing against himself. He liked change. Improvement, he called it. Whereas my father had no desire to shift.'

'Was your father happy?' Clark asked.

'I suppose so. Or limited. Or frightened that if he altered his life-style he'd do it badly and lose the bit of comfort he had.'

'Roger was the exact opposite of your father, then?'

'Oh. In some ways. My father hasn't Roger's ferocious drives. But both of them liked their bits and pieces to be good. In Dad's case it was books. In Rodge's, houses and cars.'

'But he was quite content to stay in this town?'

'Well, county. Yes, he was. It offered him all the scope he wanted. It's the right size. It has everything, hasn't it? What do you say, Tony? You're a stranger here.'

'Admirable. Two hundred and fifty thousand population. Big industrial concerns. Small firms. Plenty of the well-to-do. A university.'

'No cathedral,' Gill said with a surprising gravity.

'Except for the Roman Catholic one. But that's by Pugin.' Clark drew in breath. 'Shops, money, opportunities.'

'Does it match the South-East?'

'No, not by any means. There's more unemployment, for one thing. But I guess that meant Liz's husband had more skilled people to choose from. And property values are rising now, so that anyone into property must be sitting pretty.'

' "We all ought to be as happy as kings".' Gill, solemn-faced, mocking him.

'Except for us poor schoolmasters.'

'Poor, piffle.' Again the gin was poured, the ice dropped from silver tongs.

'Are you going to marry Jen Hope?' Elizabeth Clinton asked.

'I hardly know her.'

'She doesn't bring young men round to her friends' houses usually, I can tell you that.'

'She perhaps is grateful because I visit her father.'

'Perhaps pigs can fly.' Gillian, sharply.

'She'll look after you,' Liz argued. 'She'll not be satisfied to see you muddling along as a poor schoolmaster. What was the name of that boy she had? Crosby? Crossman?'

'I remember him.' Gill laughed. 'He escaped.'

'With his feathers intact.' The women rocked with laughter. 'Don't say we're not warning you.'

'Now just a minute.' Clark felt he must assert himself. 'Who is this man-eater you're talking about? It's nobody I know.'

'Listen to that.' Liz.

'You'll learn. Sooner or later.'

'And if Jennifer is all you say she is, why should she choose me out of all the men in the world?'

'He's asking for flattery,' Gillian said to her companion. 'You're a good-looking young man, very presentable indeed in my book. Presumably the way you think or talk suits her. But she'll test you out and drop you if you don't come up to scratch. So my advice to you is to get as much out of it as you can while you can.'

'Why do you dislike her so much?' Clark asked.

'I don't; I'm very fond of her. I'm just telling you what she's like. Perhaps the gin has made me a shade less tactful than I usually am.'

Gillian laughed out richly at that, pointed a finger.

'All this comes as a surprise to me.' Clark felt as drunk as they were.

'And it won't bring Roger back,' Liz said, in a thin voice. The other two looked at her as she sat with her hands clasped between her knees, elbows into sides, fixed eyes staring ahead. Her stillness, smallness shocked them.

'I'm sorry,' Clark said, stumbling to his feet. 'Is there anything I can . . . ?'

'Sit down, Tony,' Gill ordered. 'Liz'll be fine.'

'I shall never be fine again.'

'Don't you believe it.' Gill strode the short distance to sit on her friend's chair-arm. 'It seems impossible now, but you'll see. It's a waste, I know. Such a powerful figure, and so alive. It's wrong, somehow, out of skew. But you'll come to terms with it, Liz, because you're you. It'll take time, by God it will. And tears. And pain. But you'll do it. And in any case he wouldn't want you to grieve.'

Gillian sounded quite sober, the strength of her voice reduced, speaking her banalities as if she knew that on the twentieth repetition Elizabeth would come to accept them, and even now could dredge comfort from a reasonable voice, insipid sentiments, a humdrum presence. Elizabeth did not alter her frozen posture, did not hear, did not pretend to respond. Clark hardly dared look at the two women, locked in concern, unconcealed anguish, helpless friendship. He wanted to stand again, throw off his embarrassed lassitude, address them as from a pulpit or judicial bench and pronounce them brave, worthy, heroic. That he would not use such words, he knew. They stemmed from a simpler, more naïve age, when motive, the unconscious, the complex could be disregarded for some large, sonorous, misleading half-truth. And yet he admired the women, the one stiff in her grief, the other awkward in her unction.

Gillian was first to move.

'It's a bastard,' she said.

'You're right,' he chimed. 'But . . .' He could not continue; every egress was blocked.

'But what?' Gill in a schoolma'amish parody. 'We have to put up with it, eh?'

Both women looked at him and both were smiling.

'You're good to me.' Liz stroked the arm of the woman beside her.

'Is there anything I can do?' Clark again, helplessly. 'Could I . . . ?'

'The worst thing,' the woman continued, 'is to see the old faces around, quite unchanged, when I know I shan't ever see his again. Hugh Pearson with his simper, Jen Hope with her certainties. Dozens of people.'

'They can't help their faces, sweetheart.'

'I'm not blaming them. They can't help being alive. But they're still here, and he's not.'

The voice, Clark noticed, now had warmth, comforted against the meaning of the words. Gillian had recrossed the room, had found her glass. The talk in the next hour grew easy, though when he said he must leave they made no attempt to detain him. Out in the hall, Gillian took him by the arm and thanked him.

'You did her good,' she purred.

'I . . . ?'

'After a tragedy like that, she feels that no one in the world wants to know her, that she's a pariah.'

'It's not true.'

'It's how she feels it. She can't help what's happened. She played a very small second fiddle to Roger all along, but now he's done away with himself in that selfish, cruel way she feels defiled. You were very good with her, you encouraged her to speak, and the more she talks it out of her system the better.'

Clark suddenly knew unaccustomed, undeserved pleasure.

'You're a marvel, Gillian,' he said.

He bent to brush her cheek with his lips, but she twisted her head to kiss him full on the mouth. She grabbed his arms, holding him hard to the embrace.

'Pick the bones out of that,' she bawled, breaking away to thump him mannishly on the left bicep. 'You're a big boy now.'

She laughed uncouthly and pushed him towards the door.

X

Anthony Clark telephoned Jennifer.

'I'm on holiday,' he said. 'Fancy-free and easy. Let me take you out one evening for a meal.'

'That's kind of you.' Guarded.

'Thursday, Friday, Saturday, Sunday?'

'I'll tell you what.' She spoke in the clipped way she used to clients. 'I'm slimming. I usually am, so I don't want to waste your money on expensive food that will do me no good. I'll take Friday afternoon off, and we'll drive out into the country somewhere. I'll allow you to buy me a cup of tea, I will really. So. My house two o'clock. That gives you plenty of time to stuff yourself at lunch. Otherwise you're going to be hungry.'

'Where are we . . . ?'

'We'll decide that later.'

'Your car or mine?'

'Yours. I'll hate it but it's your treat.'

It did not feel like it. He called in on Mr Stapleton and found the old man lugubrious, even unwelcoming.

'Nothing happens round here. I eat and sleep, and that's about it. Do you play chess?'

'I'm afraid I've . . .'

'Typical. All your generation can do is listen to rock music. Bloody row. No intellectual content. Asked the young woman upstairs if she played, university scientist, Ph.D., the lot, and she stared at me as if I'd invited her to an unnatural act.'

Clark visualized it with a grin. The scruffy landlord, otherwise appearing only on rent-day, shuffling through the door with his proposition as the girl came downstairs.

'She didn't play, really, thank you. She plays that music centre of hers till the plaster drops off the ceiling. Senseless noise, neither tune nor words you can make out. And the news on television is bad, bad, bad all day. Uniformly depressing. Doesn't anybody make discoveries these days? Are we all so stupid? Or is it that they don't report them on telly, that the sadists there only allow gloom and bloody doom through their grid of pessimism?'

Stapleton's philippics rose and fell fluently, serving to console him. He invited Clark into the kitchen where they drank black coffee; the milkman had failed to deliver that morning. Another tirade of invective followed. People had no conception of a fair day's work for a fair day's pay. Clark began to argue.

'The man might be ill. And it must be difficult to snatch somebody out of thin air to take the round over. They work unsocial hours, you know.'

'It may be difficult; it's not impossible.' Stapleton followed up with a series of anecdotes in which he featured as protagonist, heroically taking over work from colleagues who had fallen sick, or gone blithely off to Greece or the Canaries leaving large loose ends. In direct, boastful fashion he described his partners' or subordinates' carelessness, proneness to error, uncertain grasp of the law or even of elementary arithmetic, and lauded his own successful efforts to set their blunders right. This put him into an almost cheerful frame of mind; his voice was strong, his gestures confident, his expression jaunty.

When Clark took his leave, saying half-truthfully that he'd enjoyed the visit, the old man stood straight, made off elsewhere for a shave, though it was now three-forty. From upstairs he shouted so loudly that Clark came running back from the door.

'Have you seen that daft whore of a daughter of mine?'

'Yes.'

'More than I have.'

Stapleton stumped higher, shoulders set in perverse delight at the uncharitable ways of kith and kin. Clark rushed from the back door into fresh air, glad to be out of earshot.

On Friday he rang Jennifer Hope's bell.

'Where's your car?' she asked.

'In the street.'

'Park it in the drive, will you? Out of the way. We'll walk.'

Certainly it was a fine October afternoon, sunny, almost warm enough for shirt-sleeves. She joined him in the drive, wearing a lightweight black coat with a multicoloured scarf. Her hair shone like a helmet. She drew on emerald-green gloves.

'It's too nice a day to be riding in cars. But the fields will be wet, and it's beginning to get dark earlier. We'll walk round the Lace Market.'

They stepped out together. When she asked about her father he recited the old man's complaints and his pleasure in them.

'You obviously please him. He grumbles, God knows, whenever I go to see him, but he grows gloomier by the minute. He enjoys reciting his old stories to you; he thinks I've heard them all, and never had an interest in them anyway. He resents his infirmities.'

'I've noticed that sometimes he walks without a limp and waves his arms about as if he's never heard of arthritis.'

'That's right. But he has arthritis, you know. He's not making that up.'

'Was he a good lawyer?'

They were stepping briskly between large Victorian houses and lime trees on their way to the centre of the town.

'I guess so. He was astute and would work long hours. His firm built up a reputation, had influential clients who would have gone elsewhere if they hadn't received a proper service. But the last twenty-five or so years it was property that interested him.'

90

The shops on both sides of the road shone, and even on this Friday afternoon the pavements were crowded. The Council House Square was bright with people, sitting, striding, watching an old lady feed pigeons; movement outmatched the afternoon sunshine as the gold-faced clock tolled two-thirty.

'This was a beautiful town two hundred years ago,' she said.

'It's attractive now.'

'Too much high-rise, fatuous building. That's our office up there.'

'It must be expensive right here in the middle of town.'

'Oh, it is.'

She laughed and pointed out a magnificent eighteenth-century house, its front spoilt at ground level with two vulgar shop-fronts on either side of the elegant doorway.

'I would never have looked up if you hadn't pointed it out.'

'You'd take me in the teaching profession, would you?'

'They wouldn't pay you enough.'

'I don't suppose they would.'

Jennifer stopped to exchange a few brief words with a smart man in horn-rimmed glasses. He carried a small leather briefcase, and smiled continually.

'Our solicitor,' she explained when they were on their way.

'Your father's office?'

'Yes. Good man. Slow, sure, but he can move when we kick him.'

She laughed at her brutality. Outside St Peter's Church on the pedestrian way a young man had collected a small crowd as he played a Mozart violin concerto to a recorded orchestral accompaniment. He performed with rare skill, his violin singing out into the wide space. They stood, watching his bow-arm and the closed eyes in a rapt face, the moving head.

'Why should anybody as good as that be busking?' she asked. 'He must have had professional training.'

'You never know. Perhaps he's between jobs. Or doing it for a bet or for charity.'

'He must have prepared for it. You can't plug a tape-deck in out in the street.'

'Sure.' He rubbed his chin. 'Or it might be temperament or health. If you're an orchestral player you have to be ready to turn out day after day, however you feel. Some people aren't prepared to do that. He might want to keep shooting off abroad. Or living on social security, and making his beer money this way. Is it legal?'

'I'm certain it isn't. The police can move him on. But I'm glad he's there. A bonus.'

A man in a long blue overcoat was speaking gloomily, waving his hands. Nobody listened or stopped. As they passed he droned, 'Jesus said, "I am the resurrection and the life: he that believeth in me, though he were dead, yet shall he live." John XI, 25. That means you, friend.' He spoke with an almost formal melancholy, expecting to be rejected. He did not raise his voice, but his eyes were open, dark and red-rimmed.

'Gives me the creeps,' Jennifer said, surprising him.

'Why?'

'I don't know. Fancy standing in the street just reciting these texts, these mantras.' She almost spat the word. 'Making no attempt to catch interest. It's an insult to us.'

'I suppose he feels it's the message that's important, not the manner. Besides, you prefer Mozart to the Bible as casual entertainment.'

'As anything else. Who said that? About the resurrection and the life?'

'Jesus, I should think,' Clark answered. 'I don't know.'

'You're as ignorant as I am.'

'Does it matter?'

Now they were walking up a gentle gradient where they stopped in front of a fine eighteenth-century house standing back from the street a few yards behind wrought-iron railings. The buildings either side came up to the pavement, shadowing the flagged yard and the small stretch of grass.

'That would be some notable's town house,' she said, 'with its orchard and gardens.'

'At least nobody has pulled it down.'

She shrugged angrily as if he were responsible for acts of civic vandalism.

'Some beautiful old houses up here,' he argued pacifically.

They moved higher, passing the Lace Centre, once a Unitarian church packed with congregations who were prepared to travel a few miles on foot, carriage or tram-car for a bit of intellectual content in the Sunday sermon, and then at the top of the rise past the City church, a square-towered cathedral-dark structure queening it opposite the Shire Hall.

'Have you been in there?' she asked, at the bottom of the steps.

'Three times in three months.'

'What do you think?'

'It's magnificent. I'm going to spend the whole day inside before too long.'

'Doing what?'

'Looking. Sketching, perhaps. Ingesting, digesting it.'

'By God,' she said, 'you take your pleasures seriously.'

As they walked round the perimeter of the church she talked of the factories, the throbbing of machines, the gas-lit windows, the clop of horses along the narrow streets.

'Would you say these buildings are attractive, or utilitarian only?' he asked.

'I'm only an accountant,' Jennifer answered. 'I find that hard to answer. I can't help thinking of the economics of it all, the money that was being made, the employment, the opportunities, and that makes me inclined to look on these warehouses with a favourable eye. One of my favourite artists worked here as a lace-designer. And the manufacturers driving off in their cabs to their Gothic brick palaces in the Duke of Newcastle's Park. Where Gill lives. Something has gone out of life since then.'

'What about the work-people?'

'I imagine that jobs on these machines would be regarded as superior. You were indoors and warm in better-lit conditions than you had at home.'

'Wouldn't it be noisy?'

'To us, yes. And the hours long. But these drawbacks are comparative. I'd like to spend a day here as it was in the years pre-1914. Merely an onlooker. And so, given that, I tend to regard these buildings more favourably. They are on the whole ugly, but they have a kind of symmetry, formality about them in this purplish brick that appeals to me. And they're not too tall, not skyscrapers.'

'They dominate pedestrians.'

93

'I suppose so. But there's always something interesting.' They'd turned into a side street. The warehouses were now a pool-hall and a night-club. The doors of both places were wide and ornate, flamboyant, more suitable to the present use of the buildings as centres of entertainment than to that of the original commercial practice. Jennifer said as much, but immediately contradicted herself. 'I have been through that door,' she pointed it out, 'and it's very attractive now. But these places were for gentlemen, in cash terms if no other, who wanted to swagger. No slipping through a side-door to a grubby reception desk. They liked the larger gestures. And why shouldn't they? One man built a chapel on to his factory so that his hands could start the day with prayer.'

'Is it still there? The chapel?'

'Yes. I've never been inside. But it's like the Japanese. Don't they often begin their work-day with some sort of communal act, only they praise the shareholders, the directors, the managers and one another and follow up with PE?'

'Is it commercially sound? Getting the troops together?'

'I guess so. And religious services weren't altogether boring to the Victorians. People went to church on Sunday for long indigestible sermons and droning hymns from choice. BC. Before cinema. Before telly. Some even read sermons at one time as they read biography now. And you'd approve of lessons from the Authorised Version, today, wouldn't you? Entertainment had a serious, educational note then.'

'Gin shops?' he asked. 'Pubs?'

'Oh, sure. There are always people who want to opt out of reality, even at the expense of a hangover. I'm not so sure I'm not numbered amongst them.'

She talked on cheerfully as they strolled. She seemed excited.

'These were great days,' she pronounced, 'if only for some.'

'And virtue has gone out of us?'

'Right.' They looked the chapel over, and noted the names of new enterprises tucked into corners of old warehouses. Brick walls were being cleaned, paintwork renewed; large, smart cars occupied parking spaces. 'If you had walked round here a few years ago, you'd have been saddened by the damp and decay. Now it's brighter.'

'Is this the place for renewal? Wouldn't they have done better to flatten it and start again?'

'It seems not.'

'But the high ceilings, for instance, mean huge spaces to be heated.'

'That can be handled,' she said. 'It's amazing what enterprising people can do. A friend of mine has taken a factory and made three colossal flats out of it, one to each floor. He occupies the top, a beautiful place, spacious, almost palatial, and with a view out of this world over the city and beyond. It's quite breathtaking.'

'Yes, but that doesn't produce anything, doesn't manufacture goods.'

'I'm not telling you that somebody should make a housing estate for the well-to-do out of this, another Dockland. My friend makes his money elsewhere. But we have these beautiful, strong, well-constructed buildings, with admirable materials, and it's a shame just to knock them down.'

'Would they do better with smaller, purpose-built factories and warehouses?'

'Many, yes. All I'm saying is that these places can still be put to use. Nowadays we need flexibility, and the floor-space here provides it. I know it costs money in heating and rates, but there are drawbacks to every kind of business venture. And when I walk round here, and see them renewing these buildings, I can't help being cheered.'

'Is that why you brought me round?'

'It's another opportunity for me to judge how things are shaping, and it's a chance for you to learn about the city. It's what establishments like yours don't trouble yourselves with, though you should. You train professional people, doctors, lawyers, yes, accountants, pure scientists, teachers of one sort and another, but they don't provide the goods that keep the economy sound.'

They argued that with a cheerful energy which increased the speed of their walking. He pressed the case of learning for its own sake; she scoffed. Then he made a plea for culture, for quality of life, a rich endowment for leisure. She admitted the principle, but warned him not to forget that these activities depended on workers producing articles others wanted to buy.

She began to jibe; all the schoolmasters she knew, clever, articulate, well-educated men, spent as much time, in spite of their claims, in staring at television as anybody else. 'They don't believe,' she said (they had paused in a narrow street of purple shadow above a long grating), 'their own fairy stories.'

He enjoyed her iconoclasm, said so.

'Do you not think I'm serious, then?'

'Of course.'

'You don't rate poor, weak women very high. I can see that.'

'"Poor" and "weak" are not adjectives I'd easily apply to you.'

Jennifer was ahead of him on the narrow pavement of a short, steep, dark valley of a street. Suddenly she stopped, laid her hands on his upper arms.

'Tony,' she said, broadly smiling, 'would you consider marrying me?'

'Now I really don't know if you're serious.'

'Try to answer the question.'

'You're very attractive. Any man would tell you that.' Clark felt at a loss. He'd enjoyed the unusual hour with her, but had no intention of making a fool of himself. He had invested too much emotional capital in Daniella to commit himself now, even if this was only her idea of a joke. 'I will tell you so.' He tried to keep the tone light.

'Anthing except "yes" or "no".'

'I don't understand your intention.'

Their pace had slowed; he was up to her shoulder.

She had walked him round this place and deployed arguments that curiously combined romanticism with hard-headed kitchen economy. Jennifer had prowled in the narrow streets between these dark-brick mills a colourful, scented figure, laughing, speaking with a quick clarity that left him baffled. He had never been sure that she had not been amusing herself at his expense. That he did not mind proclaimed her attraction. It was a pleasure to accompany her on narrow pavements, historical parentheses, flights of fancy, economic or monetarist banalities, but now she had laid hands on him to put, to pop her question. He guessed it to be a result of her high spirits, and wished he knew what had made her so animated.

'Don't worry,' Jennifer said. 'I'm not going to seduce you here and now in public.'

'I can only answer that I hadn't even tentatively considered the possibility of marrying you.' That sounded boorish.

'Tentatively? Too old? Too unattractive? Too experienced? "Thy exquisite reason"?'

'*Twelfth Night*,' he said, pleased for a moment's reprieve. 'From a drunk to a fool. Someone considers marrying when he, or she, believes the other party might entertain or see advantage in the proposal, the match. You seem, if I may say so, and I might be wrong because I don't know you very well, very self-contained. You have a job you like, and interests. You've been married and can see the drawbacks. I'd put you down in my book as satisfied with your present arrangements.'

'You're a little sober-sides, aren't you?' Bitterness etched her words.

'Be that as it may,' he used the pompous phrase, seeing advantage to himself, 'I never looked on you as one in need of matrimony to anyone, let alone me.'

'Um.'

Jennifer marched off again, he two yards behind. Her footsteps clacked between the high buildings and she did not look back. They rounded the long black east wall of the church, where she paused, crossed the road, stopped again to stare upwards at the chancel, nave, tower impressively hugely black against the brilliance of the sky.

A man appeared from one of the small entries on their side.

'Well, well,' he said. 'I hope you haven't come to examine my books.'

Jennifer made rapid introductions. Clark didn't catch the name: Dick Eames, Evans. He shook hands; the man was stout, but made of iron. He'd be in his forties but wore a smart denim suit. His curly hair had been cropped short.

'It's bad about Roger Clinton, isn't it,' he said. 'I can't understand it.'

'Nobody can.'

The man shook his head, blowing his lips out.

'I thought something might come out at the inquest, but no. His affairs are all A1. It's a bugger.' He rubbed a hand over his crown. 'You should have married him, Jen. He was keen enough at one time, after his first finished. Still, you wouldn't have stood for his hanky-pank as poor . . . what's her bloody name? . . . Geraldine did.'

'Elizabeth.'

'Who? Oh, his wife. Yes. I knew it was some bloody thing.'

'And I was married to Edwin at the time. So much for your theory.'

'Christ Jesus.' The man grinned at Clark, genuinely amused. 'That's just the way she gets after me at the half-yearly audit. Which figure do you mean? This one or this one? As if it mattered. I suppose you're one of her understrappers, are you? She's too honest for guileless old rogues like me.' The man stroked Clark's bicep with a rough unconcern. 'Can't stand here all day. Got my living to earn. Drop in for a drink one of these days, Jen. Tonia'll be glad to see you.'

He stepped into an open-topped Jaguar xjs, waving a powerful, podgy hand.

'How old do you think he is?' Jennifer asked, when the car had drawn away.

'Oh. Between forty and fifty.'

'He's sixty-three. Another of my father's associates. He's just remarried: a girl not half his age. His first wife died, of cancer; his second was killed in a speed-boat accident. And then two or three years ago he married . . .' She looked about her for eavesdroppers.

'His secretary?'

'No. His daughter's bridesmaid. They were at school together.'

'And is he happy?'

'Who is? He's the sort of chap who wouldn't show it. He has this blunt, cheerful front, but I guess he's thoroughly devious. Not to say wicked.'

'Why are you all so concerned about this Clinton chap?'

She paused outside the Shire Hall. Two gowned barristers stood on the steps in conference.

'Fear, probably. Roger was one of the successful ones. He made money because he worked hard, was sharp, knew where to go for good advice. And then he walks under a train, and I suppose we all ask ourselves, if it could happen to him, why not to us. We're a cagey lot.'

'And why's that?'

'It's the time and place. Those who go to the wall, and there are plenty, kick and scream and we hear them. Those who don't can barely believe their luck. In this place we've managed not too catastrophically even in the bad periods. Our unemployment rate hasn't been too dreadful. We've not done so well as the South-East, but now we think we're beginning to catch up with them, and we start to wonder how long it will all last. There's a feeling that our wealth and expansion don't depend on our assiduity or acumen, but on outside influences, on wars and rumours of wars, on political decisions that are not even made by our government but abroad by people who owe us nothing. So we, and I include myself because my pretty little income depends on the success of the industrial magnates, are always glancing over our shoulders for the next bit of bad news. And now perhaps we, they feel that Roger had prior notice and so closed his book.'

'I hadn't realized what sensitive plants. . . .'

'There have been some bad crashes. People in business borrow in a big way. You think you're splashing out with a mortgage or your plastic cards, but that's nothing. I've seen perfectly good profitable lines suddenly stop selling because, oh, the exchange rate makes them too expensive or some chauvinist government slaps a tariff on them, and it needs time to readjust and reorganize and the debt is too heavy to allow it.'

'You sound pessimistic.'

'No. There have been some really hopeful signs, but we can't guarantee that today's conditions will last. Of course, they could change to your advantage, but if you're walking a tightrope you don't count on it. Good fortune could topple you.'

They were now almost into the centre of the city, walking with tall, self-important Victorian buildings on their left and the Portland stone of the Council House on the right. Shops tastefully paraded their wares as singletons, a coat, a frock, a cluster of two or three hats until one longed for the vulgarity of the crowded jewellers' windows, the crammed windows of the multiple stores, even the jumbled quaintness of down-market antique shops.

'Are these making a profit?' he asked.

'That one is.' 'Marie', in old gold lettering, with a cream dress of simple cut behind the polished plate-glass. An oil painting of clouds and a pond in an ornate frame occupied one white wall. 'I do their books. They manage very nicely, thank you.'

'Do you patronize them?'

'Not often. But they know what they're about. It's run by one woman. Her husband's in the rag-trade. I'm a bit of a Marks and Sparks off-the-peg buyer, on the whole.'

They reached the town centre. Traffic seemed more frantic, crowds thicker but more volatile, breaking and re-forming.

'They're all in a hurry except us,' he said, laughing.

'Last day of the half-term break and the mothers are trying to fit it all in.'

'Where do you suggest I treat you to this cup of tea?'

She stopped, and people eddied round them.

'Our best bet is to have it in my flat. I can guarantee the taste and strength and there'll be no rush.'

'Are people just coming out of work?' he asked.

'It's a bit early, but you never know. Plenty of offices work on flexi-time. It really is crowded. Breathe deep; push on.'

Jennifer took his arm and they made progress out of the Square and uphill towards the Castle.

'This is the Norman part of the city,' she said. 'The Lace Market was Saxon, but I suppose you know.'

'I did, actually. Why wasn't there a Roman settlement here?'

'Chance. There used to be a great piece of wood in the castle grounds that was said to be part of a Roman bridge. Perhaps this district was thinly inhabited, didn't need a strong point.'

'Why?'

'You have me there. They had a fort on the Fosse Way not too far off. Just don't know. I wonder if they could sail up the river. I'll do some reading. Or you can, and tell me.'

They were now beyond the wide inner by-pass with its tally of skyscraping hotels an its islands and dwarfed trees, and were walking at a more leisurely gait past the Castle and into the Ravine, a cutting into the Park.

'Thank God it's quieter here,' she said, still holding his arm.

'Now I would have guessed that you would have enjoyed the traffic and the rattle.'

'Why, for God's sake?'

'Up-to-date, modern, go-ahead.'

'I see. I'm just thinking about what you said about knowledge for its own sake. Is there any advantage in knowing Greek or Shakespeare, apart from doing quizzes or *The Times* crossword?'

'You can't just sit in school learning to do what you'll do at work, because that might not take long, and secondly you don't know what it is you'll do. That's the case with unskilled jobs, never mind anything else. So there's much to be said for settling down to acquire vast tracts of knowledge or the keys to that. It sorts out the idle, for one thing.'

'What about interest?' Somebody could easily find grammar or long division dull, whereas they could be relatively bright about biology or craft work.'

'Agreed. That's why we have choices. I'm not saying we have exactly the right subjects. Society changes, and so must education. But I have this feeling that teachers must start up interests, give pupils a basis of knowledge worth developing even though it might have nothing to do with earning a living.'

'But schoolmasters often have closed minds,' Jennifer argued. 'If you know who Thersites is, you're in; but iron pyrites, no. Greek, that's knowledge; geology, ignorance.'

'That's partly tradition, but you could argue that the classics and literature deal with human beings, with matters that concern us every day – love, death, relationships, meetings, partings, pains and pleasures. When there's an earthquake people listen to geologists, and very interesting they are, but they are in the margin of knowledge, if that's not too condescending.'

'Couldn't you say the same about the law of gravity?'

'I'm not claiming it's unimportant, or that we shouldn't know something about it. We should. We accept it, use it, ignore it at our peril, but it won't occupy us in the same way as humanity and its concerns do.'

'You're a serious young man.'

101

'I'm ignorant. I know that.'

They were walking uphill in a street of thick-boled lime trees; potholes disfigured pavements and road, but the great houses, well back in the gardens behind high brick walls, were in first-rate order. The incline and their speed – they seemed to race against each other – made conversation difficult. Both were warm and excited by the time they reached Jennifer's flat.

They drank China tea and ate arrowroot biscuits.

'I've enjoyed our little outing,' Jennifer said. 'Did you?'

'Very much.'

'Good. I talk too much. You see, I'm most unsure what we should do with those warehouses. We nearly moved our firm up there.'

'Why didn't you?'

'Lethargy,' she answered, laughing. 'We're too busy to uproot ourselves.'

'Should you have done?'

'I think so. It would have cost us money, but we should have recouped inside five years. Those won the day who argued for the advantages of centrality, not always obvious to me.'

He suggested when they had emptied the teapot that they go to the theatre or a film.

'No,' Jennifer said. 'I shall have to shoo you away now. I've several hours' work to complete before Monday, and I'll make a start, if not break its back tonight.'

Disappointed, he could not help asking, 'Why did you take the afternoon off if you were so busy?'

'You'd like me to flatter you, would you? I wanted to talk to you and have your company. And I did, and I enjoyed it, every minute. And I hope you'll ask me again.'

She allowed him to dry the cups and plates, then escorted him to the front door where she kissed him on the cheek, squeezed his arm and left him on the wide steps, at a loss.

XI

On the same Friday evening Clark received a summons to dinner the next evening from Hugh Pearson, who apologized for the short notice saying that he and his wife had been abroad for a few days.

'It's just a small party. Clarissa's never happy except when she's organizing somebody or something. I wasn't sure whether you'd be here or not, but Jennifer Hope told me you were.'

Clark arrived with a carefully chosen bunch of flowers and a bottle of claret which Pearson inspected and appeared glad to receive. The visitor was unsure about the giving and receiving of gifts on these occasions. He had walked here, not too far, so that he would not be the first, but nobody else had arrived. Host and hostess made him welcome, provided him with sherry and an easy chair. Hugh handed him an eighteenth-century copy of *Spectator* essays, and Clark flicked through the yellowing pages, pausing at Addison's comments on recitative, the accentation of European languages and its effect on music. The chair was comfortable, the wine good; he was left alone in comfort. 'This is the way to spend your Saturday evenings,' he informed himself.

The Pearsons' house was not ostentatiously large, but well looked after and warm. The pictures seemed to have originated in some grander establishment and took up too much wall-space, were too ornately framed. Furniture was dark and heavy, but relieved by a great variety of house plants all of which flourished. Clarissa Pearson looked in on him for brief words, thanked him for his flowers and presence, rushed back to her kitchen. She wore an elaborate lace-edged pinafore almost as magnificent as her dress. Gill Wycliffe and her husband arrived to much bell-ringing, door-banging and the metallic bray of high-class voices. Hugh ushered them in to Clark's room, made introductions.

Ambrose Wycliffe was a tall, bold, straw-haired man who did not quite manage to fill his well-tailored suit. He spoke without emphasis, in direct contrast to the hearty bellowing of his wife and Hugh's quietly confident delivery. They seemed to be communicating from the far sides of a busy indoor riding-school, while Ambrose, grinning emptily, sat down as uncertainly as if he had come to the wrong house.

'Liz Clinton only went back this morning,' she bawled.

'How is she, then?' Hugh asked.

'That's it. How is she? What would you say, Ambrose?'

'Lost.' He showed his teeth. 'Stolen or strayed.'

'She's not too well, then?' Hugh, abstractedly. 'You should have brought her up. We'd no idea she was with you. We come chasing back from Paris, and Clarry says, "Dinner for a few friends, while you're still on holiday, and in the mood." I think she wonders if she can manage it.'

'I know how you feel,' Ambrose ventured.

'You like visitors. You know you do. He's been making eyes at Liz all the week.'

'I've been out, away, working like a dog.'

'A good job,' Gill answered him. 'Or I wouldn't have answered for the consequences.'

Hugh led Gillian, at her importunity, off to the kitchen. Ambrose, handling a large gin, said he was sorry to have been out when Clark had called.

'Is this a busy time for you?'

'All times are busy. And now I'm old enough or mad enough to get involved with the RIBA and local societies, so if I'm not sitting bored at committee meetings in all quarters of the Midlands, I'm haring down the motorway.'

'Do you not find it congenial?'

'No. But somebody has to do it, and so it might as well be a man with his head screwed on the right way. Me, in short.'

His smile became more toothily asinine.

'I see.'

'I take it Jen Hope is your partner this evening?' Ambrose, coughing slightly.

'That's news to me.'

'That's the impression I had from Gill, if I was listening properly. She brackets you two together, rightly or wrongly. I guess she's a bit envious.' Ambrose spoke with enormous diffidence now, as if the topic was only marginally interesting. Clark said nothing, determined not to commit himself. The other man, undeterred, embarked on a long-drawn-out, inconclusive anecdote which, as far as Clark could judge from the unemphatic asides and the muttered narrative, purported to show how foolish architects could be on the subjects where they had expertise. As the man talked, Clark thought him shrewd, calculating, puffing out this colourless small-talk as he summed up his companion. Wycliffe would make a nasty enemy. The voice dribbled on.

The door-bell pealed and Hugh Pearson greeted Jennifer in the hall, showed her after a time into the drawing room. She was dressed strikingly in a short black and red dress which left the shoulders bare and was certainly not from Marks and Spencer. Had she worn a tight black hat she could have been Columbine. Both men stood; she refused to drink and sat neatly.

'Where's Gill?' she asked.

'Giving Clarissa a hand in the kitchen.'

'How are you, Ambro?'

This led to another low-key account, this time of a professional quarrel over the design of a school. Jennifer questioned the architect sharply; Wycliffe answered at ease. Neither made any attempt to include Clark in the conversation. Pearson appeared again to order them into the dining room.

'Where's Deirdre?' Gillian enquired, bustling in with soup-plates.

'Upstairs. She won't appear.' Clarissa ladled from the tureen.

'Did she go to France with you?'

'She did not.' Grim.

'My, Jen, you look stunning. Don't you think so, Tony?'

The soup quietened them. The roast lamb was delicious. Gillian had kept up a kind of banter all through the main course. Clark noticed that neither she nor Jennifer drank wine, and that Hugh Pearson was already the worse for alcohol. He seemed to hesitate, in action and speech, and frowned as if he had lost his glasses or his head ached. Clarissa queened it as she served. The conversation concerned mutual friends, locking Clark out. Nobody appeared to notice. He, sitting between the diligent Clarissa and the loquacious Gillian, ate more slowly than usual, masticating, putting his knife and fork down, lifting his glass with infinite care, making no attempt to intrude or impress. He felt uncomfortable. Hugh was now deeply into a story, mainly in French, about some incident on their holiday. The table roared at the climax, which Clark did not understand. He laughed with the rest. Ambrose attempted to cap this with some long-drawn-out history of a Corbusier building and Mediterranean weather. This lasted until the pudding; the two older men laughed loudly, beyond measure, flushed with wine.

Clarissa swooped on Clark in a quiet interval.

'Do you remember Helena Noakes? You met her here.' He did.

'Fair. Hair in a bun. A solicitor.'

'That's right.' Clarissa wheeled away from him. 'Her husband has cancer.'

'Badly?' Ambrose.

'Can you have a good cancer?' Hugh laughed ridiculously loud.

'They've started him on further treatment this week. Radio-therapy, I think.'

'Has he been ill long?' Clark, now in.

'Well, he's had an operation. Not too long ago. Can't be.'

Clark did not remember him at the barbecue, said so.

'I don't think he was there,' Clarissa answered, 'but we didn't know he was ill. He was a very good cricketer, wasn't he, Hugh?'

'Oh, yes. Blue at Oxford.'

They disposed of the invalid, and Gillian questioned Clark about his skill at sports. Hugh mentioned that the young man was an excellent swimmer.

'You never told me that,' Jennifer said, her first remark directly addressed to him.

'You know very little about me,' he answered stiffly.

'That's quite true.'

Clark watched the company with care. Gillian led the talking, interestingly, never short of a lead. Clarissa sat larger than life, encouraging Gillian as if she were a trusted servant: Hugh and Ambrose were willing to be amused and to amuse each other; Jennifer seemed subdued, as if she wished to be elsewhere, quite at variance with the brightness of her hair and clothes. She and Clarissa spoke equably one to the other, though he remembered Deirdre's remark that Jennifer was *persona non grata* here. Ambrose was now telling how he had once played the organ in St Paul's Cathedral.

'That's rather a public place for a practise, isn't it?' Hugh.

106

'I didn't play loud. Or anything beyond my capabilities. I couldn't manage it at all now.'

On the way out to the drawing room Hugh Pearson dropped and broke a plate. His wife appeared from the kitchen.

'I guessed it was you,' she said.

'But smiled in case it wasn't.' He snarled suavely.

Hugh and Ambrose took brandy with their coffee, Clarissa Drambuie; Clark already dizzy with a surfeit of table wine, joined Jennifer and Gillian in abstinence, earning a rebuke from Ambrose.

'I hate it when you youthful puritans put us aged hedonists in the wrong.'

'One more glass of that brandy and you won't know the difference between right and wrong.' Jennifer.

'I have great difficulty now.'

Clarissa questioned Clark about his impressions of the town. Was it as he expected? In what ways was it better? Did he like the people? Would he be prepared to spend the rest of his life here?

He answered soberly enough, won favour. He talked about his trip with Jennifer to the Lace Market. She brightly joined in.

'The trouble with that place,' said Ambrose, slowly, in slight, drunken difficulty with consonants, 'is that it's become popular. Rents are rising. Landlords who bought a few years ago on spec, at rock bottom, are making a packet.'

'As they deserve.' Gillian.

'And are they going to kill,' asked Hugh, carefully enunciating his words, 'the goose that is laying their golden egg?'

'A possibility. Jen's father and Rodge Clinton had a fair-size holding there. They bought when the buildings were nearly worthless.'

'Did they foresee the present development?' Clark.

'Ask Jennifer.'

'I can't answer for my father, but I greatly doubt it. They might well have had some scheme of their own on hand, but just happened to be luck.'

'You don't give your poor father much credit?' Hugh.

'He's good with his own affairs, or was. And would have

hedged himself round against disasters, but I don't think he would have guessed with any accuracy what would happen there. I may be wrong. I may be underrating the man.'

'Why don't you ask him?'

'I don't think he's all that interested now. And I'm sure I'm not. Besides, I doubt whether he'd bother to give me an answer. We don't . . . I'm not giving away secrets . . . altogether hit it off.'

'It surprises me,' Hugh said, 'that he's lost his interest in his financial affairs.'

'My father and my grandfather both spoilt the end of their longish lives wondering how to keep the estate up,' Clarissa affirmed quietly as if to smooth a quarrel. 'Death duties and inflation and the ruinous wages one had to pay for the most menial tasks, even then.'

The hostess talked at length, the first time this evening, and to some effect for Clark found himself feeling sympathy for the noble lords in their troubles.

The Pearsons had seen a Racine play, *Phèdre*, and an amateur performance of Alfred de Vigny's *Chatterton*, extraordinarily good, during their short stay in France. They compared French acting and direction with English, and Hugh quoted at length a speech from Corneille's *Le Cid*. His voice had a remarkable strength and timbre in French, and he seemed moved. Clarissa nodded and said that when Hugh retired, the sooner the better, Deirdre would be off their hands and they'd retire to France.

'For good?' Clark asked.

'To live and die there. Unless, well, unless. . . .'

'You don't like Beechnall?'

'No, not if you press me. I've spent more time here than in any other place now, and I've had enough.'

'Why didn't you move?'

'Hugh was happy, well, comparatively. The schools did the children adequately. We found interests. We were cushioned.'

'What do you say to that, Hugh?' Gillian asked, intervening.

'It's exactly right.' His voice was sharp now; he had abandoned the drink-ridden slur or the high rhetoric of France. 'We haven't achieved a great deal. Our family has been brought up; I've made a fair job of my department, kept standards

108

higher than in most equivalent institutions, but it's a small puddle.'

'But not muddy?' Ambrose asked.

'I wouldn't even claim that. I've done about what was to be expected. When I was Tony's age, or a bit younger perhaps, I felt capable of anything, everything. Now I know that it isn't, wasn't so.'

'What had you in mind?' Ambrose pressed.

'I don't suppose I could have changed the world. And if I had been more ambitious and moved into administration, become a headmaster or a director of education, then I'd feel equally unsatisfied now. At least in the classroom I actually achieve a good result or two, whereas at best as a head I'd only have made it possible, or easier, for somebody else to do the classwork satisfactorily. It wouldn't have suited my temperament. I've not done as handsomely,' he paused on the word, 'let's call it academically, as I should. I've produced a few textbooks, I'm not ashamed of them, but I could have done more, and of higher quality. No, that's wrong. I could have done the book on Stendhal I've always been playing with. I'm half idle, really, and that's worse than bone-idleness, because you've written something. You've partially eased your conscience.'

'And is that all?' Gillian said.

'No. I've cooped Clarissa up here. Looking after my children.'

'And you.' Gillian.

'And me. When she could have done very much more. Clarry could have made her way in the world. In business. Like her brother. In fact he wanted her to join him just after we left university, but no, we were in love, we must marry. We knew best. And so instead of being a millionaire she's a school-master's wife in a provincial town.'

'Is that right, Clarissa?' Ambrose, mischievously solemn.

'I sometimes think so,' Clarissa answered, 'but I should have married someone in the end, anyhow, and it would, I suppose, have been different. But,' here she paused, 'I look sometimes at Sidney's lot. Especially when I'm feeling down. He's inherited the title, and has the money to keep the estate up for one more generation, but he's never there to enjoy it; he lives in London, and he works himself to death, and he's been married three times because he can afford divorce. His children compare unfavourably with ours, and there is this, oh, element of culture in our home. Sidney has access to more concerts and theatres, both by proximity and by bank account, than we have, but I guess we see and hear more than he does by a long chalk. And ideas come up and are occasionally discussed in this house.'

'There's no idea more interesting than money,' said her husband.

'That's because you've never had enough of it. The marvellous thing about the artistically inclined, people like you for all you say, is that everything or everybody else seems more important or fascinating. They live through the frustrations caused by what they think they lack.' Clarissa laughed, slightly hysterically. 'Is that true?'

'Ambrose?' Hugh, pleased with himself or Clarissa.

'Absolutely. Never satisfied. That's your artist.'

' "For ever roaming with a hungry heart",' Clark quoted.

'Exactly,' said Ambrose. 'Especially in my little trade. The trouble with architects is that they tend to repeat. Originality is troublesome. In my view our greatest twentieth-century architect is Lutyens, and he cloaked his originality. But we . . . on the whole . . . we . . .'

'If Ambrose is about to start denigrating his own profession then it's time we went home,' said Gillian. 'Besides, it's late. I've never met such slow eaters.'

'Except your first husband,' Ambrose smirked.

'He wasn't an eater at all. He played at it.'

The party did not break up, but continued with a discussion of health food, unit trusts, childhood memories, indoor plants, air travel, Brazil (where Ambrose was to attend a conference), the teaching of languages, the function of the police. Clark said little, surprised that they did not expect him to speak. Exchanges were quick, never quarrelsome though occasionally malicious; they often dropped a subject at its most interesting point. It was, Clark decided, a kind of demonstration of friendship, clannishness; each enjoyed the company of the others, but would have done so without the assistance of food or alcohol.

They stood about in the drive, talking with force as if they had met only minutes before after a long interval. Midnight struck from the Council House clock. When the Wycliffes and Jennifer Hope offered lifts to Clark he refused and strode off through the warm October darkness far from pleased with himself.

XII

Clark was glad to be back into the routine of school.

He thanked Pearson (he had written a note to Clarissa) for his hospitality, but his senior thanked him in return. The man looked far from well, with dark pouches under his eyes, his cheeks drawn.

'It does us good to have some young people there. We're interbred. The same few friends going over the same old topics. It doesn't do.' He turned away, then back suddenly. 'Are you and Jennifer getting on well? She seemed subdued.' Pearson rubbed his cheek with embarrassment. 'I'm fond of Jen. She has a great deal going for her.' He walked quickly towards his classroom. Clark thought the man would have been easier saying what he did in French or Spanish.

Gillian Wycliffe surprisingly invited him to the opening of an exhibition on Friday evening.

'Ambrose is in Brazil now, or en route. I don't want to go on my own, and I know Jennifer's away because I asked her if she'd any plans for you.'

'You surprise me.' He spoke almost rudely.

'I don't want to upset her; it wouldn't be worth it. But I could do with an escort. And yours is the sort of male pulchritude which appeals to me.' She mocked him, he knew. 'I will pick you up.'

The gallery was situated on the ground floor of an odd-shaped Victorian house not far from where he lived. Gillian, dressed to kill, parked in what had been part of the front garden, and led him towards an ornate entrance lit by two lamps on the patio. A small, highly polished brass plate, 'Dencos Gallery', was the only advertisement.

111

'Do you know anything about pictures?' she asked.

'Nothing.'

'When you come to buy a house what will you do, then?'

'I shall be so busy paying the mortgage off it'll take me all my time to keep the walls clean and tidy, never mind hung with masterpieces.' She rocked comically. 'I'll come and ask you.'

'What will Jennifer say to that?'

'I'm not Jennifer's slave.'

'Tt, tt, tt.' She clicked at him, and taking him by the arm led him inside into the resplendent light of the hall. A blonde young woman took their coats; a young man in evening dress ushered them towards the wine-table. They helped themselves.

Gillian sipped, grimaced and led her companion on. The exhibition was mounted in a large oblong room off the hall, decorated in a tasteful but darkish green below the frieze. The highly decorated plaster ceiling swirled purely white above them as they helped themselves to a typed catalogue: Paintings by John Worth, R.A., Enid Delaney and Helmuth Wallis.

'Not many by John Worth,' Clark said, glancing down the paper. 'Three.'

'Surprised he exhibits here at all. He lives in London. Has done for some years.'

'By God,' said Clark, 'they're expensive. I'd need the room round 'em for that price.'

'Somebody will buy them,' she said. 'Let's go and find them. Ambrose has two, an oil and a drawing. He's a good draughtsman is Worth.'

They had, however, paused before the first painting in the exhibition, 'Attention, Angels', by Helmuth Wallis, a Professor of Fine Arts at the Polytechnic. It was lightly painted with a great number of crossing or converging straight lines, the intervening small spaces shaded in unevenly and the whole surrounded by a fuzziness of fugitive whites and greys.

'Well?' Gillian demanded.

'It does nothing for me.'

'Do you always take this stance of an unimpressed provincial?' She sounded angry. 'For instance, most of your colleagues wouldn't have said what you did about the price of those Worth paintings. Whatever they thought, and probably

112

they have no more money than you, they'd have nodded and kept mum. They would like to appear able to afford them.' She waited; he kept quiet. 'But not you. And now you dismiss this.'

'Right. I'll smile for you. And do my best to look affluent.'

'There you go again. You and your colleagues would pay several thousands for a car and its upkeep. Is a car more valuable than a picture?'

'You can't go to work or on holiday on a painting.'

Gillian pulled a face, inched on towards the next Wallis, a kind of blue and woolly tangle, a ravel, entitled 'Nocturne'.

'Good at titles, this man,' Clark said.

A stout party with a grey goatee and a pink bow-tie bore nautically down on them breathing out 'Ah' like a mountain sheep. This was the gallery owner, Andrew Kitts. Gillian made the introductions. 'You teach my son in Lower Fourth,' said Kitts, and turned eyes upward to describe the mounting of the exhibition.

'What about the John Worths?' she asked.

'Far end. In all their glory. I've sold one already. The others will be gone by tomorrow.'

'To whom?'

'Jim Warburton.'

'Didn't know he was interested. Good for him.'

'How did you persuade Worth to show?'

'I knew him when he lived here. And I insisted he could charge metropolitan prices. And lowered my commission. Worth it to me; they're an attraction. His agents are sharks, but he hasn't changed much. Quiet sort of man, interested in painting, works very hard. And he's well-to-do now. I set up his first exhibition. Ah. Here's Helmuth. You know him, of course.'

Wallis was as portly as Kitts, more heavily bearded, and thoroughly jovial. He joked about his pictures, his job, his wife's pretensions, his corns. The 'Attention, Angels' was the result of studying vapour trails. He admitted that at one time he would sooner have been a pilot than an artist, but he said he had been found incapable of putting a plane safely to earth. 'Not eyesight, judgement,' he whispered. The man demeaned himself, Clark decided. Nervous and excitable, the artist made out he was attempting or achieving very little. He did not believe it, could not, but felt that he could win social favour by decrying his effort. Clark did not like it.

They were joined by other cognoscenti, no introductions were made, who talked of anything but the pictures. Clark betook himself to Wallis's third, this time a combination of irregular ladders or scaffolding rising from a meadow and set out against an eggshell blue sky. The title was 'Extension'. Two small maiden ladies stared at the picture with him.

'I can't say it's horrible,' said the first, sotto voce.

'It doesn't mean anything.'

'Perhaps it's not meant to. They say a good picture is just as satisfactory looked at upside down.'

'If I thought that, I'd never look at a picture again.'

They glanced nervously at Clark, as if he perhaps were the artist. He assumed a rapt deafness.

'Three hundred and eighty-five pounds. A funny sum. Oh, no, it's not that one.'

'That's three hundred and fifty guineas, dearest.'

'Is it? Dirt-cheap at half the price.' A giggle, hastily extinguished. Clark did not correct their arithmetic.

They whispered on, ladylike, to the next.

The three coalesced again before another of Wallis's lines and coloured spaces. Clark, more interested in the spinsters, stood behind them, ears pricked. All three stared. The right-hand lady turned and, snatching off her glasses, gasped and looked away from Clark. The two shuffled on out of his reach. Talk from the Gillian group increased in volume; there importance resided. They laughed out loud, in the presence of art.

Clark reached the Worth pictures in a place of honour at the end of the room. Each was widely framed in gold, though the largest was only a foot by fifteen inches. The oil paint was rough, heavily daubed on, with a knife or an iron-hard brush, and made little sense from close up. Two seascapes and a low mountain. Clark stepped back a yard or two and the pictures dropped into immediate if unusual sense. He retreated another yard, elbowing a young man behind him in the process. Both apologized, dusted themselves down.

'These make the rest look pretty feeble,' the young man ventured.

'Good frames.' Clark.

'You don't like them, then?'

'Let's say,' Clark tapped his catalogue with his fingernails, 'I wouldn't be prepared to pay this sort of money for them.'

'Oh, I haven't that sort of wealth. But if I had I'd risk it. There's a sort of integrity about these. No show. There's overall design and a marvellous colour sense; and there's vision; he's used the paint to convey that, but something beyond. You can tell there's wind; the clouds, y'know, the breakers, the sea-horses, and it's all moving, in both senses. A painting's static; one second's glance is frozen, but this suggests the next second, and the one after, and one's imagination is stirred, and not only one's visual imagination. Aural. I can hear the wind, because its direction's so precisely caught.' He stepped across to indicate this with his index finger. 'A modern miracle.'

'The colour,' Clark answered, contra-suggestibly, 'isn't realistic, isn't natural, is it?'

'I'd argue that with you. That's one reason why Worth's so good. He sees exactly. Then, of course, he has this marvellous hand to match his eye.'

'You're a painter yourself, I take it?'

'No. Amateur daubs. I'm an architect.'

'Did you know Worth when he lived hereabouts?'

'No. That was before my time. I know people who did. My boss, Ambro Wycliffe, for instance.'

'I came along with Gillian. He's in Brazil, isn't he?'

'Yes. He's away a great deal these days. He's quite a notable in the administration of the profession now.'

'Is he a good architect?'

'Oh, sure. He knows what he's about. Not original, but can spot originality. And that's unusual. He's done one or two good things. Have you seen that little Newcastle library, or an even better one in Frankfurt? And that Catholic church in Kent? Very good of their kind. He was working with a young married couple. She was a genius. Really. And Ambro made it possible.'

All the time he spoke the young man kept his eyes fastened to the three Worth paintings, as if he could not bear to waste one minute's viewing. There was something impressive in this scrutiny, as if he were two people, one talking everyday sense, one lifted heavenwards. He was older than Clark had at first thought.

'And what does he say about Worth?'

'What you'd expect. Quiet type. Lived out of the way somewhere. Made a name with his "Entry into Jerusalem", left for London, and hasn't looked back.'

'Nor come back?'

'No idea.'

The voice was abrupt, putting an end to tittle-tattle.

'You two know each other?' Gillian arrived from nowhere.

'By chance and collision,' said the young man.

'Anthony Clark. Louis Spencer.'

They shook hands, making fun of Gillian.

'What about these, eh? Good?' Spencer asked her of the Worths.

'Give me a moment.'

'I wish I had the money.'

'Yes. I like them. He's not afraid to experiment.'

'Within prescribed limits only.' Spencer laid down the law. 'That's his strength. He's a first-rate draughtsman and an outstanding colourist. He knows which way to turn in the sense that he never attempts the incredible.'

'Is that good or bad?'

'It depends on the man, his personality. Of course there are those who say he's too bound, but there are always critics who'll come up with any balderdash you choose. Worth's a real painter. He sees, takes it in, arranges it in his mind and then brings this enormous talent to bear. And do you know what this talent is? It's putting paint on canvas. There are thousands, millions of ways of doing that, and Worth always chooses the right one.'

Spencer lectured on, caught up in himself trying to understand the effect of the pictures on him. He was excited, though his voice never exceeded a middle-class propriety.

Gillian had joined another vocal group, whooping and gesturing.

Spencer accompanied Clark round the rest of the paintings. He thought little of Wallis, but hoped Enid would make a name. 'She'll never be a Worth, but she has something to show

116

us; more than you can say of Helmuth.' When they reached the end, Spencer shot outside, to return with two more glasses of wine. 'To soothe our ravaged throats while we have another squint at those Worths.'

They pushed their way down the gallery which was now both crowded and noisy. Clark could not see Gillian, who did not obviously need him any longer as an escort. He listened to Louis Spencer's account of Kitts's start in the art-dealers' world, of Ambrose Wycliffe's wedding to Gill. At one point he introduced Clark to Enid Delaney, a small, bird-like woman in a black dress. She dipped and bobbed like a courtier, and smiled, but said nothing, hair slightly untidy.

'I'll come round to see you,' Spencer told her, 'when this is over.'

'Thank you,' she whispered, and darted away.

'What does she do for a living?' Clark asked.

Spencer, still looking at the Worths, explained at length.

Another half-hour had elapsed before Gillian approached him again.

'You haven't been bored,' she said. No question of interrogation about that.

'Interesting. I spent a good part of my time looking at the Worths.' She grinned. 'Under instruction.'

'From Louis Spencer? You could do worse. Clever, thoughtful young man. Are you ready for home? Now you can go straight back to your place, or come with me for a drink. But I warn you, I shall be in no sort of state to drive you back. You'll have to get a cab; there'll be plenty.'

'Which do you prefer?' he asked.

'I hate men who can't make their minds up.'

'I'll come home with you and see your etchings.'

'I'll show you Ambrose's Worths if you're so interested.'

It took Gillian another twenty minutes to detach herself from the crowd. Each time she said goodnight an exchange of information or questioning broke out, most if it unintelligible to Clark, who stood at her elbow smiling brightly.

'Thank God,' Gillian said, once they had reached the car. She drove carefully, pointing out buildings of interest. She and Jen united in their efforts to educate him. Back in her drawing room she poured large whiskies. 'We need this to strengthen ourselves after all that pretension at Kitts's.'

'Why do you go, then?'

'I can't expect perfection. One will find the odd gem amongst all the dross.'

'And tonight's example.'

'There were two actually, but they both need so much explanation to you that it would wear us both out. I haven't the energy.' She had kicked off her shoes and was massaging her feet. 'Would you do this for me?'

'I'm no expert,' he answered, surprised, but knelt down and gently rubbed the grey tights round her feet. She drank half her whisky. His hand moved above and below.

'That's good. A bit rougher,' she ordered. 'Make me feel it.'

He continued his ministrations. She murmured pleasure and thanks. Her position was now abandoned and with her dress high he could see to the top of her shapely, strong, parted legs.

'Don't stop,' she said. 'I'm enjoying this.' There was nothing seductive about her voice; she spoke with her usual horsey brusqueness. He stroked on. 'You're allowed to have a drink.' He rose, took a sip of excellent whisky. She drew down her dress, put her feet to the ground. 'You have the touch. For sure.'

'Let's go and look at those pictures while I'm capable of standing.'

She drained her glass, led him across the hall and into a study. As well as a desk there was a large, adjustable architect's board at which she pointed.

'I hate that damn' thing.'

'Why?'

'It's so big, and modern, and stark. And don't tell me it's useful. He never uses it now. He did at first, but not now. I tell him, "It's a talisman," I say. "Perhaps you're right," he answers, and unscrews it and moves it up and down just to annoy me.'

'Poor old husband,' said Clark.

She took his arm; she seemed shorter still, perhaps because she was shoeless. 'The Worths.'

The painting, an oil, was of a winter wood, three feet by two.

118

Trees leaned, spread branches, bright green in the foreground, dark behind. It had a kind of realism, but seemed dominated by patterns, significant shapes, contours of light.

'It's quite early,' she said. 'Soon after he came out of college. He's good, isn't he? I wish Ambrose'd hang it somewhere else, but no, he hogs it to himself.' Gillian had produced keys and was unlocking a drawer. 'Here's the other thing.' She un-wrapped a folder, and handed him a pencil drawing of a young woman sitting at a table marking exercise books. Sparely drawn, the figure seemed both static and energetic, concen-trated for the moment on spelling errors or mistakes in arithmetic but with a suggestion that the girl would leap up at any moment and swear at or argue with the artist. A title, 'URSULA', in block letters stood above scribbled initials.

'I wish I could do something, anything, as well as that.'

'Exactly.' She smiled. 'Exactly.'

'Did he ever work this up? Paint it, I mean?'

'I've no idea. I've not seen it if he did. You can teach, Tony; Hugh says so. Worth couldn't. Or not very well. Perhaps he'd be better with adults. He could perhaps show interested people how he'd do it.'

She re-wrapped the drawing, closed the drawer sadly.

'Back to the booze.' She led the way. 'I'm fed up,' she informed him over her shoulder as she slopped whisky into her glass, waved the decanter in his direction. He shook his head.

'Why, pray?' Facetious as he could.

'I'm bloody fifty. I'm doing nothing. All day and every day.'

Clark resumed his seat, sipped, looked up.

'This is one of the most beautiful rooms I've ever seen,' he began. 'So is your hall. It's a little gem. Presumably you're responsible.' Immediately he became uncertain; perhaps Ambrose had worked on it.

'So I'm a museum curator,' she said, 'but without a public. When I was married to John, a parson's wife with four children, I was rushed off my feet with parish duties and school journeyings and cooking and the rest. And I had a horse I rode. Every minute was occupied. Some twice over.' She giggled at her own expression. 'But though I had plenty of energy I often felt dog-tired by the end of the day. And I complained. Perhaps

119

I'm one of nature's grumblers. It wasn't what I wanted to do, I'd committed myself to the life, and there I was. Couldn't escape. Not idle; the very opposite.'

'But what did you want to do?'

'There's the rub. I just didn't, don't know. I'm no good at anything much. I ride well, I've been doing that most of my life. I suppose I'm good in bed; John taught me a fair deal there, but by now I'm losing such looks as I had. I don't panic easily. Give me a job and I'll make something of it. I support Ambo, who's a big-wig at his work, and sometimes I travel with him. He needs looking after, I can tell you, but if I wasn't there, he'd manage for himself. And I'm fifty. Life's rushing past me.' She laughed out loud. 'Isn't it bloody pathetic?'

'No,' he answered, 'not at all. But what do you want to do?'

'I've no idea. I started too early on the marriage round. It doesn't pay; not for me, anyhow. I can't paint or write or even garden properly. I supported John as hard as I could, though I hadn't much faith, in any sense. Now where am I? We're well-to-do. Within reason I can choose to live as I like, but I don't know what I want.'

'Friends?'

'Yes. Acquaintances. I'm not fond of anybody, or not very. And they don't ask me to do anything for them. If they did, I should be annoyed. And so I follow foolish fancies, like that Beech House jaunt. Anybody could see that it wasn't suitable. But, no, I chase about, and drag Jen into it.'

'If you were in America or Switzerland you'd be consulting an analyst.'

'I'm consulting you.'

'An amateur.'

'But good-looking, and an admirable stroker of feet. Would an affair be in order?'

'How do I know that?' Clark answered. 'Would it be worth it? How would your husband look on it? Apart from the relationship, you'd have to give all this up.'

'I suppose so. We've been married six years. It's all I deserve. He's not mad keen on sex. He enjoys it, but he can do without it. I guess his sexual energy's always been pretty low. I think I've taught him a thing or two.'

120

'He wasn't married before?'

'No. An old bachelor. He was forty-four when we married. And from that time his career took off. He'd done good things before and built up a strong firm, and so he might have done just as well without my help. I tell myself it isn't so. The fact that he has a wife who can dispense hospitality makes him the right sort of figure to hold responsible positions. That and his other virtues.'

'Who are this man and woman he employs, or has in partnership? Louis Spencer said that woman was a genius.'

'They're the Stockdales. And Emma is certainly very good. I don't know about genius.'

'How old are they?'

'Getting on for forty now. They're both partners.'

'Is Spencer?'

'Yes. He's the anchor man in the office when Ambo's away on foreign assignments or architects' committees. He's good. Talented, I mean, as an architect, not just an administrator. He was responsible for the alterations we made in this house, not Ambrose. And his wife is a nice woman. Shy. Doesn't go about much. Not my type.'

Gillian stood, walked a few steps this way and that on the Turkish rug in front of the hearth. She pointed to the decanter. Comically, stiffly.

'My only friend.'

Now she knelt alongside him and laid her head in his lap.

'Stroke my head, Tony, please. Gently, for a start.'

He did as instructed; she circled his legs with her arm, tightly at first, then in relaxation.

'Thank you,' she said, 'that will do. We musn't get too excitable. Jen wouldn't like it.'

'Why does everybody connect me with Jennifer?'

'Because she's fond of you.'

'She doesn't say as much to me.'

'Does she need to?' Gillian yawned, widely, not covering her mouth. 'You're keen on her, aren't you?' She playfully patted his genitals and stood to resume her pacing of the rug. 'She's bound to be careful.'

'Why?'

'Bad experience. No, not her husband only. She's only just recovering. But you should ask her, not me. She'll tell you in her own good time. You're interested in her, aren't you?'

'She's eight years older than I am.'

'That's nothing. Nothing at all. She'd make you an ideal wife, in that she'd push you on in the world. She's young enough still to have a family.'

'Surely she can do better than me.'

'Why do you say that?'

'I'm a schoolmaster, in a depressed trade, and low down on the scale. Even if I do well, I'll end up where? Headmaster of some out-of-the-way place. I don't want to go into administration or inspection.'

'You, young man, don't know what you want until somebody like Jennifer gets her hands on you. . . .'

'And shapes the inert clay?'

'Exactly. Jennifer, if I know her, doesn't just fancy you either for your bright eyes. I know you're young, and presumably lusty,' Gill giggled again, 'but she sees more in you than that. She's looked about a bit in her time. What I mean is that she knows what's what in her, our, your sort of world.'

'This is all very fine and flattering,' Clark said. He enjoyed this, the whisky slightly blunting his judgement. 'But, but, but. She doesn't say anything to me. Why?'

'Feminine diffidence. Have you said anything to her?'

'No, not in that way.'

'What do you expect? But she goes about with you. She gave me an account of the pair of you traipsing round the Lace Market that made me think of young lovers on a May morning. I'm telling you.'

'Why do you see all this so clearly when I can't?'

'You don't allow yourself. That's the top and bottom of it.'

The conversation meandered on until midnight. She kissed him passionately, rubbing herself against his loins before turning him loose. He walked home singing, not sober through dark streets, the tune that drunkenly repeated itself in his head, 'O Waly, Waly.'

I leaned my back up against an oak;
I thought it was a trusty tree.
But first it bent, and then it broke,
And so did my false love to me.

As he walked he lectured some wide-eyed, imaginary inter-
locutor that one sang the songs of broken love best when one
had first caught the plague. 'Methought it did relieve my
passion much.'

XIII

November brought an early fall of snow, and the back
playground in which the staff and Sixth-Formers parked their
cars was fringed with thin white where wheels and footsteps had
not churned the surface to black mush and puddles. Outside it
was almost dark, and though school had finished ten minutes
earlier people still foraged about in the lighted corridors.

'Ah, Mr Clark.' The Headmaster's voice, rich and steely.
'Are you busy? Or can you spare me ten minutes?'

They walked along together, the Headmaster wondering
whether this early snow presaged a hard winter, a white
Christmas or a mild slush in January and February, the months
he disliked most. He spoke in clichés, but impressively, his
voice as bland as the smooth, grey hair, as polished as the toe-
capped shoes.

'Sit down.' They were in his office, his 'study'. His desk had
been cleared, its green leather top glistening. He sat well back,
legs crossed highly, right ankle on left knee. The silk socks were
unwrinkled, the large white fingers interlaced.

'I'm glad I've seen you. I ought to have spoken to you before
this to ask how you were making out, but reports indicated you
were shaping well, and so it wasn't exactly urgent to talk to you.
I have my spies out.' He smiled, blank and handsome. 'But it's
very necessary to ask the man himself.' He unlocked his huge
hands, placed the fingertips together. 'What do you think of
us? Or, how are you settling down here?' The Head's face,
creased by a smile, showed neither friendliness nor interest; he

stared into the far corner of the study, his appearance hard and unrevealing as a well-polished sideboard.

'I'm enjoying it, sir.'

He never had addressed the Head of his last school as 'sir', but here it seemed proper. Some of the older members of staff called H. D. W. Short 'Headmaster', at least in public.

'Go on.'

Clark compared and contrasted his work with that at his former school. Here standards were higher, people more alert, in agreement about objectives though livelier in discussion on how to achieve these aims. Short listened, smiling, cat-faced.

'Inter-departmental rivalry?' he murmured.

'That's so in all schools. Or at least those which are doing the job properly.'

'You approve?'

'Within reason. I can easily see that it could grow beyond bounds.'

'Does it, here?'

'Go beyond reason? I've no evidence. But I've been here less than a term.'

'Um. I'm not setting you up as part of the espionage system.'

The Headmaster seemed almost sleepy, or preoccupied as he questioned Clark, who answered diplomatically, about the Head of his Department, and the use of drama, about new ideas of teaching, what were the advantages of learning Latin, or poetry by heart. Short slipped from question to question unemphatically, listened politely, once or twice raised crucial objections, was scathing about the teaching of mathematics, his own subject, in the majority of schools, even good ones. Clark admired the cross-examination because it was wide-ranging, thorough, clever and courteous. Short was no fool.

'How do you get on with Thompson?'

'Well.'

'Good. He should be thinking about a move now. He won't make much more progress with us.'

Clark said nothing, wondering if the Head intended him to pass the message on. Thompson did not speak favourably of Short.

'You're friendly with the Pearsons?' The Headmaster pursued his way.

124

'Hugh's been very kind to me.'

'Yes, yes. Of course. And Miss Hope?'

Clark started with surprise. How in hell did he know that?

'I see her sometimes. I met her through her father.' He described the carrying of Stapleton's shopping-bags. Short's expression did not change as he heard his colleague out.

'These people are well-to-do,' Short intoned in the end. 'They're well-connected. Clarissa's father is a baron, not a life peer. Her friend, Mrs Wycliffe, is the granddaughter of an earl. They are also connected in what I could call the aristocracy of money. Like Miss, Mrs Hope.'

'I don't understand you, sir.'

'In what way, Clark?'

'It seems, well, silly, if I put it into plain words,' he stuttered his diffidence, 'but are you warning me off, against these people?'

'Warning? Why should I do that? No. Not really.' The Headmaster stroked his smooth cheeks, no whit put out. 'I'm telling you, for your good I hope, that these are wealthy people. There is private money on both sides with the Pearsons, for instance. Now,' he brought his brown eyes down to the level of Clark's, 'they take you up, make a fuss of you, invite you to their homes. That's not surprising. You're a very personable young man and making, as far as we can judge, a most successful début here. All I'm saying, in the mildest possible way, is that you shouldn't raise expectations too high with them. They'll enjoy your company, but if it suits their purposes they'll just as quickly drop you. Does that constitute a warning? If so, so be it. They may not neglect,' Short smiled, coughed at his word, 'you. I hope not.' He coughed again artificially, a large doll. 'A nod is as good as a wink. . . . But there, that is enough. I've perhaps spoken out of turn.'

His benevolent blandness denied his word.

'I have enjoyed this exchange with you, Clark. We've picked a winner in you, as I knew we had. If at any time you wish to consult me,' he stood, walked across the parquet floor to lift down scarf, topcoat, trilby hat from the stand, 'on this or on any other matter, don't be afraid to do so. Now I must delay you no longer.'

125

Short had opened the door, and waving the young man out into the corridor with gentle, flapping motions of the left hand.

Clark wished him goodnight and hurried away to the common room, which stretched dimly empty. He stared round and shivered.

Why had the Headmaster issued the warning? Clearly he had received favourable reports from Clark's Head of Department, but from whom had the rest of the information come? The young man sat down on the edge of a chair; the caretaker had not yet begun his evening clear-up and the place appeared shabbily littered. No chair stood in place; tables were out of skew; only one bar-light shone. Clark was certain how the unfavoured Thompson would answer his question: the Headmaster felt himself excluded from the Pearson circle, and took his revenge childishly by issuing this unfounded caution. Clark gathered his belongings, found himself standing in the urinal, listless, bemused, mindless, tweaked by vague premonitions of evil. He pulled himself together, buttoned his coat to the collar, made his way out to his car by a side door. In the bitter night he lost himself again, standing by the car door, keys in hand, making no move.

Slightly cheered by Mrs Mackenzie's liver casserole, he marked a set of exercise books and then sat down to re-read Book I of Spenser's *Faerie Queene*. He would not himself have chosen this as an A-level set text, had never looked at Spenser at University, but had inherited this from his predecessor. When he had proposed to change to something else, Maddison, his Head of Department, had quietly demurred.

'I wouldn't if I were you, and I'll tell you why. One, the boys will feel aggrieved that they've done work for nothing. Two, it's a very good examination subject. It consists of plenty of small interesting episodes and the overall aim is easily grasped. You can talk about the Nicomachean Ethics or holiness or temperance and abstinence or whatever, Greek names and all, and it suits our types. Put them on to D. H. Lawrence or Virginia Woolf and they're more puzzled. They like their good and evil in small, digestible gobbets, at least for examinations. And if they have a seasoning of symbolism, allegory, dark conceits to sprinkle they know where they are.'

126

'Don't they with Lawrence? Know where they are?'

'No. Nor will you, I suspect. Nor will the examiners.'

Clark read in front of his hissing gas-fire, only half concentrating. He had a quotation from Dryden to hand for an essay now that his pupils were well launched: ' "For the rest his obsolete language and ill choice of his stanzas are faults but of the second magnitude." Discuss.' He wondered what the boys made of the Red Cross Knight. Did they approve of a hero who was not constantly victorious, who himself needs rescuing, who is put to training in a hard school? One pupil had already argued in favour of a Batman figure, always ready, never at a loss. Clark had argued that Spenser's approach was nearer life, that even the most gifted needed help or instruction. His class had seemed removed, distant, almost patronizing. They had acquired the correct snippets of knowledge, the telling quotations to score distinction marks on their answers, but the poet had little connection with their day-to-day problems. 'He is still intelligible,' Dryden had claimed, but Spenser rang few bells for them. Clark felt much the same. A poet's poet? Mm. Spenser represented some less subtle attitude towards the difficulties of living. Could that be true? Well, Freud and the like had muddied the waters, and to our benefit.

Mrs Mackenzie tapped at his door.

'It's Mr Stapleton,' she said, 'on the 'phone. Could you go down? He seems not well.'

The pair processed downstairs. Stapleton spoke hoarsely; he had fallen, but fortunately near the telephone. He explained, not well, brokenly as if pain sabred the cohesion of his thoughts, where Clark would find the back-door key.

'You haven't chained or bolted yourself in?'

'I don't think so. I'm not sure.'

'Lie still then. I'll be there inside ten minutes.'

Clark returned to his room, stowed his books into his briefcase, bundled into his overcoat, and made for the front door. Mrs Mackenzie was ready with advice: he was to be careful, the streets were glassy. He must ring back if he needed help.

Frost sparkled on the road. Piled snow was dirty and rocklike. Twice he almost fell, but skidding saved himself. He found the key, made his way into Stapleton's kitchen which was lit but empty.

'Hullo. Where are you?' he called out.

'Here.' A faint voice from the hall.

Clark rattled out, and there by the telephone table Stapleton sat, groaning but upright.

'Now what's the trouble?' Clark asked, clicking on further lights.

'I fell.'

'But rose again. What's the damage? Is anything broken?'

'How in hell do I know that?'

'Good sign. I'll dodge out and make you a cup of coffee. Just sit there.'

'I want a pee.'

'I'll bring a bucket in. Don't get shifting about yet.'

He did as he promised. Stapleton said he could manage.

When the coffee was brought in, the bucket emptied, the old man zipped up, Clark fetched himself a chair.

'Are you warm enough?' he asked.

'We'd do better in the kitchen.'

'Hang on here until you've had your coffee. How did it happen?'

'I was just out here. . . .'

'Doing what?'

'Walking about. Christ, man, I'm allowed to walk round in my own house, aren't I?'

'Provided you do it in safety.' Clark felt reassured. 'Go on.'

'One minute I was right as rain, the next I was down flat on my face. I lay there. Then I found I could move and so I dragged myself over to the telephone. I hoped one of these bloody lodgers upstairs would hear me groaning, but no fear. Living their own lives. My 'phone book was open by chance at C, I'd rung George Chettle the builder earlier in the evening. I saw your name, c/o Mackenzie, knew you didn't live far off and rang you.'

'Is Jennifer at home?'

'I've no idea. She wouldn't want to know, not unless I'd broken my neck. She'd just order me to fix myself up in sheltered accommodation, or employ a full-time nurse or housekeeper.'

'Mrs Mackenzie has offered to look in.'

'Who's she?'

'My landlady. You just mentioned her. She took your 'phone call.'

'I don't want women. I've had enough of their interference. I'd soon had enough even in the days when I could find myself a bit of pleasure with them.'

Stapleton grumbled continuously as he drank slowly, once ordering Clark back to the kitchen for the biscuit tin. Ten minutes later Clark led him out, moaning and cursing, to his seat.

'Have you plenty of food now? The roads outside are like glass. You mustn't venture out on any pretext.'

'This is the age of the freezer, my young friend. Modern technology and the siege mentality.' Stapleton had recovered his poise, grinned, spoke cheerfully. 'I needn't put my head out of doors for three months.'

'I'll tell Jennifer you've had a fall.'

'She won't want to know. And if by some freak of chance she does she'll be down here and on me like a ton of bricks to do this, that and the other. Are you thinking of marrying her, young man?'

'It hadn't crossed my mind.'

'Had or hadn't? Oh. I see. You be careful.'

'Should I make a good son-in-law?' Clark asked, unseriously.

'Son-in-law doesn't carry much weight or status as her husband. If I saw Hope socially a dozen times after their wedding it's as . . .' His voice trailed off, and he thinned his lips. 'He was too busy with his own concerns. That made two of us. Mark you, it suited her at the time. He was well on the way to the senior partnership; he saw she was properly promoted in the firm. Again, I've no doubt she earned her keep. She knows her way about.'

Clark sat on for twenty minutes, listening, before he rose to leave.

'Are you sure you'll be able to get into bed?'

'No doubt. With the usual struggle, I expect. The reason I rang you was because I was frightened I'd broken something. Now I haven't, I'm right as ninepence.'

Clark swilled the cups, donned his anorak.

'I'll let Jennifer know.'

'You do.'

There had been no word of thanks, and the old man chuntered on to himself even though his rescuer had closed the door.

Jennifer expressed brief gratitude before inviting him round.

He called on Saturday. The winds had swung to the milder west, and it drizzled; snow had melted. Jennifer seemed to be cooking.

'I've been out at work all week, and this morning, and now I comfort myself playing housewife, baking jam-tarts, rock buns, flapjack.'

'Do you enjoy it?'

'I suppose so. I wouldn't do it otherwise.' Her kitchen smelt delicious. 'Haven't seen much of you. Are you busy?'

'Always plenty to do. This is my first term.'

'Is it a good place to work?'

'I'm pretty sure it is. Old-fashioned in some ways. There are computers and up-to-date labs and so on, but emphasis on instruction and testing seems unalterable.'

'Don't you approve, then?'

'I'm in two minds. Though that's not unusual with me. No, there are all sorts of bright schemes in the junior part of the school, but come the examination time, back to mark-grubbing. It doesn't knock the spirit out of them, though. They'll score their ninety-five per cent by doing as they're told, but they argue like blazes outside exam syllabuses. We have some really bright boys.'

'Wouldn't it be better if you had girls as well?'

'In some ways. My last school was co-educational. Its standards were nowhere near as high, I think, but it was nothing like as selective.'

'And the staff?'

'They're very friendly.' He thought for a moment; she sat torpid. 'Shall I tell you something? In confidence?'

'I love secrets.' Her face was immediately bright. 'Out with it.'

'Short, the Headmaster, grabbed me the other night to ask me how I was shaping. And amongst other matters he warned me to be careful in my dealings with the Pearsons, the Wycliffes and with you.'

'Careful? In what way?' She did not appear unduly interested.

'He suggested that you were very well connected. . . .'

'They are. I'm not.'

'And affluent as I wasn't. I was a bit shaken and asked him to dot his i's and cross his t's, but he wasn't having any of it. He had nothing against you all, but you were above my star and would drop me whenever it suited you, and so I wasn't to raise my expectations. They were his words, I think. It surprised me.'

'Why?'

'How did he know I had anything to do with you? He must have talked to the Pearsons, or Gillian, or you, wouldn't you say?'

'Hugh Pearson, I'd guess. I know Harley Short, and Tessa, moderately well.'

'And have you crossed him in some way?'

'Not at all. He just doesn't want you chasing after us, throwing your money away, and neglecting your work. He doesn't want you dazzled by us.'

'Is he a good judge of character?'

'He's no fool, is Harley.'

'So he's right, is he?'

'I don't say that. No.' She yawned. 'Do you mind making us a cup of tea? Earl Grey bags into the flowered tea-pot. I'm knackered.'

Clark asked for precise instructions before going out.

When he returned Jennifer sat with her legs tucked under her, shoes off, reading. He poured.

'That's saved my life,' she said, sipping. 'I don't know what to do with that bloody father of mine. I suppose if I had any charity in my make-up, I'd take him in. If that's the expression.' She laughed, not at her ambiguity but secretly as if at something else. 'Or move the pair of us into one of his houses. He has plenty.' Now she frowned. 'But I don't want it and I don't suppose he does either. So I do nothing about it.'

131

'He's not helpless.'

'Not yet. But it won't be long before he is, and then what?'

'What do your brothers say?'

'Damn-all, as you'd expect. They get on with their respective careers, and never a thought of the old man or me except how much he's going to leave them. They flatter him at intervals, of course. They know which side their bread is buttered.'

'Both,' Clark said.

'I beg your pardon.' She seemed genuinely puzzled. 'Oh, I see. Yes, I suppose so. The country's filling up with old people we don't know what to do with.' She passed her cup across; he stood. 'Ought I to feel bad about it?'

'Never mind "ought". Do you?' he asked.

'Not really. I'm too busy to trouble myself.'

'Then why talk about it?'

'Because, dear Anthony, every time I see you it reminds me of my father. There's a man who visits him, as I don't. Sometimes I think my brothers and I just stand around, waiting for that dicky heart to give up. Do you get on well with your parents?'

'Moderately. I can't stand too much of them.'

'Do they know that?'

'My mother does. But she feeds me, and rams advice down my throat in a hurry, and tells me when I'm married we'll only too glad to shuffle the children off on to them.'

'And your father?'

'He does as he's told. He's busy, and acts old, though he's not much over fifty yet. But he's always been a bit of a fuddy-duddy.'

'And who are you like?'

'My mother. In looks and temperament. Why do women always take their shoes off?'

Jennifer looked wide-eyed, then laughed.

'They're lighter than men's, more cramped. And women have more sense than men. If their shoes hurt, they kick them off.'

He told how he had massaged Gillian Wycliffe's feet.

'Goodness,' she answered mildly, 'I hadn't realized what things you get up to. Do you want to stroke mine?'

132

'Do you need them stroked?'

She thought about that, biting on the nail of her left index finger.

'Not really. But if it gives you some satisfaction, here they are.'

Clark did not move.

'That's not very flattering,' she grumbled. 'Would you give me another cup then?'

'It's your third.'

'Aren't I allowed more than two? That's why I told you to use the large pot.' She pointed at the tray. 'Are you not having another? Please yourself. Come and sit here.' She pointed to the floor by her chair. 'Bring a cushion.'

Clark obeyed, though he did not find the position comfortable. Jennifer began to stroke his hair, but perhaps because she did it with her left hand he found it neither soothing nor enticing. Now she pulled his head back towards her and fondled his cheeks.

'You like women, don't you?' she asked distantly.

'Very much.' Primly.

'Clinton was bi-sexual, you know.' Her hand kept up its kindness. 'I sometimes wonder if that wasn't the reason for his suicide. I'm only guessing. Emotionally he was always in a mess. He couldn't help himself. In some ways that was the secret of his success. He'd work like blazes, take on and manage impossibilities because of his frustrations elsewhere.'

Her hand played in his hair; he had leaned over and stroked the outside of her thigh. Their movements were leisurely, almost asexual.

'I don't think we'll ever find out what really drove him to it. His life was such a criss-cross of muddle and close shaves and emotional disasters. All except financially. There he was steady as a rock.'

'Didn't his erotic adventures cost him money, then?'

'Yes. But only to a small extent. Well, within the limits of, oh, his petty cash. And people never tried to blackmail him, or, if they did, wouldn't get far with it. He was a rough character when he wanted.'

'You admired him?'

133

'Yes,' Jennifer answered, 'yes, I suppose I did. He wasn't my ideal, by a very long chalk. But, yes, I did. He told you what he wanted, and grabbed it.'

'And that goes down well with you?'

'I wouldn't say that. Not always.'

She ceased caressing his hair to drink her tea. For some reason she tapped the bottom of the cup on the rim of the saucer as if to provoke memory. He could hear her breathing, not excitedly, deeply.

'He was friendly with Hugh Pearson, wasn't he?'

'As far as anyone can be with Hugh.' Bitterly, but softly. 'He's only half a man. Oh, he's fine in the Sixth Form explaining about the imperfect subjunctive or what Corneille understood by duty, but he's feeble otherwise. That's why he's hung around here so long.'

'And Clarissa.'

'She doesn't mind. They both drink.'

'But if Hugh had gone away to a more responsible job, wouldn't that have caused him extra stress?'

'Possibly.'

Clark stroked her thighs, boldly rested the butt of his hand on her mons veneris outside her dress. She did not appear to mind, even notice.

'And Gillian Wycliffe?' he asked.

'What about her?'

'Why should she be so bad for me?'

'Money. Bloody money. That's what Harley's worried about. He lives on his salary and hoards. Tessa's the same. They can't understand people using wealth for enjoyment. They're rainy-day types, but don't ask me why because I don't know. Never had a great deal, perhaps. Or had some financial crisis in their childhood. He thinks Gill and the Pearsons will encourage you to splash your cash around.'

'On what?'

'Bottles of whisky, expensive pictures, holidays beyond your means. They're all the same to Harley. Hasn't he lectured you yet on plastic temptation?'

'Not personally. I've heard him speak about it.'

Now his hand was under her dress and lace-edged petticoat,

134

stroking the rough smoothness of her tights. She allowed it for some time then suddenly, fiercely, grabbed his hand through the material of her dress.

'Not now,' she said equably. 'It's nice but I'm too fagged out.' He moved away, and she gave an account of her week's work, the long hours, the incapacity of some businessmen, their foolhardiness. 'You'd think some of them wanted to end up in prison.'

In the end she stood up.

'What are we going to do with this bloody father of mine?'

'Nothing, for the present.'

'That was prompt.' She patted his arms, smiling with sarcasm.

'That's what you want to hear. And it saves trouble for the moment.'

'Not without brains,' she said.

He stayed for another half-hour before she shooed him out.

'What are you doing this evening?' he asked.

'Staying in to pamper myself. I shall read.'

'What?'

'Oh, Henry James or P. D. James. All grist to the mill.'

She kissed him quite affectionately out in the hall, but he felt certain that as soon as the door shut behind him, he'd be dismissed from her mind.

XIV

On Monday morning, as Anthony Clark prepared to set off for school, the postman delivered the mail.

'Lucky today,' Mrs Mackenzie called to him. He scanned his three letters: a bill for books, his mother's weekend screed and a faintly green, long envelope in Daniella's handwriting.

'Interesting?' Mrs Mac now knew him well enough, she thought, to make fun of him.

'Moderately.'

'I can't see you blushing.'

He smiled, slipped them into his anorak pocket and made his way out to the car. He liked to arrive in good time, especially on

Monday, so he'd have ample leisure this morning to deal with his correspondence before the scholastic day began.

Sitting at his desk in his empty form-room, he left Daniella until last. He'd expected the bill; his mother was unusually brief because she had spent most of Friday nursing his father who was in bed with 'flu. A bad patient, he'd had her up and down stairs all day. She concluded that he seemed no better on Saturday morning when she was about to go out shopping and to post her bulletin. Clark decided he would 'phone her that evening.

He carefully slit the envelope of Daniella's letter.

One sheet, folded so that he could not see the writing. He paused, mildly excited, warning himself to expect nothing. She'd perhaps left a book in his keeping or wanted somebody's address.

Dear Tony,

    I don't know how to write this. I feel a fool, and I am.

    My infatuation with Jonathan lasted really no more than a fortnight. It's done completely now. Even while it was on I knew I'd made a wrong decision.

    If you still feel anything for me at all after my inexcusable behaviour, perhaps you would write. I realize I have not the slightest claim on you. It has cost me a great deal to take this decision to write to you. Perhaps you think, 'so it should'. Please let me know one way or the other. With love,

                                    Daniella

One side of neat writing in best fountain-pen ink, properly punctuated and with a double squiggle under the last 'a'.

Clark breathed deeply, read the plain letter slowly again, returned it to its envelope, extracted and reread it, carefully folded it, tucked it away.

Smug triumph dominated. That aberration hadn't occupied the silly bitch long. He remembered her white energy on the tennis court, in minor operatic roles, in bed. Daniella's body was beautiful, a golden pallor, strongly slim, scented, fulfilling. He could have her back if he so wished. If, if, if. But. He drummed on his desk-top, thrusting his chin into the palm of his other hand. Outside the sky stretched blue, with shower clouds. So much for last week's snow. He stood, looking out of the window down at the playground. The first bell whirred; a straggle of pupils clambered the steps. His own door was flung open, and five twelve-year-olds pushed in together. The leader, a mischievous boy with auburn hair, bowed deeply in his direction.

'The top of the morning to you, sir.'

'Ah, Snaith. I see you have qualified once more as a fancied entrant for the thick-ear stakes.'

'Yes, sir.'

The boys grinned, sorting out their books, old-fashioned desk-tops up. Nobby was in a good mood. Ready, they folded their arms waiting. The day's work began.

At one o'clock Clark sat at lunch with his friend Thompson who had wasted his weekend on an archeological site near Hadrian's Wall.

'Couldn't do or see anything much. Everything saturated. And snow about still. And the fellow in charge knew damn-all about it.'

Clark realized how much Thompson was enjoying this complaint and took pleasure in it with him. The man had learnt a great deal, and acquired a thick folder of information, had bought a book, had met a couple of interesting people, and yet felt bound to present his satisfaction in grouses. Clark encouraged him, and they were laughing together as they left the dining-hall.

Hugh Pearson observed them.

'I'm glad somebody's pleased,' he said.

'Aren't you?' Clark stopped; Thompson moved boorishly on.

'Monday. No. I'm a long-weekend man.' Pearson smiled, attractively. 'Done anything interesting?'

Clark said a word or two about Stapleton's fall. His companion ushered him, frowning, into the small book-lined room where he taught scholarship pupils.

'It hardly seems any time since Ernest Stapleton was a vigorous, self-sufficient man. Sit down. You'll join me in a cup of coffee, will you? Or do you prefer the common-room bath-brick?' He busied himself with a percolator. 'Don't suppose you know what bath-brick is; they cleaned kitchen knives with it at one time.' Pearson moved delicately. When preparations were over he sat down, tugging at the ends of his pullover. An MA gown hung on the back of the door. Nobody wore academicals these days. 'I hear that the Headmaster has been warning you against me . . . amongst others.' He bared his teeth.

'News soon gets round here.'

'Jennifer Hope had lunch with us yesterday.'

Clark, displeased, sat in silence, not helping out. The percolator bubbled.

'I shouldn't let it worry you.'

'It doesn't.' Ungraciously.

'Short cannot understand why someone with all my advantages, as he describes them, should be content to remain here as an assistant master. There must be some failure of character, or nerve.'

'And is there?'

Pearson wagged a finger, beautiful teeth together.

'Of course, though I am not likely to infect you with my lack of ambition. I guess I am rather an awful example of how not to act.'

Pearson chatted on, gently maligning the Headmaster, until the coffee was ready. Clark noticed that there was a small refrigerator in the cupboard. Typical. The coffee smelt and tasted delicious.

They drank in a friendly silence, so amicable indeed that Pearson could peruse a pamphlet without appearance of rudeness.

'I shall have to push you out now,' Pearson said gently when they had finished their second cups. He stood to walk the three steps to the door. 'Don't take Short too seriously. He's a hierarchy man. You're doing well here. Maddison says so. And Short, to give him his due. You've made an excellent impression in that you do your job, inside school and out, properly, without any untoward cult of the personality. I like you for that. You don't show off, you don't go out of your way to draw attention to yourself, and yet you're there, having a good

138

influence. Old-fashioned, eh? Clarissa said as much to me only yesterday. "He has a real quality." Those were her words.'

Pearson closed the door silently behind his young colleague. He had spoken with the easy authority of an Oxbridge combination room; you may take it or leave it, as you please, but I have the truth. Clark guessed that he now made modest addresses to the whisky bottle to sweeten his afternoon's lessons.

'This is my day for good news,' Clark thought, legging it along the corridor. He stopped at the top of a stone stairway in this the old part of the school, by a Victorian Gothic window which looked out on to a shrubbery, dark laurel bushes, privet and box hedges, cotoneaster, chaenomeles, mahonia, rhododendron, camellia, senecio, philadelphus; he had learnt the names from his mother. He saw no boys on that side; the wrought-iron gates were closed, the tall, black, ornate railings delicately forbidding or foreboding to the avenue beyond. The gardener and a cloth-capped assistant moved together along a gravel path, the subordinate a respectful foot to the rear. Large trees shadowed the margins.

' "I am a part of all that I have met",' Clark quoted ironically to himself. He did not know whether he spoke out loud or not, but a passing prefect nodded and smiled affably in his direction.

Clark reached the common room, but before he had the chance to sit down his colleague Thompson was pointing at him and thumbing in large mystery towards the door.

'Our beloved Headmaster wants words with you.'

'What about?'

'He did not confide in me.' Thompson pulled lugubrious faces. 'Trot on. "Praise waiteth for thee in Sion".'

Clark knocked on the Headmaster's door. He could hear voices. He tapped again. This time the electric board signalled 'engaged'. He went into the office where the Head's secretary drank a cup of coffee and leafed through *Country Life*.

'The Head wants to see me.'

'I know.' She managed a smile. 'Mr Grant's in there now.'

'How long will they be?'

Again she smiled, her hand smoothing an already polished page.

'I just don't know. Tell you what; I'll fetch you when they're done.'

He thanked her; she returned to splendid property, he to Thompson's mimicry of disappointment and despair, his 'Grant us, o Lord', his bitten fingernails.

Ten minutes before the first afternoon bell the secretary appeared looking neither right nor left.

'The Headmaster will see you now, Mr Clark.'

He followed her through the office and into the study, where Short sat stone-faced pulling at the skin of his jaw with the left hand. With the other he waved impatiently towards the chair, presumably vacated by Grant. Clark sat. The Head seemed somewhere else, gloomily preoccupied. Suddenly he brought both hands down heavily on to the top of his desk.

'This won't take long. A niece of mine, she wants to study science, failed English GCSE last summer. Would you give her a lesson or two? Inside the next fortnight? I know what you're about to say; I've already said it to my sister. But.'

'What school is she at?'

Short screwed his face sourly, named a state school in the county.

'Was the teaching poor?' Clark asked.

'I shouldn't think so. The fault will lie with the girl, I guess. She's clever enough, but she does as she likes.'

'Does she read?'

'I doubt it. I know, Clark, you can't promise anything, but what they want is this, a short course of four or five lessons with an expert, so that he can see what's wrong and begin to rectify faults. I named you. A good-looking young man might jolt her into effort. But will you see her twice this week? We'd make arrangements, if you agree. I've told my sister that this is grossly unfair on you, that you are fully occupied, but women are . . . Perhaps you'd do it as a favour to me? Charge the full price whatever that is, but you will not, I insist, in any way cross me by refusing. It is entirely up to you. It's a ridiculous enterprise, but then one never knows. What do you say?'

'I'll do it.'

'Good. I'll ring my sister, sing your praises.'

They briefly discussed suitable evenings. Short took notes. Clark was to drive over.

Even by the end of the afternoon he was still delighted with himself, circling the Head's proposal and Daniella's letter. After dinner he tried a draft.

Your letter surprised me.

I think we had better be cautious for the present. It would be too easy to fall into easy, fatuous, self-deceiving promises on paper. When we actually see one another then we can reach some sort of conclusion. This may seem grudging or a poor start to a new relationship, but your first letter left me sore. I shall be home for Christmas. Or a weekend sooner than that. Tell me what you think.

That had the right, distancing effect. He locked it away with his passport and birth certificate in the strong-box inside his portmanteau at the bottom of the wardrobe. Daniella must wait.

Next morning as Clark left his car a colleague, George Frensham, came across the playground-cum-car-park towards him. Clark had the impression that the man had been waiting. Frensham was big, six foot two or three, broad-shouldered with it; his face seemed battered, with the ugly nose broken, but the brown eyes shone liquidly bright.

'Morning.' Standard public-school accent. 'I wanted a word with you if you don't mind.'

They walked towards the outside steps together.

Frensham, who'd be in his early thirties, taught in the Modern Languages Department, had made one or two forceful and sensible interventions in staff meetings, but had not spoken to Clark before this morning.

'I would like your advice. I asked Hugh Pearson and he suggested you.'

'Go on.'

'I've written a novel. At least a first draft. I'd like your opinion. It's done on my word-processor so you won't have trouble with my handwriting. But it's rather long. Five hundred pages or thereabouts. It's an imposition, I know. But Hugh said you read novels. I've asked Ted Wakelam at the University to read it, and a literary agent in London who was

141

at college with me. Then I'll compare what the three of you say.'

'How long did it take you?'

'Four years off and on.'

'And are you pleased with it?'

'That's it. I don't know. I've spent time on it to the exclusion of, well, other matters.' He laughed, ruffled his short, dark brown hair. 'That's why I want you to be honest: I've sweated at it. But. . . . Will you?'

'Yes, I will.'

'Thanks. I'll deliver it tomorrow. I realize you're busy. But perhaps you'd finish it over the Christmas vac.'

'Do you want a written report?'

'That's entirely up to you. Give me your honest opinion.' He coughed, thanked Clark again, and turned off before they reached the common room.

Clark was flattered. Ted Wakelam, a senior lecturer at the University, was intelligent, a well-regarded poet, left wing and not afraid to speak his mind, in public at least. Hugh Pearson exchanged a word or two during the lunch-hour but did not mention George Frensham, who failed next morning to hand over the novel as he had promised.

Over the telephone Clark set the Headmaster's niece an essay which was delivered the next day. It now became clear that the girl's parents wanted four or five lessons before the girl re-sat her exam in eight days' time. When he reported out at Edwalton with the marked essay Mrs Blair greeted him with enthusiasm. Her husband did not appear.

He sat down with Imogen at the dining-room table. She was a well-formed, blonde young woman in a cream dress that made her almost matronly. As he explained how many marks she would have scored in the examination, and why, she sat dumbly, not looking at him, acknowledging only grammatical slips or unintentional spelling errors with a short intake of breath or shrug. As he showed her how the essay could be expanded to the examiner's pleasure, she sat still as if pop-music played in her head drowning his advice.

'You're a scientist, aren't you?' She nodded. 'I'll give you a list of headings. Total length, type of sentence structure, paragraph size and so on; all the things that will bring your bacon home. We haven't much time. I shall expect you when you next write for me to have paid attention. You're clearly intelligent enough to do that. And for God's sake try to choose a subject you're interested in or know something about.' Again she shrugged, barely perceptibly.

He spent the rest of the hour working with her, she grudgingly, on a précis. She seemed to have only the vaguest notion of what was expected, or gave that impression. 'You summarize what the passage is about, and cut the illustrations even though they're much the most interesting parts in your opinion.' She raised her fair eyebrows at such heresy, but quickly toed the line when he began to hector her. 'We haven't time for philosophical justifications,' he said. 'We do as we're told.'

He set another essay and précis from a paper he had brought along. Imogen rose, gathered her file.

'You'll do,' he said. 'Thank you.'

The nipples stood out proud under the fabric of her dress.

'Any questions?'

She shrugged. Mrs Blair was waiting in the hall. The girl went gracelessly upstairs without a further word.

'What do you think?' the mother asked.

'I can't guarantee anything in this short time.'

'No, I realize that. I'm willing to keep her away from school for a week.'

'For goodness' sake, don't. I'll be back the day after tomorrow. Just see she completes the work and I'll mark it in the lunch-break on Thursday before I arrive.'

'I'll do just that. I don't think Harley much appreciates my using him as a messenger.'

' "Diseases desperate grown by desperate appliance are relieved." '

'You think we should have noticed this before, don't you?'

'Somebody should.'

Mrs Blair expressed satisfaction at this, and thanked him with something of her brother's rat-trap lack of expression. When he refused her offer of a drink, she quickly sped him through the front door.

Clark felt displeased. Though the girl was, for whatever

reason, a borderline case, she was intelligent enough and with a few weeks' coaching would walk through the exam. He had not won her confidence and had once or twice savaged her, not the ideal for a first lesson. Still, they had left him little time for finesse.

When the Headmaster delivered the second essay, together with the précis and the rest of the paper answered, he did so personally and enquired about Imogen's chances.

'Touch and go,' Clark said. 'I'll do my best. And obviously she's doing some work.' He flicked the papers. 'Her parents see to it that she's buckling down to it.'

'My sister will make sure that she follows instructions.'

'I had to lean on her a bit.'

'Lean?' The Head's face, well-shaven, grew inquisitional.

'I had to insist, speak sharply, if you like.'

'She wasn't cooperative?'

'Not really. Not rude or badly obstructive, but hardly forthcoming.'

Short stroked his thin chin.

'It is often claimed that men who teach in single-sex male schools are either too sentimental or inclined to bully when they come to instruct females.' He smiled bleakly, almost with a sneer. 'We shall see.'

He took his gleaming white collar and thin, black-haired hands quickly away.

'And a merry Christmas to all our readers,' Clark cheered himself. He had no idea what the Headmaster meant; probably he had established superiority to his own satisfaction and no more than that.

In the evening Clark wrote to Daniella. It was soon done.

Thank you for your letter, which certainly (crossed out) surprised me.

I don't know what to think, but suggest we leave matters as they are for the present, and arrange to meet in the Christmas vac. That's not long now.

This may seem grudging to you. It does to me, and I admit it, but your decision to throw me over still makes me most uncertain whether there's any future in a relationship

144

between us. I think I shall know better when I see you. Exchanges of letters can be misleading.

Yours sincerely.

Clark did not feel proud of these sentences, though they expressed what he thought. Suspicious and vulnerable, he left the letter unsealed so that he could change his mind in the morning.

He did not, and posted the unaltered missive on his way to school. He glowered at the pillar-box. 'So much for the open mind,' he said out loud as he thrust the letter in. Two passing girls opened their eyes wide.

XV

On Sunday afternoon Anthony Clark sat reading.

He'd spent Saturday morning in town and had dedicated the rest of the weekend to a close look at George Frensham's novel. The author had handed over two volumes, in red folders, with a shame-faced mumble, 'See what you make of it.' He had backed away, awkwardly.

The novel was set in Africa at some time in the second half of the nineteenth century. Two white men, missionaries, had completed a trek through a fearsome forest and had arrived at a clearing where a preliminary palaver was taking place between one of their porters and the village elders in a language neither white man understood. Their translator and factotum was equally baffled; it was only by chance that the party included a man who could speak this dialect. The discovery in this place of a group with an unexpected language both intrigued and frightened the missionaries. They said in plain, slow English what they wanted to convey; their head boy translated into Swahili with explanations in Rwanda and this the bearer, a young frightened lad who tossed his head as he spoke, put to the chief and his advisors. Then followed the process of translating the answers. Both Britons spoke Swahili, but the version used this day seemed twisted, not immediately comprehensible, needing explanation, minute elucidation on everyday terms.

145

Frensham was in no hurry, did not court easy favour from the reader, often gave first a translation of the Swahili, then the translator's translation, and finally the missionaries' gloss or discussion. This seemed laboured at first so that Clark had to drive himself to read, and then reread. He looked ahead to see when this first chapter ended; it occupied eighty-seven pages. By page eighteen Clark had been convinced; one saw how Frensham had distinguished between his characters by speech, by rhythm or idiom or metaphor. He wondered whether the writer had managed this by constant small revisions, or whether white-hot imagination had lit these subtle distinctions first time round.

On page twenty-four Clark found himself considerably annoyed when Frensham had broken off the palaver and had begun to describe the journey over the last few days which had landed the party in this clearing. The writer's knowledge was clearly immense: flora and fauna were brilliantly described, unknown exotic birds exactly named, sounds conjured; foreign heat, sweat, sun, darkness and discomfort made instantly, palpably lively. Clark was impressed but sceptical. Frensham had either lived in Africa or had researched with dazzling thoroughness, but an English reader was no expert in African matters, could easily be bamboozled by misinformation confidently handled, and in any case Clark felt himself like St Paul's Athenians (he taught Scripture once a week and his task this term concerned the journeys, with maps, of the Apostle to the Gentiles), constantly on the watch for some new thing. If, he often asserted, a writer had any talent out of the ordinary, he could describe one man in a provincial street saying good morning to another and no more and yet enlighten the perceptive reader to the human condition, without recourse to the alien or the remote. He regarded Frensham's expertise with suspicion, made a sarcastic note or two.

But within ten pages the author had won his way once more. These descriptions of place or atmosphere were directed with such method, such force, though subtly, that they served over and over again to distinguish between men. The younger missionary snatching off his hat in a clearing of sudden, blinding sunlight, or standing on a stone directing with immense confidence the passage over a rough stream of his men who not only did not understand him but had crossed such a place a score or fifty times to his one. The bearers heard the brassy, Anglian, Anglican-foreign Swahili and picked their way as they had always done. The older man took all this in but concentrated on his fatigue, his diarrhoea, weakening in the boiling shadow.

The pages stalked magnificent.

Though Frensham offered a sentence or two about the characteristics, or background, or temperament of the missionaries it was unobtrusively done, but on second reading Clark noticed such pointers were placed where there might have been ambiguity; the writer took care of his reader but his great strength lay in his rare ability to make action or scenery underline the fears or intrepidities or foolishness or intelligence of each man. Clark made another admiring but suitably subfusc note.

George Frensham was in the Conrad class. His power was both frenetic and yet finely, delicately controlled.

Clark read on into the small hours, woke early to continue, completed his task soon after lunch. He straightened his notes, wrote a conclusion, and packed them away with the typescript for a second reading in the Christmas vac.

As soon as this was done, he poured himself a glass of Scotch, and took to the comfortable arm-chair. The book had unsettled him unexpectedly so that he took to alcohol before walking out. The grey afternoon offered no sort of welcome. Whisky brought him little comfort.

The last three hundred and fifty pages of the novel had disappointed compared with that ferocious first chapter and a half. Now the book depended more largely on the tale, the attempts to pass impenetrable jungle at an ill-chosen season, shortage of food, the death of an elephant, three separate attacks by hostile tribesmen, a clash with a pioneer group of Muslim missionaries, with European pirate traders. Men died in two dreadful accidents bloodily detailed. There was no treasure found; this was no *King Solomon's Mines*; no sex interest with she-deities or native princesses, and Frensham, as in his opening pages, kept to his habit of breaking off from a

147

narrative he had firmly running in the reader's mind as if to test his own skills. At one point during an admirable account of a river crossing while the party was under attack from both banks, Frensham diverged on a long, seemingly arid dissertation about some religious controversy which had occupied the elder missionary. What Biblical authority was there that Christ had died for us, instead of us, for our sins? It had little relevance to the two or three desperate hours with ropes over and in the river, concerned as it was with unimportant, forgotten arguments, while Darwinian heresies about the age of the earth and the placing of fossils marginally hovered. Nothing was certain any longer. It bore no strength as a symbol, either of the old man's limited understanding or error, or even the results in a hundred years' time after his courageous establishment of missionary schools and colleges which would turn out in the end students who accepted godless European science and its consequences without so much as a qualm. The minds of their grandchildren would fester because they had somehow deserted the African heritage instead of incorporating it into, making it a larger part of Western cosmologies. These were not exactly dull pages, but Frensham seemed to be determined to dot every 'i' of these ancient controversies, to stress their importance, to make Bishop Colenso the equivalent of Montaigne or Pascal or Newman, a Wyclif, Hus or Luther.

And yet Clark could not be sure.

So powerful had been the effect of the first hundred-odd pages that he was perhaps left incapable of understanding, responding to the new challenges Frensham set down. The reader had been numbed, anaesthetized; he could stand only so much manipulation, so that when the writer turned elsewhere with equal power the battered auditor could only back away, whimpering, justifying his own weakness by accusations of falling-off on the part of a writer who grew too rigorous to be borne.

Clark sensibly made a further note after he had finished the whisky, put on his coat and walked out. From Mrs Mackenzie's sitting room, forbidden territory, he could hear the sounds of a television football commentary. Noisy as the programme seemed, even behind two closed doors, Mrs Mac claimed it as suitably soporific.

The streets darkened already under grey skies as he walked fast. Excited by what he had read, by the favourable judgement he'd deliver tomorrow to the author, Clark seemed above, outside himself. Here alongside him at work existed a notable mind, an outstanding talent, and he had not known. He remembered how at his last school a quiet, intense, muscular young man who had turned up for a joint training session one evening proved to be a famous Welsh international.

Clark saw it as his duty to express exactly his admiration for Frensham's achievement, but he realized that unless he spoke carefully, his criticisms, for example, his view that the second part of the book did not match the first, would take priority. He must establish that Frensham had won a place in the highest class, was already a potential equal with Fielding, George Eliot, Conrad, Bennett, Lawrence. They had produced, each one, an *oeuvre*, but . . . It was a privilege that he, Anthony Clark, had chanced to be on hand, to herald the phenomenon, to convince the author of his place and value. To the walking figure all this seemed unlikely, the product of whisky rather than of judgement. He waved his arms as if haranguing a crowd.

A car drew up at the kerb. Jennifer Hope. She called him over.

'What are you doing in these parts?' he asked as he bent to the lowered window.

'Making up my mind to visit my father. Get in and come with me . . . if you've nothing better to do.'

He obeyed. They drove sedately towards Stapleton's house, talking little. Jennifer said she hated the onset of the winter.

Stapleton took long enough to let his visitors in. He was unshaven, and his face discoloured, puffy, cut.

'What's wrong?' Jennifer pointed. 'What on earth have you been up to?'

'I've not been fighting. That's one thing for certain. Another fall. I'm bruised all down this side.'

The three hovered round the kitchen table until Jennifer made an enquiry about investing in a property. Immediately Stapleton changed. The collarless, stubbled tousle-head ordered his daughter into the drawing room, instructing Clark to make tea. When he carried the tray into them, the father with

149

eyes closed ridiculed some proposal she had put. . . . His voice was not strong, his minatory finger crooked with arthritis, but he was certain in his mind. Jennifer thanked him with ironical politeness.

'I don't like to see you throwing good money away.' Stapleton.

'I'll do my best.'

'It's on a par with a bet on the Grand National.'

They drank their tea. Clark cleared away and washed up while Jennifer consulted her father again. From the kitchen the young man could hear their rapid, unintelligible exchanges. The only understandable words were, 'No, no. I've told you,' in a loud squeak from Stapleton.

When Clark returned Jennifer was on her feet, buttoning on her coat. They left in a hurry.

'That was soon over,' Clark said, outside in the dark.

'I feel like a dish-rag.'

'Did you get good advice?'

'I asked him about something I'd no intention of doing, and he rubbished me.'

'Why?'

'Why what? Because it gives him the chance to lord it, and I can judge how he is. It's no use offering him either sympathy or soft soap. Ask him a question and see how he shapes.'

'And did he do well in the test?'

'Oh, yes. Though I didn't like the look of his face. He seems very unsteady on his feet.' They stopped at the end of Clark's road. 'Are you doing anything important? Will you come home with me?'

'It's my free evening. We forage for our own tea.'

They drove in silence: Jennifer, preoccupied, could not sit still as she drove, but fidgeted. She led him indoors as if she was now sorry she had invited him.

'Do you feel like eating?' she asked brusquely.

'No, thanks. Sit down and relax.'

She snorted, shot out to the kitchen, put on the kettle. When she returned with a tray she seemed calmer, kicking off her shoes, tucking her legs under her on the settee.

'I'll be mother,' Clark said, rising.

150

'It's a bastard.' She pointed to where he was to set her cup down. 'I work so hard all week that when it comes to Sunday I don't know how to spend it.'

'Are you away next week?'

'Yes. Not far, but a very large concern which demands some senior person there.'

'Are you good at it?'

'Of course. They wouldn't have made me a partner otherwise. I had to be better than the men.'

'But your husband . . . ?'

'He's the worst anti-feminist of the lot.' She smiled, sipping. 'It's quiet here tonight.'

'Isn't it always?'

'No. There are party-givers somewhere in the street. Usually at weekends. Their bass thumps, enough to lift the tarmac.'

'They must be quite some distance away.'

'At least a hundred yards, yes. But they still make themselves heard.'

'Does nobody complain?'

'I expect so. The police come round to steady it down.'

'Who are they?'

'No idea.' She straightened her back. 'Come over here and sit with me. And while you're up just press that end button, will you?' She pointed.

He did so, and Vivaldi mildly filled the room.

She leaned against him, but tentatively, examining the polish on the fingernails of her left hand.

'Are you comfortable?' she asked. 'Can you reach your tea?'

'Perfect.'

She kissed him on the mouth, but with no great show of passion.

'Now you have lipstick on your face.'

They attended to their cups, and then he kissed her. She responded warmly, slipped under him.

'That's nice,' she said in due time. She spoke ordinarily after the torrid play of mouth on mouth, body on body. 'Pour us another cup, and then we'll go up to bed. We're in no hurry, are we?'

'You speak for yourself.'

151

Upstairs they made love, not altogether satisfactorily, and then lay naked under her duvet holding hands. When he raised his head, painfully, he could make out a watercolour of clouds bundling over a green, breaker-capped sea. Jennifer's eyes were closed and she did not speak. He thought perhaps she was disappointed, but dared not question her.

'Who did that picture?' he asked in the end.

'My mother. Shut up, will you?'

Within a minute she had fallen asleep, smiling. He dozed with her.

After the nap, they made love again, and this time she grew noisy, shouting sometimes obscenely, pulling his hair, digging her nails into his back; yet she seemed, as she did her violence on his body, to neglect him; it was more like an exorcism or sacrifice than an act of love. Again she lay in her silenced world, he beside her quite still in the strange bedroom. Her oblation.

She slapped his thigh, narrowly missing his genitals.

'That was good,' she said heartily. 'Let's get up.'

She dragged the duvet off, swung her legs and began immediately to dress, her back to him.

'You use the bathroom first,' she ordered. 'Last door. You'll find towels.'

He shuffled nakedly out. It seemed right. When he had washed and dressed he found his way down to her drawing room where he cleared the tea-tray and picked up a magazine. Nearly half an hour later she came down, bathed and in a black, simple, expensive dress with a white collar.

'Are you hungry?' she asked.

They decided on salad sandwiches which he helped her to make, slicing tomatoes, washing lettuce and cress. She mixed mayonnaise which he refused. 'Brew the coffee strong,' she ordered.

Clark felt pleased with himself; the brown bread was delicious, the coffee almost heady, and his mistress sat statuesque a yard or two away. She did not say more than a few sentences, and this silence, bearable as they ate, left him uncomfortable, suspicious.

'Do you know George Frensham?' he asked.

'Yes. Slightly. Why?'

He began to describe Frensham's novel, with enthusiasm. She continued to eat, slowly, chasing crumbs round her plate, as he spoke. When he had finished she completed her sandwich, put down her plate and, delicately masticating still, signalled for more coffee. She thanked him with a nod. When she had cleared her mouth she straightened the skirt of her dress and said, rather formally.

'His grandfather was a missionary, I think; his father a colonial administrator, and he was born out there. I seem to remember his telling me that his first language was Swahili or some African dialect.'

'Is he married?'

'Yes, but he's homosexual, I suspect. I don't know what his practices are. He's older than he looks. I was at university with his younger sister. That's how I got to know him. She had kept in touch, and introduced me a year or two ago when she came up here.'

'Is he a friend of the Pearsons?'

'Not that I know of. He wouldn't suit either of them. He's a big, rough bear. They like bland, cultivated types. Like you.' As she did not smile Clark did not know how to take this. 'You say he's talented?'

'Very.'

'Will the novel be published?'

'It ought to be. If there's any justice. It's very powerful.' He began again to sketch the scenes, its scope and strengths. She listened, her face smooth, hands still.

'I don't know about you,' she began when he had finished, 'but I tend to be over-impressed when I know little about the subject-matter or the setting. I'd be more likely to be dazzled by, let's say, incest in the Sahara or soldiering in the jungle or the trenches than by the love-life of an accountant in Beechnall. Now there seems some error there, some failure of judgement. It ought to be the writer's observation or grasp of life, his literary skills that count. Don't you think so? Not the far-fetched or far flung?' She spoke with the steady ease of a Sixth-Form mistress returning the Latin proses.

Clark sat still.

There was no tenderness about Jennifer, no intimacy. She

seemed friendly enough, pleased to talk with him, but without any intimation of close regard. Their love-making was discounted: from her attitude he might have been a plumber who'd sorted out some difficulty or, better, perhaps, a doctor called in and chatted to once he had given advice and written his prescription. Jennifer in some measure tested him to decide whether he came up to scratch.

His sense of sexual triumph held pride of place, but uncertainty lurked. Whether he read into the situation what was not there he did not know.

This doubt remained when they had finished eating and had taken to gin. Jennifer retained her superiority, seniority almost, pulling rank; of the shouting, pouting woman on the bed, nothing remained. At quarter to midnight he said he must go; she made no attempt to detain him, though she said she would stay up to watch television for another hour.

'And I shall walk home,' he said.

He took her in his arms by the door, dominating her but only temporarily.

'That'll be enough for tonight.' She broke away.

'When shall I see you?' he pressed.

'I'll 'phone you when I've sorted these next weeks out.'

' "Don't call me, I'll call you" .'

'Something like that.'

Jennifer accompanied him out into the darkness.

'No party tonight,' he said.

'No. And it's not raining. I can call you a taxi if you'd rather. I've drunk too much to drive you.'

'Don't worry. The walk will do me good.'

She waved, formally, queenly.

Puzzled he set off down the drive.

XVI

The High School term ended at full pelt for Clark.

He helped make up each night for the school play, attended the carol concert, the Headmaster's social evening for parents, two staff meetings and an afternoon concert, and kept up his

154

teaching as well as writing 'short reports'. Examinations would be held next term. He'd need to think about his papers.

'They exact their pound of flesh here,' he complained to Thompson.

'That's why parents will spend their hard-earned cash on us.'

He'd passed twenty minutes with Frensham, but that had proved unsatisfactory. The novelist had appeared abashed by lavish praise, had become gruff and laconic. Clark, not put off, had insisted on reading out his notes and underlining his compliments. Frensham, shuffling his feet, had seemed better pleased when the reader had said that there had been something of a falling-off in the second two-thirds. He had nodded vigorously. That's what critics were for, in his view: to make disparaging remarks.

'That will need re-writing?' he asked, humbly, almost eagerly.

'I don't know. Perhaps I'm wrong. With your permission I'll spend some more time on it this holiday. Have you heard anything from Ted Wakelam?'

'No. But he's always busy. And very slow . . . if not bloody idle.' Frensham leered, malice in his expression for the first time.

'Your job this holiday is to get it off to a couple of big publishers or agents. Look out addresses. As it stands, with not one word altered, it's magnificent.'

'I'd like to spend some more time on it.'

'Never mind what you'd like,' Clark laid down the law. 'Put it into the public eye. If you want to do more writing, as you should, start a new novel.' Clark enjoyed his ephemeral position of power. 'You have one thing to learn above all. Confidence. You're very good. You have to understand that. And practise to keep the standard.'

Frensham removed his huge bulk, smiling shyly, shoulders hunched in apprehension. Clark sat a few minutes proud and amazed at his own temerity.

The last day ended without ceremony. The pupils left early in the afternoon. In the lunch-hour a prefect had invited him over after school to a house in a nearby avenue for a 'last glass of sherry'. The place was a white, early Victorian, perhaps

Georgian, mansion where some dozen Sixth-Formers sat in a beautifully furnished drawing room over two bottles of sherry. Clark chose the dry, and listened while two bright-faced young men whom he knew by sight but had not taught enjoyed themselves explaining, and providing examples of, Kant's analytic and synthetic judgements. They spoke with a clipped zest, and deferring tried a time or two to involve Clark. He admitted his ignorance, and asked for explanations, which they supplied willingly. In return he gave them an anecdote about an old man in Cambridge who had supervised him and who claimed he had criticized Wittgenstein for some social gaffe and lived to tell the tale. The great man had glowered over the rebuke and finally had pronounced, 'You are right there', and then gone on to exercise his mind over some other niggling matter which was temporarily obsessing him.

Clark refused a second glass, excused himself, and drove to his lodgings. He had made arrangements with Mrs Mackenzie to stay until the morning of Christmas Eve. That would give him time to complete his greeting cards, buy the last few presents, not a difficult undertaking, and to think about Daniella.

The girl had replied to his letter implying that she would willingly wait for his instructions. She wrote both naïvely and gushingly, apologizing for acting so badly. The letter switched bad to worse. Now he had to make up his mind. He'd spend the four days over Christmas with his parents, and then had arranged to visit an old college friend, newly married, in Hampshire. They had invited him to take Daniella down with him.

It seemed sensible. There'd be abounding talk and drink galore, so that the sociable excitement might give them time to heal their rift. Whether he wanted reconciliation on such terms he could barely say: he needed to see, to listen to Daniella first. He was even unsure whether he should invite her over to his parents' home on one of the days of Christmas. His mother would not be pleased. Daniella had permanently blotted her copy-book there.

He completed his Christmas chores. He had earlier bought four excellent modern prints of small Bonington watercolours and had them framed for Gill Wycliffe and Jennifer. He wrapped them in holly-bright paper and delivered them. Which two should be Jennifer's? It was difficult. In the end he chose one, 'The Quais and Institut, Paris', and picked the second at random from the wrapped three. Immediately he knew he should have decided on 'The Doge's Palace, Venice', but was too proud, or ashamed, to reopen the packages.

First he drove to deliver to Gillian.

In darkness a bald man held the door open. Clark announced himself, said he could not stay but was invited into the hall. He had not recognized Ambrose Wycliffe. The long fingers traced a flat curve of brightness with a thin cigar, richly scenting the air.

'Not allowed my whiffs when she's at home,' Ambrose said, sourly amused.

'Won't she smell it when she comes in?'

'Of course. But she can't do anything about it. Too late. "The moving finger writes and having writ".' He laughed again, scribbled with the cigar, and accepted the presents, balancing them, hand against hand.

'Your wife has been very kind to me in my first month or two here.'

'Oh, yes. Has she? I'll tell her so.'

'She'll know.' Clark felt that some such stiff answer was required by this eunuch's voice.

'Of course she'll bloody know. Won't you sit down for a few minutes, have a drink?'

Clark explained that he was driving, and had another call. Wycliffe did not argue, thanked him again. The visitor looked about him.

'A beautiful house, this,' he said.

'Yes, it is. But it is Gillian who made it so. People give me the credit because I'm an architect, but it's she who has the real eye for the matching of colours or how much wall-space is to be taken up by a picture, or what furniture will enhance the good characteristics of a room. She'll discuss it with me but she knows her mind.'

'You admire your wife.' Clark did not know why he came out with the judgement. Perhaps the elegance of the surroundings overawed him into formal frankness.

157

'I am lucky. I'm the typical self-cosseting bachelor, fussy and narcissistic. She has changed me radically, never mind my house.' Again the thin, goatish chuckle.

Clark stood upright to his six-feet-one, suddenly delighted. He held out his hand. Wycliffe grasped it softly, held, then released it.

'There is no advantage in change.' Wycliffe talked as if to himself. 'Only in change for the better, in improvement.'

Clark thought he'd continue, in the Roget tradition. Amelioration. He grinned behind his hand. Wycliffe did not seem to notice.

'Thanks very much,' Clark said, stepping off for the door.

'I will give her the present. Pictures by the feel of them.'

'Boningtons. Prints, not real.'

'Before you go, would you like to see a real Bonington? I can lay my hands on it in a second. Wait there.'

The man left at speed, returned with a small, square package which he unfolded. Cliffs, beach, a distant sea, three small figures. It was lightly painted, almost colourless, except for a splash of scarlet on one of the men.

'Richard Parkes Bonington,' Wycliffe said. 'Here, grab it.' Clark did so, nodding his head, not knowing what to say.

'Why don't you frame it?' he asked.

'Can't hang everything, and it's a bit small to hold its own on a wall.' He appeared to savour the rhyme. 'You need it right under your eyes. I've known that all my life. Belonged to my great-grandfather.'

'Was he a collector?'

'Of sorts. Mostly Victorian etchings. I don't like them, though they fetch money now. But he owned this and two little Turner sketches in watercolour. He bought them somehow. Settlement of a debt, don't know. Very modestly, anyway. He was an architect.'

'Runs in the family?'

'Neither his son nor my father followed.'

He rewrapped the painting with great care, tissue and oil-treated covers, but carried it casually to the door.

'I'm sorry Gill wasn't in. She will be disappointed to have missed you.'

158

Clark liked the man in spite of appearance, thin voice, pallor. They shook hands again.

He drove round to Jennifer's and pressed her door-bell, wondering where he'd leave the packets if she was not at home. She came out almost at once, invited him inside. She wore a white blouse and a pair of check slacks, suitable only for the golf-links. Her dining table was littered with papers.

'Don't breathe, or you'll blow something away. Never offer to do work for a friend. This is a small business, at loggerheads with the tax-inspector. I'm just about sorting it out. It's taken three whole nights already.'

Clark presented his present. She looked and felt, eyes narrowed, distraite.

'What are they?'

'Little prints.'

'Thank you, Tony. I have a present for you, but it's not yet wrapped. I was well ahead of myself, and then this. What a mess.'

'Will you be able to clear it up?'

'Not really. She's disposed of or mislaid too many vital bits and pieces of information.'

'Dishonest or just careless?'

'A bit of both. But all's not lost yet. The inspector will be so pleased when I present something that makes sense that he'll accept it. Or that's what I hope.'

'And next year? Or will there be a next year for her?'

'Oh, yes. She runs a profitable business. Is very good at it.'

'What's "it"?'

'Making and marketing rather good clothes. A real talent for colour and shape.'

'That's what Ambrose Wycliffe said about Gill.'

He described his visit, spoke favourably of the husband.

'I know what you mean,' she said. 'Yes. Just keep talking for a quarter of an hour and give me a rest from this chaos. I haven't been able to sit down to a proper meal since I started. Never be kind-hearted.'

Clark began again on Ambrose Wycliffe. She listened standing by the fireplace.

'Good,' she said in the end, 'I'm glad you like him. The

159

epicene appearance is against him. But he's clever, and amusing sometimes, and extremely knowledgeable on all sorts of subjects. And, moreover, he's well-to-do. Gill knows her way about.'

Jennifer asked where he was to spend Christmas, said she was going away to a hotel in Bournemouth, 'just like an old lady. I shall walk if it's fine enough, and drive if it isn't, and eat big meals.'

'But why Bournemouth?'

'The epitome of bourgeois *gemütlichkeit*.' She laughed at her own words. 'Easygoing good nature. And it's expensive, so I shall be boiling cross if I don't get my pound of flesh.'

'Your metaphors are in a fine old mix.'

'That's enough of that, young Clark.'

'What's your father doing?'

'Yes. Go on. Trouble the vestiges of my conscience. I don't know. My eldest brother invited him down to Kent for the holiday, but he wouldn't go. He'll sit about.'

'Have you bought him a present?'

'I have. A tape-recorder. He won't buy himself one. And a recording of some poems.'

'He'll like that?'

'God knows. It'll give him something to do. One never knows with him. It may set him off on a craze, but on the other hand he may never take it out of the box. It was the best I could think of.'

She then said she must begin work again. When he asked for how long she'd be at it, she said she'd finish at midnight. At the door she kissed him, briefly, dryly on the lips, promising to drop in his present at Mrs Mac's before he left. She thanked him, stroked his upper arm, but he guessed as soon as she shut the door she'd frown, sigh and be immediately immersed in her task.

He stood for a moment in the hall of her house, dimly lit, but wide and free from dust. It needed a large, brilliantly lit Christmas tree at this time of the year to relieve the solidity, the greyness, the shadowed alcoves. He looked back at her door, uncertainly. He ought to rush back, insist she stopped work. All he had to do was to walk four steps and tap the door. He did not do so. He had bedded this woman, but found out nothing about her. Once he reached his parents' home he'd write her a letter so that when she raced back from the South Coast she'd find amongst the two late cards, the dozen pieces of junk mail that had been at the bottom of the postman's bag for a fortnight, a real piece of writing. He left the hall, stood on the ground outside. He'd do better to write the letter to her father. Old Stapleton needed stimulation; she apparently did not.

'My trouble,' she had informed him, 'is overwork. I've the necessary energy, and I like the money, but I ought to be doing my local history, or going to concerts or traipsing round picture galleries or, oh, foreign spas.' She had laughed at these, her old-fashioned expressions. 'Instead, I play about with figures on bits of paper.' She had coughed and then told him to beware of promotion as it killed humanity.

Back at Mrs Mackenzie's he found his landlady and one of the schoolmistresses decorating a small Christmas tree in the dining room. He was invited to join in.

Mrs Mac explained why she needed the tree, its provenance. Clark was instructed to plug in the chain of electric lamps, but when he did so there was no result. He tightened each bulb, tested each wire as best he could and was rewarded.

'I like a man about the house for these jobs.' Mrs Mac warmed to him.

The schoolma'am, who had another day to work before term's end, smiled vaguely at him. She seemed worn out, or shy of him, and dropped her eyes when he spoke. Though she'd be in her twenties, she was dowdily dressed, looked older. Both women smelt of scent, heavily used.

On the completion of the tree-decking, Clark was ordered up the stepladder to fasten paper garlands from the corners of the room to the wooden circle in the centre from which the electric light flex hung. Mrs Mac had one short red, yellow and blue elaborate length left and this they fixed in two equal loops above the mantelpiece. Mrs Mackenzie, expansive, made them sit down for a celebratory glass of sherry while she explained how she would spend Christmas. On the day itself she'd be alone, eating sparingly, reading, occasionally turning on a suitable programme. Here she listed the many unsuitable offerings which

161

she would disregard. Boxing Day was to be spent with her old neighbour and friend, a widow, Mrs Priest, who lived out at West Bridgford. She would need to watch the buses most carefully, as there was only a skeleton service, but she had checked; she always did. Mrs Priest invited in a blind lady from up the road for her Christmas dinner. On the Saturday following Mrs Priest would arrive here at noon and stay until eight; it demanded two bus routes and she was approaching eighty. 'Otherwise,' she concluded, 'refurbishment. That washing machine will be gurgling all day.'

She insisted on pouring second glasses of sherry. The schoolteacher said she came from Manchester and could get back home on the day she broke up, but had decided against it. The second schoolmistress appeared and was pressed into sitting with them. She was not loath, and told them a joke about a lion and a missionary. Mrs Mac capped it with another equally feeble. All four did their best with laughter. Mention of the missionaries led the landlady to say that she would appear in church either at midnight mass or on the morning of Christmas Day, and from this she expounded her view that our society had forgotten the religious significance of the holiday and commercialism had swamped all other considerations. She needed no help on this, though the two other women agreed and crooned muted agreement. Clark amused himself trying to guess the next platitude, but found no logic in Madam's discourse; anecdote tumbled over assertion in a ruthlessness of banality.

In the end Clark rose and said he had one or two small jobs to do that evening, a flat lie. The schoolma'ams were immediately on their feet. In a flurry of thanks they left Mrs Mackenzie with her four empty glasses to wash.

'God,' said the first on the top landing, 'does she never stop?'

'She's lonely,' the second whispered.

'Was there a Mr Mackenzie?' The first, mischievously. 'He'd be glad to go.'

They looked at Clark apprehensively, but he nodded pardon and peace. They made for their respective beds, with compliments of the season in case they did not meet again.

Clark arrived at his parents' home on Christmas Eve in time for the heavy evening meal prepared for the men. His mother grilled him about his work, and he sat idly answering questions. 'What sort of man is the Head?' 'Do you see much of him?' The invitation to coach Short's niece was commented on, favourably, at length. The two schools where he had taught were contrasted, and compared with his own day school. His mother was at her best; she had plenty to do, but was adequately prepared and on top of her tasks. No subject loosened her tongue like education. Slightly flushed, she talked, she probed, she pronounced; her menfolk encouraged her.

Mrs Clark was momentarily dashed when he asked permission to use the 'phone to call Daniella. That period was over in her mind, but she recovered sufficiently to offer the girl hospitality at any time. 'She'll be going down to her parents' home, won't she?' 'I doubt it. She doesn't see eye to eye with them.' Mrs Clark glanced steel-sharp at her husband who studied the ceiling jovially, but the mother carefully closed the door on the conversation.

The exchange with Daniella struck no sparks. The girl had come up to London, to stay in the flat of a friend who was away over the holiday. Yes, she would be pleased to drive over on Christmas Day for lunch; she had made tentative arrangements but they could be cancelled. It would take her no more than an hour, if that, as there'd be little traffic. Daniella spoke cautiously; he could not tell, either from tone of voice or sentences, whether she was excited at the prospect of seeing him again. She would arrive at twelve midday.

'We haven't bought her a present,' Mrs Clark said. 'We never expected . . .'

'There are plenty of bits and pieces in this house, Sheila.'

'Such as what?'

'Knick-knacks. Rings. Brooches. You choose one; I'll polish it up.' Father Clark obviously looked forward to the advent of Daniella.

The parents, up and about early on Christmas Day, brought breakfast to their son in bed.

'You need the rest,' said his mother. 'And it keeps you from under my feet.'

His father looked in.

'Compliments of the season,' he called. 'I'm just looking round for something to keep me out of your mother's way. When I've shaved, she's set me to polish the furniture. Always have the house reeking of Mansion when you expect visitors.'

David Clark sat on the side of the bed and talked about his wife. She'd been a tiny bit off, nothing serious, but he'd insisted she'd gone down to the surgery for a thorough check-up. Nothing wrong, the doctor had said.

'I don't know whether it's because she has too little to occupy her. She chases round the house, and cooks as if I needed a banquet every night. Then she hasn't many friends. She doesn't drive and she won't learn. I talk about WEA and the like, and she's all smiles and agreement, but she never signs up.'

'You're worried, aren't you?'

'Yes and no. We're getting to the stage in life where people are beginning to drop off.'

'You're fifty-three. That's not old.'

'But we can't guarantee, as you can, that all the people we know roughly our age are still alive. It'll get worse, I expect. And it makes me that extra bit anxious.'

'Work's all right? You're not thinking of early retirement?'

His father had managed a small suburban branch of a bank for the past fifteen years.

'That's another thing. I've been at Market Street now for long enough, and didn't want, didn't expect, to move. I did apply for other jobs when you were a boy, at home, and though they interviewed me, I didn't get appointed. I don't know whether I was serious or not. I didn't put in for everything, I picked and chose . . . and paid the penalty. But,' here Clark's father slapped his knee, and then stroked it as if he'd hurt himself, 'just at the beginning of November, not long after you'd been over for half-term, they sent for me and offered me a much larger branch, twice the size, in Kentish Town.'

'And? Were you surprised?'

'Yes, I was. I'd run my place well enough. And I also had the impression, right or wrong, that the people higher up the line hadn't much notion how the likes of me went about our business. They knew the high-flyers, the people always up for interview, or those with pushy backers, because they had once been like that themselves. But the little man in the trilby hat,' his father had never even owned one, 'they didn't understand. I did my job well, and didn't want to shift. As you know, in a bank the size of ours there are plenty of places for honest journeymen. So, yes. It came as a surprise. I hadn't applied. I was invited.'

'How come?'

'You have me there. We'd had a couple of inspectors in during the summer, and they'd been pleased enough. But. . . . I just don't know. In the ordinary way they'd appoint a young chap in his forties, younger perhaps, even a woman nowadays. Whether they'd had trouble in this place and want to import some sort of father figure, or whether one of these inspectors had said I wasn't employed to the limit of my ability I don't know. It's never happened before. And how the word reached somebody of sufficient importance to change the bank's policy is another puzzle. But I was sent for, and interviewed, and last week offered the post. It's a mystery.'

'You'll take it?'

'Yes. I talked it over with your mother and decided to accept it.'

'That's not what's upsetting her?'

'I don't think so. She doesn't like change, any more than I do. But no. We can stay here. I can commute. And I shall be better off, better pension prospects and all the rest of it.'

'But what about the work?' the son pressed. 'Do you look forward to that?'

'More to do, perhaps. More risks to be taken. But that's a side that's never bothered me much.' The son, straight in his bed, had never before in his life considered his father's difficulties, the decisions he had to make, the judgements. He wished he knew more about banking. 'If, of course,' his father continued, 'it's been a matter of clashing personalities, that will be more tricky. But I've seen it before; I've had some.'

'This is great, Dad. It really is.'

'It's a bolt from the blue, that's certain.' The father grinned. 'But if they're making the right decision they should have made it fifteen years ago.'

'You don't hold it against them?'

'No. And the people who decide are not the same from year to year. And for every appointment they make there'll be a dozen applicants, all of whom will give satisfaction in their different ways.'

'I can't tell you how pleased I am for you,' Clark said. 'When do you start?'

'Third week in January.'

'Is your successor appointed?'

'Yes.'

'A young man?'

'Not very. About the age I was when I took over.'

'Will this be your last move?'

'Two months ago I'd have said I'd serve my time out in Market Street. Now, God only knows. I'd think so. I'm dizzy.'

His father talked on at length about the difficulty of fetching people in from other parts of the country because of house prices, and even embarked on a fantasy in which self-important managers lived 'above the shop' as in the old days. The prospect of new opportunity had clearly stirred his imagination. His manner, his gestures, voice, vocabulary were as before, old-fashioned, slightly down market, that of the grammar-school product with a stiffish collar because his own father wore none for work, but his mind was leaping inside the rigid limits that years of suburban life had drawn. The old man wouldn't be chasing blondes, or throwing parties, or taking to religion or even package holidays, but he had changed. Clark himself felt elated.

When later Clark talked the move over with his mother he found her view different. 'Your father's got his due at last,' she said. 'It's late, but better than not at all. He's clever. When he took the banking exams he was always top of the class, but he wouldn't go hawking his merits through the streets.' Clark grinned at the metaphor. 'He should have had this move twenty years ago. Oh, well, not quite. It doesn't do to exaggerate.'

'And what will happen to him next?'

'Nothing much if I know them,' his mother answered. 'It's quite a big promotion, but he's not been made a member of the board.'

166

'How will you spend the money?'

'We're very comfortable as we are. We live within our means. I suppose we could move into a bigger house, though this one's ample for just the two of us. We can change the furniture or redecorate all through the place, but there's no need.'

'Clothes? Holidays?' the son hinted.

'Your father's always been generous, has not begrudged me anything. No, we shan't go mad on spending sprees. Your father might invest it. He knows about such things.'

'That won't do you any good.'

'No, but you'll benefit.'

'You might live, Mum, another forty years. It's likely.'

'I don't like to be called "Mum",' she said, with a snap. She was as pleased as her husband; he was sure of that. Why she had not mentioned any of this, however guardedly, in her letters was a question easily answered. She had not expected anything to come of the interview. Her little husband would bow out with no ill-feelings while some young fly-by-night with half his brains would snaffle the job and the kudos.

Clark, pleased with the news, sang in his bath, about the house. 'O, come, all ye faithful/Joyful and triumphant.' By midday he sat ready in his best for Daniella's arrival.

She looked, he admitted it, extraordinarily pretty, with her fair curling hair, the oviform earrings, the pastel-green neckerchief, the matching tights, the cream dress. Good enough to eat, he thought. She kissed him, rather timorously and clumsily, not on the lips, and sat down on the edge of a chair, a glass of sherry in her hand. Father Clark made a fuss, hovered, drank in her perfume, hummed his happiness tunelessly. Daniella and Anthony discussed health, his new job, and he enquired about their mutual acquaintances. She seemed jerkily nervous, looked about her as if for some inspector who judged her performance. Just under the lower lip she had a spot, or cluster of small blemishes, obscured for practical purposes by her make-up. Mr Clark, half-way through a long anecdote about a colleague who spent his holidays driving through France merely to sample the cuisine, was called away to the kitchen to help with the final stages of the meal. Clark could easily imagine his mother's exasperated lecture. 'They need to have a bit of time together, not listening to your blather. They had a bad quarrel. They must have done.' The poor man would be detailed to set the starched serviettes in their silver holders, which he would do with extraordinary neatness and speed, and then sent off to see the dining-room table was properly laid. He would carry out these tasks, but keep glancing at the closed door of the drawing room where the young people sat.

They were easier now; perhaps the sherry played its part.

Clark had given an account of his time-table, pupils, Head of Department, colleagues, the Headmaster and now, finally, Hugh Pearson. Daniella, knees clasped as she leaned forward, eyes bright, was prepared to be impressed. He, entertaining, wondered whether he should invite her to Hampshire, to the Lumleys. He had no idea as she faced him, pretty and pleased, not a word out of place.

He described Gill Wycliffe, Jennifer Hope, Ernest Stapleton and their homes, the town and its attractions, the Sixth-Formers discussing Kant in their leisure-time, the concerts. Daniella kept bright eyes on him as if he had returned from Fatehpur Sikri, Goose Green or Tasiussaq, her lips slightly parted, her teeth pearly. She looked young compared with Jennifer, vulnerable but unnoticing; the word 'puppy' came into his head. Her fingernails were long, tinted, polished in the delicate, unmoving hands.

They received the call for lunch with a formal fumbling to feet, self-recovery.

Mrs Clark had excelled herself. They all, except the mother, emptied plates piled with Christmas fare. 'Leave room for your pudding,' the hostess warned, but both then took second helpings as Daniella laughed out loud. They drank muscatel.

'We'll have a few minutes' rest,' Father Clark said, tapping his paunch.

'You will not. And let my sauce spoil.'

The turkey was wheeled out, still plump with meat, and the pudding arrived, was topped with blue flames organized by the older Clark. They ate small portions this time, but not slowly. The dark sweetness, the white sauce tempted but no one passed a plate for more.

168

'Cheese, now?' Mrs Clark, almost boisterous. She had eaten quite sparingly, her son noticed. 'Fruit? Coffee?'

'Oxygen,' said her husband.

Daniella cleared away, and the men washed up. Clark realized how little there was; his mother had cooked and cleaned together. Dizzy with a small, post-prandial port, he realized what a remarkable woman she was, said as much to his father.

'Yes. She has her points,' the old man replied, short of Christmas spirit. He belched politely.

They sat round a gas-fire and gave and received presents. The Clarks had produced from somewhere a beautiful little casket, with thin gold bands and divisions. Smooth, polished, cold, it looked like alabaster to the young man but he was not sure. His father showed equivalent ignorance.

'And what should you keep in that?' he asked.

'That's your choice. Cosmetics or small sewing aids or jewellery.'

The father blew his lips out, but was glad.

Clark's present to the girl was a handsome travelling bag she had talked about just before their break-up. She had bought him a complicated wristwatch which he had seen advertised in the quality papers and had wondered who invested in such offers. All seemed pleased, he and father with their shirts and sweaters, mother with her book on annual flowers, her necklace, her two-piece, her blouse.

About four, Daniella surprised them saying she had to return, that she had another call to make, and asked Clark if he'd like to come with her. Surprisingly his mother encouraged the idea, though his father asked how he'd get back.

'I'll go in my own car,' he said. 'Follow Daniella.'

His father shrugged. The mother insisted that they had another cup of tea before they left. No one could manage the offered slice of Christmas cake.

Clark insisted that Daniella gave him the address and directions in case he lost her during the journey. In fact he had no difficulty, the roads were comparatively empty with traffic lights changing for no one. They arrived in a little over half an hour, had some trouble parking, but walked together in darkness to the friend's flat which Daniella had borrowed.

169

The place was small, two rectangular oblongs, sitting and bed rooms, a cramped square of kitchen, and a bathroom and lavatory with, as Daniella put it, 'standing room for one'. The rooms smelt both stuffy and damp, and the plaster on the walls was painted a dispiriting acid yellow. Daniella stamped round opening windows vigorously, quickly had the gas-fire hissing and the electric kettle on.

She sat him down in an arm-chair, handing him the *Cambridge Encyclopaedia of Language* to occupy him. From the bedroom he could hear her making a 'phone call. When she returned with tea, she said, aggressively,

'I'm not a liar. I had to come back.'

'Go on,' he said, mildly and intrigued.

'I promised to deliver Aileen's Christmas present to her grandmother. I couldn't do it yesterday. She lives ten minutes' walk away in an old people's complex. When we've had this we'll walk round; at least I shall; you can please yourself.'

'I'll come with you.'

'Thanks. I don't suppose I shall be long. I don't know the old dear. Never met her. But Aileen had to dash off. She's in Paris until the New Year. And left me this chore. I've just 'phoned to see if it's convenient. You needn't come. You can stay here.'

'I've said I will.'

Daniella seemed uneasy, uncertain, and this showed in a sharpness of speech, a brusqueness of movement. The flat was enough to dishearten; she'd taken it over to be near him, and hated it. He would as soon have spent his holiday in a telephone kiosk. Dismal sounds of occupation could be heard from the other tenants and owners. He asked what Aileen did for a living.

'She teaches. She's clever; she'll get on. She's a deputy head at thirty. She'll move in a year or two, sell this at advantage, and then buy a decent house elsewhere in the country with the proceeds. She was Head of the Foreign Languages Department at my first school, befriended me. Then moved up here. She came from hereabouts. She's ambitious and bright. First at Queen Mary's, brilliant MA in her spare time. She'll be a somebody.'

'Her next move?'

170

'Headship or the inspectorate.'

He could not tell whether Daniella liked or approved of her friend. That she admired her was clear, but there were reservations.

'Is she married?' he asked.

'No. Not likely to be. It would stand in the way of her career. She's had men friends. In some ways she's a continental intellectual. I'd guess, no, it's silly to say this, it really is, she'd sooner speak her mind in French than in English. It's more precise, or forceful, or cutting.'

'Is it?'

He began to describe Hugh Pearson, who, though scholarly, spent a good part of his holidays in France where they had a country cottage, seemed a paradigm of the product of the English public school.

'He's utterly superior, but quite unambitious,' he told her as they walked along the not well-lit streets. 'He'd make a good headmaster or director of education, even, but he has never put himself out. He leaves promotion to lesser men.'

'I'd like to meet him.'

'Quite likely. If you came up. He's been very kind to me in his distant way.'

'What is it about us,' she asked, tucking her arm into his, 'that makes these notables want to look after us?' She seemed easier out here.

They walked along discussing their two older colleagues. Aileen, from a working-class home, had forced her way upwards, stylishly passing exams, making herself known, determined that one at least of her background should reach the top of her profession, influence decisions there. She worked all day, without sparing herself; she bullied and cajoled, blackmailed or impressed. There would be no holding her. The flat, with its ugly, bitter walls and cramped discomfort was typical. It offered her warmth, the means of cooking a simple meal, a desk at which to write and plan, a bed to flop on to late at night. A tigerish activity would make her known. Yet underneath this magnificence of effort, this ferocious intelligence there existed, no, was the source of her power, the small, dark child led twenty-five years ago into an

171

infants' school classroom for the first time in her life and there had opened her inward eyes.

Clark's Pearson seemed quieter, more enigmatic. Unlike Aileen he had no need to demonstrate his cleverness; it was expected of him. He'd done well at the university because his family had always done so, because of earlier advantages such as being brought up bi-lingual, and because his interest was caught. He had married into a higher stratum of landed gentry than his own, and since some private money made the relationship financially comfortable if not affluent he had, for social reasons, become a schoolmaster and done the job adequately. Pupils and colleagues respected him, even when they considered him old-fashioned; he put up with their egalitarian notions and taught with such success that enemies felt themselves unable to compare themselves with him. On the other hand, he made no attempt to apply for more prestigious positions. He'd condemn that adjective.

'Why's that?' Daniella asked.

'Something in his personality perhaps. Some failure. Or it might be that he wants to perfect what he's doing. Or perhaps he feels himself above the battle. He has enough; why scratch and scrape for more?'

'Does he live in a big house?'

'Not really. Decent. Substantial. In a very good residential area. Fine, long stretch of garden. First-class carpets, furniture, décor. Marvellous pictures. Stately home stuff.'

'And his wife?'

'I don't know her well. An Honourable. But quiet, like him. He never appears to lay the law down. And yet he's respected. He knows everybody of importance in his subject. Oxbridge professors, chief inspectors if that's what they're called, notables of university presses, members of the government and the top échelons of the Civil Service.'

'Did he tell you this?' Daniella laughed at him.

'He did not. It's mainly those who dislike him, or fear him, those who think he came out of the ark. They rubbish him like this, but you can tell they envy him, wish they had the same advantages.'

'What about his department? How does he keep them in order?'

172

'No need. He's a good picker, they tell me. His people don't stay long, three or four years, and then off to positions of power. If such exist in the educational world. And he chooses his next high-flyer.'

'How did you come to be in favour with him?' Again the mockery in her voice.

'Don't know. Can't tell.' That was right. 'But when you come up and meet him, you'll find him a very polite, shy, tallish, handsome man with this neat head of curly, public-school hair, who won't force his attention on you, won't try to be witty at your expense or try to impress you. You'll admire his suit and his shirt and his shoes, if you've an eye for such things, and his hands. He hasn't even got this haw-haw voice, clear at two hundred yards, though his wife's a bit that way. If you met him for five minutes, you might be attracted by the outward appearance, he looks like an aristocrat, but not by anything he's said to you. After an hour or two you'd be amazed by how much he's taken in, how much and how accurately he's used inference. If you confessed you'd just murdered your mother, he wouldn't turn a hair.'

'My, Tony! You're enthusiastic.'

'Yes. But it's not until I've had to begin to tell you all about it that I've realized quite how remarkable Hugh Pearson is.'

'You must have known. I knew how much better by several miles Aileen was than anybody else there.'

'I didn't. Perhaps I'm obtuse. Or cynical.'

'We ought to be grateful that such people are still found in the teaching profession.'

Daniella had demonstrated her superiority over him. As they entered the shadowed yard of the old people's complex, Wesley House, Clark drew her to him, kissed her lips. She returned his kiss, but not wantonly, with suspicion.

'We're late,' she said, 'and I hope you haven't spoilt my make-up.'

He rubbed his lips and she examined her face in a small hand-mirror as they entered the cramped foyer, almost as dimly lit as the yard. A barely decorated Christmas tree occupied one corner and darkened garlands criss-crossed the ceiling. They rang a bell at a guichet marked 'Enquiries'. Nobody answered.

They looked about them. A worried, grey-haired woman came into the hall.

'Could we see Mrs Owen?' Daniella, unusually small-voiced. The woman screwed her forehead as if this were a question beyond understanding. She gasped, collected herself.

'We're just rounding them up. For entertainment in the dining room. Television and a few recitations and a round or two of bingo. What name did you say? Owen? I don't know if she's gone in yet.'

'We shan't be too long. We've just brought her this present. From her granddaughter. We'll hand it over and then she can go to your party.'

The woman consulted a printed list.

'Owen. Number thirteen. Granny Owen. Oh, yes, I know her. Follow me.'

She set off, led them in a corridor round one and two half sides of a square. There was no evidence of other movement. They could discern no great rush for the entertainment.

'Thirteen. Here y'are.' The woman knocked. 'Mrs Owen. Mrs Owen? Are you there?' A small crow or croak inside in answer to the cockney questions. 'Are you decent? You never know with these old dears. Are you, then? Your granddaughter's brought you a present.'

The door opened, and a wrinkled woman eyed them, upwards.

'Mrs Owen?' Daniella spoke firmly. 'Aileen asked me to give this to you. I'm sorry I couldn't bring it before.'

'Better late than never.' The grey-haired woman, socially.

Somehow the party of four stuttered into the room, which was tiny with a table and four chairs occupying the larger half, one arm-chair, a cactus or two, a television set. No pictures decorated the wall, only an oval mirror above the mantelpiece and gas-fire. The place was warm, from a radiator, well-lighted, with patterned, drawn curtains, but comfortless. Clean, it had no humanity about it, a space into which one had packed the chipped furniture from an old woman's house, where it now stood cheap and solid on the golden parquet floor. Carpets were remnants, cut down from former use and edged. Inside one could smell the disinfectant of the corridors.

174

The grandmother, recovered, thanked them. She asked after Aileen, said she was not surprised she was spending Christmas in France, she always did. 'I thought at one time she'd marry a Frenchman. She brought one or two of them home.' She was a good girl. Daniella added that Aileen was clever, would make a name for herself in the sphere of education. 'She took after her father. He could have been anything if they'd have given him half a chance,' the old lady said. She insisted on being introduced to Clark, and asked if he was going to marry Daniella.

'It's a possibility,' he conceded, pleasantly.

'She's very, very pretty.' Mrs Owen spoke as if Daniella was not there. 'But these days young people don't bother about weddings. They just live together.' He feared more questions. 'I don't know that that isn't better. Just like that daughter of yours, Mrs Smith.' The worried woman blushed, and frowned.

Clearly the old woman's memory proved too good, too unacceptable for her comfort. Clark wondered why Mrs Smith had been so grudging in admitting that she knew Mrs Owen. Perhaps the complex was troubled by visitors, officials from the DHSS, local do-gooders, con-men, potential muggers, petty thieves; though surely, not on Christmas Day. Clark found amusement in the thought that he and Daniella, however well-dressed for festivities, appeared as suspicious characters.

Mrs Owen talked about Aileen, and her family. She spoke in neat, well-presented sentences; obviously she had all her wits about her. She had placed the present, a square box in silver and scarlet-striped paper, topped with a rose of ribbon, on her table. She shook her bent forefinger at it, telling them she'd leave the pleasure of opening it until she returned from the 'concert'.

'There's some bingo,' Mrs Smith comforted in misjudgement.

'I shan't win that. I'm never lucky.'

'Why, you had one of them 20ps in your Christmas pudding.'

They laughed. Daniella wished Mrs Owen good night, repeated her name again. They shook hands with compliments of the season. Mrs Smith warned the old lady to prepare herself for instant entertainment, stumped ahead of the visitors to the main entrance.

175

'My word, she's kept her senses.' Daniella. 'Aileen said she was ninety.'

'Too sharp for her own good, sometimes.' Mrs Smith.

Gloomily, she let them out into the darkness of the yard.

The young people walked away in silence, broken a hundred yards on by Daniella.

'Thank God I'm out of there. I'd hate it. Pokey little hole.'

'But warm, and there's company, and somebody to call on if you're in trouble. And you have your own bits and pieces round you.'

'What bits and pieces?' the girl snapped. 'That bloody old extending table?'

'What did Aileen buy her?' he asked pacifically, a few paces on.

'No idea. It was there wrapped when I arrived, with a note directing me where to deliver it.'

For the rest of the journey Daniella seemed quite out of sorts, either silent or complaining. She allowed him to take her arm, but unwillingly. He tried to find out what her operatic society was performing, and when, but that led to further short sentences, ejaculations, of disgust at incompetence and rife favouritism. He did his best with an account of the violin recital and a sing-for-yourself *Messiah* he'd attended. She merely quickened her pace.

At the flat she invited him in, clattered about making instant coffee, but asked if he'd like a piece of Christmas cake. All these preparations she made in her outdoor clothes. When she put his plate in front of him, he stood and took her in his arms. She allowed him to kiss her lips, then twisted her head away. Her body was limp.

'What's wrong?' he asked.

'Nothing. I feel off. I've got the curse. I don't know. I hate this flat. It's as comfortable as a tube station. God, I thought Aileen would have. . . . Anybody as clever and knowledgeable as she is. It's worse than a bloody dog-kennel.'

She removed her coat; both sat down to eat the thick slices. He left his icing and marzipan until last. He gave her details of his day or two in Hampshire, invited her to join him. When she refused, she did so aggressively, putting him into his place,

176

naming her duties. They fell to silence, and good cake. She made no attempt to talk.

'This hasn't been very successful,' he said, wiping the last crumb from his lip.

'What hasn't?'

'Our meeting, reunion.'

'Hasn't it?'

Anger mounted, but he kept his voice steady.

'It seems not. No.' He placed emptied cup neatly on his plate. 'Are we going to meet again?'

'That's up to you, isn't it?'

'I don't think so. You were the one who broke it off before, and asked then to make up. You've not made me exactly welcome.'

'I feel very off today.'

'I'm not so sure that that's it, but I'm in no position to argue.'

She fidgeted, but looking at him, in a combination of fierceness and fear.

'More cake?' she asked. It sounded sarcastic. 'Another cup of coffee?'

He waited. Nothing came of it. A cheap alarm clock ticked over-loudly from behind him. He rose and carried his crockery into the kitchen. When he returned she sat exactly as before.

'That's it, then.' He lifted coat and scarf from the back of a chair. He had carefully folded them. Hers had been dropped to the floor. In no sort of hurry he wrapped his scarf round his throat, shrugged on his short driving coat. 'I'm sorry,' he said. No answer. 'I didn't come up to scratch.'

'It's nothing to do with you.'

Again he waited for an explanation. None came. He checked the buttons of his coat. They were properly fastened.

'Goodbye, then.'

He held out his hand. She reared, dragging in breath, subsided and began to cry. Caught out, he stepped across, knelt, placed a hand in the crook of her left arm.

'What is it, Dan?'

'Leave me alone.'

'No. I can't just go out when you're like this. What's wrong? Perhaps if you try to tell me about it, it won't seem so bad.'

She continued to cry, half-heartedly. He resumed his seat, facing her but not looking directly at her. After a few minutes

177

she felt down to the hand-bag which she had dropped with her coat, unclasped it, rummaged in it, to take out a small square of handkerchief with which she dabbed her eyes, blew her nose. She crumpled the handkerchief into her hand, and sat strongly upright.

'Well, then,' he began. 'Is that better?' No effect. 'Please, Daniella, tell me what's wrong.' Nothing. 'Will you?'

'No.' A sniff, a further dabbing. 'There isn't anything.'

'Wrong, you mean.'

'Oh, for Christ's sake. I've got a cold. It's the time of the month. I'm tired. I'm cooped up in this horrid flat.'

'Come to Hampshire with me.'

'I can't. I've promised to visit my parents. It's nothing. I just feel so miserable. I thought meeting you again would set me up, but it hasn't. Your mother doesn't like me. And there's nothing in it for you and me, is there?'

'That's partly my fault.' He answered slowly, as if preventing her from speaking rested her, gave her the opportunity to recover. 'I was, well, doubtful, not very forthcoming. We used to laugh a lot, and make fun of people, and then suddenly you drop me. It shook me. And so I come back suspicious.'

Her eyes brimmed. She rubbed at the reddened end of her nose. Her skin was waxy, delicate. She shook her head.

'I'll go home tomorrow, Boxing Day, and then I'll perhaps sort myself out. I must think. Thrash it out. And I'll let you know.'

'Will that take a long time?' he demanded, but gently.

'If I can't make my mind up, it'll mean "No", won't it?'

That seemed sharp, intelligent enough.

'Is there anything I can do for you now?'

'No. I don't think so. I shall put the electric blanket on and go to bed.'

'Do you want me to ring you? At your mother's?'

She smiled at that, like a well-behaved small child.

'No. Let me sort myself out in my own time.'

He sat for a few minutes longer in his coat, knees together, very still, giving her the chance to change her mind. She did not.

'I'll be on my way, then. You have my parents' 'phone

number. This is the Hampshire one.' He tore a slip from his notebook, wrote. 'I'm there from the 27th. In the afternoon.' He put the paper on her table.

''Bye, then.' He stood, put out a hand. She moved, brushed his fingers with hers.

'I'm sorry,' she said, looking at her feet.

Clark let himself out, sat downcast in his car, fastening and unfastening the seat-belt. He was not surprised, and yet the Daniella he remembered, the golden girl, laughing her way through the antics of her operatic society, mocking her colleagues, riotously active at disco or in bed, sure of herself, of life, of him had changed into this dumb, dim, morose zombie. And he was not surprised.

''Twas Christmas Day in the Workhouse,' he said out loud, but drove quietly off. There were more people about than he expected, more cars, one group of young revellers singing arm in arm across the pavement.

He waited at the traffic lights, wondered what his friends in Beechnall were about. Jennifer was in Bournemouth. The Wycliffes would be at home, both with large volumes, glasses of port, not saying much. The Pearsons would have their children about them, skimming above the surface of the earth, nobody happy, but all warm and not sober. 'Hark the herald angels sing.' Not here.

His father had left the gates open. He parked in the drive. Nine-forty-five. He let himself in.

'I didn't expect you so soon,' his mother said, rushing out into the hall.

'No.'

XVII

Clark enjoyed Boxing Day with his parents.

They ate well; he walked out with his father in a dull, almost muggy afternoon, and the old man named the prices of properties. Later, his mother held a long, loving cross-examination about his first term at Beechnall Boys' High School; both her menfolk, one unexpectedly, had succeeded as

179

she wished, and she celebrated. Oddly, Anthony himself quite enjoyed the conversations, and at the end of the day his dad, a man of few gestures, patted him almost expansively on the upper arm.

The two days in Hampshire he spent at work. The Lumleys had decorated a fair amount of the interior of their new home, and a large part of the good furniture, stored for some months in a parent's upper room in Hampstead, arrived at much the same time as the visitor, who helped his host lug it about the house. He had then helped with the polishing.

Meals were huge and bucolic. The Lumleys, Clark, the furniture man and his schoolboy son (these two were on holiday all week, but Charlie had somehow managed to 'borrow' a pantechnicon from work, and had drummed up assistance at the London end) sat down to potatoes, cabbage and stewed beef, red wine, and jam roly-poly with white sauce.

"Aven't had this since I was a child,' Charlie instructed his son. 'You can keep your Christmas turkeys and puddings. This is food, boy.'

The two left, belching, soon after five, a litre bottle of the red plonk in the cab as a reward for father's abstinence during the meal.

'I'm glad I couldn't drink too much,' Charlie confessed. 'In my view wine detracts from the food.'

'What a puritan,' Beth Lumley said as the pantechnicon rattled away.

Clark took his leave after late breakfast on his third day.

'I'm sorry we've made you work so hard,' Beth apologized.

'It was quite unintentional,' Denis added. 'This removal we organized at the very last minute. A bit of pocket money for Charlie, tax-free. And his boss, if I have the story right.'

The dashing about, the changing of mind, the elbow-grease, the quick lunch-time trips to the Silver Swan, the one long afternoon walk had suited him exactly. The fiasco with Daniella barely occupied him. The Lumleys asked if she was coming, were told she had to visit her parents, and that was that. They were as content as his mother, who had asked three or four blunt questions ambiguously answered, to allow her to drop out. The Lumleys were trenchermen and conversationalists,

180

holders-forth rather, and they filled his head with their concerns. Denis, a solicitor, had become partner in a firm in Alton, and Beth had achieved a fortunate transfer to a tax office not half an hour's drive away. And they had achieved their ambition to live in the country. Denis had been considering for some months an offer from an old college friend whose father was about to retire and they had almost decided on a 'very decent' house when this eighteenth-century cottage had come up for sale. They felt favoured by the gods, though they wondered how a couple of townies like them would manage to keep their three acres of garden and orchard under control.

Clark was delighted as he drove back to his parents'.

His trousers were stretched; two of the nicest people he knew had been especially fortunate and were making the most of it. They were two or three years older than he was; Beth had taught with him in his first year but had married at the end, moved to London, decided to employ her mathematics in the Civil Service, and now they had managed what they had always wanted, or as the careful Denis had it, 'what we think we want'.

They'd have clever children and rosy apples, Clark decided, and do good by stealth and take advantage of no one. The world seemed a better place for their success.

His mother was waiting for him.

'A lady rang you from Beechnall.'

'Who's that, then?'

'Jennifer Hope.'

'What does she want?'

'To speak to you. Very polite and very nicely spoken. She asked if you'd ring back straight away as it was rather urgent.'

'Did she say. . . . ?'

'No, she did not. She left these two numbers, home and work.'

He tried both. No answer from her flat; a secretary muttered that Mrs Hope had been into the office that morning. He shrugged away, announced the lack of news to his mother cheerfully appearing with coffee and chocolate biscuits.

'Keep trying,' she said cheerfully. 'It's urgent. Rather urgent.'

181

She began to ask questions about Daniella, put two and two together.

'I don't think she's the one you're looking for.' Mrs Clark sounded self-satisfied.

'We shall see.'

'If you're not sure, the answer's "No".'

'If only it was as easy as that.'

'What does that mean?'

'Nothing. Another oracular utterance.'

'You're as bad as your father. He thinks I understand nothing except cookery and ironing shirts. There was something about that Daniella that was, well, not right.'

She was launched. He half-listened, wondering why Jennifer would ring 'rather urgently'. His father had gone back to the bank to clear up the year at his old branch. His mother chattered at, not to him; Daniella was rejected every half hour; the two days in Hampshire were inspected and an enquiry or two made about Jennifer Hope. The school and his prowess there were praised. He tried three times in the ninety minutes before lunch to contact Jennifer, ran her to earth at home just before two o'clock.

'Oh, is that you, Tony?' she spoke breathlessly.

'You sound a long way off. I've been trying to get you ever since I got back.'

'I'm sorry. I had to be out. Things are. . . . I've some bad news for you.'

He did not speak, waited as she did.

'It's Hugh, Hugh Pearson.' Again the pause, which she allowed to prolong itself beyond all reason. His mind scrabbled for sense. 'He's dead, Tony. He died.'

That snatched his breath. He could not utter.

'He fell on Christmas Eve. Down the stairs. An awful, awkward trip and hit his head on the newel-post. Terrible, Clarissa said. You could hear it all over the house. They were all on their own. He was unconscious, of course. White as a sheet. Clarissa ran next door, and fetched the neighbour in. By that time Hugh was coming round.'

'Did they call a doctor?'

'No. Hugh wouldn't allow it. He was all right, he said. He

182

was dizzy, and very shaken, and couldn't remember anything, but they put him to bed. Apparently he slept.'

'I see.'

She made him wait again, as if she herself had to come to terms with her news sentence by small sentence.

'Clarissa made him stay in bed on Christmas morning, and he seemed not too bad. He got up about twelve and had a bit of lunch. He seemed, as she said, very quiet, a bit disorientated, and it wasn't until later in the day that he began to feel really ill. Tremendous headache and nausea, vomiting. She sent for the emergency doctor this time, but you know what it's like on Christmas Day. The neighbour, a man called Cross, owns an electrical business, came in and he rooted some other doctor out, somebody he knew, lived near by, and he sent straight off for an ambulance.'

'Was that long in coming?'

'I don't know. Anyhow they took him in, and she and Jack Cross followed in her car. None of the children were over for Christmas. They were very good in casualty but the scanner wasn't working. If it hadn't been Christmas Day somebody might have done an exploratory operation. I don't know. He died on Boxing Day.'

'Was she there?'

'No. She'd stayed most of the time, and had just gone out for an hour, when he died.'

'Is there an inquest?'

'Yes. After the post mortem.'

'So we don't know when the funeral is?'

'Probably next Tuesday. It depends. What the coroner. . . . He wasn't sober, Tony.'

'When he fell?'

'No. Can you come up?'

'When? For the funeral?'

'Can't you come before that?'

'Yes, if you want me to. I'll just have to find somewhere to stay. Mrs Mackenzie's gone up to Scotland for the New Year.'

'I've a spare room. Can you come tomorrow?'

He made the promise and she put down the 'phone without further talk. He sat, chin on chest, for twenty gruesome minutes before he went to explain to his mother. This time her questions braced him, forced him to take a hold on himself.

'How old was he?'

'I'm not sure. About Dad's age.'

He talked to her about Hugh as if the man still lived, with the same warm admiration he had expressed to Daniella. Pearson had been kind to him, exceptionally so, it seemed, in his distant, hoity-toity fashion, but he was, if Clark was honest, an unsatisfactory man. Only half-finished. Wasting his talents. Too good for the rest of humanity. Over-fond of the comforting bottle. Hand-brake never quite off.

This was not exactly true.

Because Hugh Pearson was unusual for a schoolmaster, from a higher social level, with as many talents and advantages as drawbacks, he had impressed his younger colleague. Had Hugh been suddenly transferred to a diplomatic post, or a university French Department, or some superior quango, be it on arts or health, he would not have seemed out of place. Presumably he'd have to learn his way around, but he'd appear comfortable, amongst equals; his accent, tone of voice, cut of clothes would give the appearance of a right man in the right quarter; whatever self-doubts existed would be hidden. Hugh was clever, but had not driven himself hard for years. Effortless superiority, tolerant irony, a great future behind him, no rivals near the shabby seat, these were the insignia of Hugh Pearson. Those, and the bottle, the hip-flask.

Clark said nothing of this to his mother, explained how Pearson had recommended him to the Head as a suitable tutor for his niece. She added glosses by the dozen. Later in the day he heard her explaining to his father that Tony had had this terrific shock, that a distinguished colleague and genuine aristocrat had died suddenly after an accident, that their son, considerably shaken, was returning early and with propriety for the funeral. 'So be careful what you say to him. I know you, now, David. Just think before you speak.' His father proved himself perfect, muttering that he was sorry about the news, and asking if there was anything he could do. At that he left it.

A further call at the weekend from Jennifer said that the funeral would now be early Tuesday morning and invited him to come over Sunday evening, but not until seven as she wouldn't be home before that. The inquest had been a formality, verdict of accidental death. There had been a piece in the evening paper which had distressed Clarissa who otherwise was taking it well, managing to contain the histrionics of her children. The widow was not making plans; she'd take a holiday abroad once this was over. She was marvellous, really, unlike herself, on top of everything.

Clark found that by the next morning he had come to terms with Hugh Pearson's death. He barely thought about it. His mother had been out and bought him a magnificent white shirt and a black tie. 'You'll need these, you'll find.'

'You're cheerful.'

'This is no matter, Tony, for joking.' She had pleased herself. 'One has to look on these things as they are.'

His mother liked nothing better than having two men to mollycoddle and command.

'You don't realize,' she told her son, 'how upset you are. Death's played little part in your life. Your father lived as a child through the London blitz.'

He allowed her ministrations, and the accompanying sermons.

'How's Dad shaping up,' he asked, 'now he's about to move?'

'On edge. All the time. Haven't you noticed? Small portions at meals. Everything to hand. I've even cleaned his shoes this last day or two.'

'Is he scared, do you think?'

'There's nothing wrong in being nervous. It makes you that bit more alert and efficient. He doesn't like change, but he's prepared to put up with it if it means he will shape well or make money. And it's my part to see that it's comfortable at home. Easily digested meals, no minor snags, plenty of encouragement. What they call on the telly "pipe-and-slippers". Don't think I like sitting listening to complaints about how careless so-and-so is or how the standard of personal service is falling. Oh, I like bits of scandal or tittle-tattle. But your father's grouses are as much likely to be caused by his uncertainty as by some flighty young miss's slap-happy manners. He hated computers; he was brought up in the days of hand-written ledgers; well, not quite, but, you know. . . . Now he loves these new machines. Revels in them. I pull his leg sometimes. "Any time anything's wrong these days, you blame the computer," I say. "Not me, Sheila," he answers. "You will find faults, odd electrical failures and so on, but the mistakes come from the two-legged brigade more often than not." Hardware and software, oh, he loves it. He's clever, is that father of yours, Tony, but he needs looking after. And pushing.'

'And that's where you come in.'

'You may laugh.' His mother shook a wicked, unusual finger of mockery at him. 'You'll be the same. It takes two to do a job properly, especially as a couple gets older. That's why, in my opinion, so many marriages go wrong. Women are so keen on their careers they don't look after their men.'

'The feminists wouldn't be pleased to hear that sort of heresy.'

'I agree with feminists in so far as they want the value of women's work recognized and recompensed properly.' She thumped her second verb. All the time she chattered she continued with her work, moving with quick steps from pastry board to sink to cupboard. 'Looking after a man and a family is probably the most demanding, stressful work there is. But because universities don't give degrees in it, it's not recognized.'

'Would you say that my dad and I were particularly difficult specimens?'

'I don't suppose so. Not for a minute. You're neither of you idle, for a start. You're both prepared to learn, and you'll do your best, and that is often very good. And the pair of you think you're considerate.'

'And aren't we?'

'Within limits. For men.' Her mixer whirred, delaying her conclusion. 'But I know that in this next month or two I've got to cosset your father, and encourage him.'

'And polish his shoes.'

'You can mock, but yes.'

'And if you didn't do all this, he'd make a hash of his new job?'

'I didn't say that.' She held up a floury hand. 'He'd manage,

186

but at a personal cost; torn nerves, an ulcer maybe, a shorter, less pleasant life. Your father will retire within the next dozen years, and I want him to be in one piece, not a complaining invalid or a miniature urnful of ashes on the mantelpiece.'

Clark relished his mother's blethering intelligence. She understood her *modus vivendi*, her place in the scheme of things. He said as much, not without a twinge of apprehension. She twisted her lips.

'Oh,' she said, 'you're just like your father at your age. You think you're young, and tough and resilient and can take this Mr Pearson's death in your stride. But I doubt it. That's why a show-off like Daniella Smart's no good for you.'

'She's not just a pretty face.'

'Oh, she knows her way about; I don't deny it. But she doesn't appreciate you enough. And worse, she's not prepared to try. *You* must set *your* stall out to please her. That's her view.'

'What happens if a woman's cleverer than the man? Or has greater earning power? It's possible.'

'In that case it will appear and then people can make the adjustments. It's not so in her case. I knew I was nothing like as clever as your father, but I had virtues that complemented his.'

'You realized this from the word go?' he asked.

'Don't be silly. I had to learn it the hard way. I thought I was just as quick and capable as he was, and in some ways it might have been so. But he was the long-distance man. He had stickability. I know what you're going to say: that he hasn't lived up to his promise. Well, I don't know about that. I'd have been satisfied if he'd retired at his present level, which is what I expected. But somebody at the bank has noticed him and now rates him properly.'

Clark thoroughly enjoyed his mother's haranguing. She seemed to think straight according to her lights. He had never admitted this before, even to himself, and tried to account for his change of view. Perhaps, he decided, David Clark's unexpected promotion had lifted her so that she had created a credible mythology to fit the facts. He did not know. He was impressed as he had not been when he lived at home. That was the reason: absence. His mother, in her plethora of words, had proved herself a woman of substance.

On the Saturday, the day before he left for Beechnall, he received a letter from Daniella.

She was in bed at her mother's with 'flu. She could not write at length, but said that her illness was perhaps the cause of her oddness on Christmas Day. 'I can't say I felt ill, only saddened, or numb. And depressed.' When she was better, and she felt like death warmed up now, perhaps he could drive across to see her. She was sorry. With love.

He telephoned, spoke to her mother, whose voice was not unlike her daughter's, and explained that he had to go back early to attend the funeral of a colleague. Mrs Smart said she thought Danny was improving, but she was still upstairs. She was very run down. He said he would write from Beechnall.

On the day he left he and his father took a stroll before lunch. The Christmas trees in front windows flashed coloured lights in vain. On a dull day, streets were empty. Clark praised his mother.

'Yes, she has her ideas,' his father answered. He seemed unenthusiastic.

'But they're not right?'

'She has theories about people and how they live.'

'And they're wrong?'

'Hard to say. I can't easily judge, and I don't suppose she can. But she's interesting to listen to, sometimes.'

'But don't you have to decide at work, who you'll lend money to, and who not? Aren't there con-men trying it on with you, for instance?'

'Some, I suppose. But they have to provide references or collateral security and mostly we know them as customers.'

'And do you ever make mistakes?'

'I expect so. But I'm a hard case. If I'm uncertain I'd say "No". I'm not there to take vast risks with huge sums. That's done elsewhere.'

'So you don't subscribe to fancy theories about human behaviour?'

'I expect I do. We all must, in a rough sort of way. I'll tell you one thing I do think. People don't tell the truth very often. They always make their side that little bit more glowing or attractive than it really is. I tend to deduct a fraction or two. In

188

plain language, I don't believe them, when they're even basically honest people.'

'Does that make you a cynic?'

'No. A back-street bank manager.'

'It must have worked, otherwise they wouldn't have promoted you.'

'You're kind to say so.' That made him glance sharply at his father whose expression did not change. The old man had a sharp dryness both attractive and threatening.

'And what about my mother's theories?'

'Your mother likes to talk. Last night, for instance, she gave me a thorough run-down of all she had said to you yesterday morning.'

'Improving it as she went along?' Clark could not resist this.

'I expect so. Though I've heard these ideas before. They don't grow in seconds. She tries them out and modifies and so on. Your mother's trouble is that she's under-educated. No, that's wrong. She thinks she's under-educated, that she missed something vital. When we used to visit you in Cambridge she carried on for days about what a privilege it was for young people to be educated there in places where teaching and learning had been going on for hundreds of years.'

'And?'

'Romanticizing. These college courts and the Backs are all very fine, but if a professor there writes a book to explain his ideas clearly that's good enough for me. I can read it.'

'Would you say my mother was clever?'

'Oh, yes. And it's a pity that she never had full educational opportunity, but then how many of us do?'

'You greatly admire her?'

'Of course I do.'

'And I never noticed it. I wonder why that was.'

'Young people,' his father's voice grated, 'never make head or tail of their parents. Adolescent differences spoil them. It makes them turn their heads or shut their eyes. Even later. I tell you, I've only just come to terms with my father, and he's been dead for getting on thirty years. We just don't want to look. Just as children don't think of their parents having sex. In the same way they can't regard them anything like sanely. Look at these

189

notabilities in the Sunday newspapers talking about their fathers and mothers. You never read such fiction. Hide, hide, hide. Though to be truthful, the parents speak just as ridiculously about their children.'

'I've decided my parents are clever.'

'You've come to your conclusion because you escaped early.' His father apparently accepted his judgement. 'You've not lived at home full-time since you were nineteen. I was under parental influence until I was married at twenty-five and then I didn't live far away. We visited every Sunday, for instance. My mother was always round.'

'And that was bad, you think?'

'No. No worse than a good many other scenarios. All it means is I didn't find it very easy to make judgements about them. They were on top of me. Or to correct the bad conclusions I couldn't help reaching.'

Clark gave his father an account of Ernest Stapleton, their first meeting, the old man's relationship with Jennifer, the inability to cope with old age.

'How old is he?'

'Seventy-five.'

'Not decrepit. Or shouldn't be. And you say he has money?'

'And property. A great deal.'

'Playing with finance keeps some men lively. Does he deal with his transactions entirely himself?'

'That I don't know. What seems sad to me is that he clearly realizes that he's going downhill.'

'Yes, I suppose so. I've not quite reached that point yet.'

'I should think not.'

'When I listen to old people,' said Mr Clark, in his superior, modest, managerial tone, 'the one thing that strikes me is that past events, big troubles or trivial nothingnesses alike, are bearable, even good, because they've been lived through. "We got over it, we managed" seems the motto. The catastrophe's complete, and they're alive to tell the tale. You know, Tony, when I think about that it ought not to be so, but it is. We often judge on selfish grounds. It didn't disable us. We struggled through. That's the criterion.'

'My mother said you lived through the blitz as a child.'

'Our house wasn't hit but some in the street were.'

'And has that had an effect?'

His father, smartly stepping out, rubbed his chin, then fiddled in his pocket for a packet of throat pastilles, one of which he offered to his son who accepted it. Mr Clark helped himself before carefully rewrapping cellophane and closing the cardboard flap.

'Soothing, these are, I find.' He sucked. 'An old-fashioned taste about them. You feel they're doing you good, though I don't suppose they are. They're strong; they ought to cure you.' He cleared his pastille-scoured throat. 'The blitz now. I was four when the War started, ten when it finished, so I can remember well enough. The whistling noise as the bombs came down, for instance, and the crump and shake of the explosions. We used to have all sorts of cock-and-bull tales about how to distinguish the sound of German planes from ours. And whether or not a buzz-bomb was going to hit you.'

'Were you frighened?'

'I try to remember that. I suppose I was, but it's left no deep mark that I can recognize. They carried me down from bed at first. Sometimes we crowded in under the stairs in a kind of cold pantry and at other times we made for the cellar. It depended on the accepted wisdom of the time. We didn't have an Anderson shelter out in the garden. I don't know why. My grandparents had one, with shelves and bunk-beds.'

'It didn't leave too many traumas?'

'That I can't say. Without the bombs I might have been quite different. I don't know. It's not that I can't remember. I can. If somebody encouraged me to write my childhood memoirs there'd be plenty there. The bedrooms opened up. Pictures still hanging on the walls up there. It seems impossible. We all went to see the Empsons' house, I was at school with Jack, and it was just a big smoking hole full of bricks, and wood and rubbish. But I can't say I have bad dreams, for example, or that I have ever had them. Perhaps my temperament was such that I could put up with what I saw and heard. I'd think I was slightly nervous now. Perhaps if there had been no war, I'd have been quite without nerves. I don't know. There are such people. How can you possibly tell? All I can claim is that my experiences have never been anywhere near incapacitating me, as a bank employee, a husband or a father, or anything else.' He grinned at his son.

'Are these memories of yours vivid?'

'No. Dim. Faded. But that's because I never think about them. If I did they'd be clearer. Just this morning as I've been talking to you I've remembered one or two things I haven't thought about for years, and so I imagine bits and pieces would come flooding back. If I encouraged them. But I don't.'

'Yes.'

The pair walked along in silence, the son six inches taller than his father.

'I often tell myself,' David Clark began again a short street away, 'that I'm missing out on all these opportunities, dismissing them, not taking advantage of what's happened to me.

'Psychologists say nowadays that those who are capable of repressing horrible memories, such as those of Auschwitz or Belsen, are those most likely to do well, not to suffer from nervous trouble.

'When I was young they used to tell us the exact opposite, that those who buried their bad memories away from their conscious minds were the kind who suffered mentally and who weren't sorted out, until hypnotists or analysts disinterred the original horror, exposed it to conscious view.'

'That boils down,' Clark told his father, 'to what you said before. Those who have the temperament, the necessary physical endowment to get rid of the memories and forget them can do so without trouble. Others can't. Do you think it's in part genetic?'

'Don't ask me. Who am I to come to conclusions?'

His father spoke gently, ironically. 'All humans are different, we know that.'

'And must be treated as individuals.'

That seemed to satisfy, or at least to silence by its banality. The older man's steps minced, twinkling to keep up with his son's longer strides. His polished toe-caps gleamed.

'Talking of treatment of individuals,' the father said, 'your Ma is delighted with the pair of us.' The use of the form 'Ma' intrigued; neither man would call her that to her face. It disparaged her judgement, was meant to, introduced irony.

192

'That's something, then.'

'There you are at this posh establishment of yours. I hear her boasting. "Academically one of the best in England. And one of the oldest." And you're part of the action.' David Clark breathed deeply. 'And I've been snatched up into promotion. And that was as likely, in her view, as your being made headmaster of Eton or Harrow.'

'What about your view?'

'Surprise. Can't understand it. It's pretty unusual for anyone of my age and status to get this sort of offer. Even with the housing situation in London there are plenty of well-qualified, younger people, the right age, to take over this kind of branch, I'd have thought.'

'So you can't account for it?'

'No, not at all.'

'You've not met and impressed some notable? Or made some suggestion or improvement, or worked up such a profit that it's brought your name out in lights?'

'No. My place is well run, and always has been. I applied for such promotion in my early forties when I expected to stand a chance, but got nowhere. I didn't apply for everything. I've explained this before. It was clear to them that I wasn't desperate to move. That told against me.'

'And are you looking forward to it?'

'I shall earn more, finish up with a bigger pension. Knowing your mother, we shall probably up sticks and buy a more expensive house. But I'm comfortable as I am. The new job doesn't frighten me. It won't present any more difficulty than the other one. Different, yes. If I'd been ten or twelve years younger, I'd be more likely to want to introduce changes there. But perhaps that's what they're after. A stick-in-the-mud. To see if we're any less profitable than those under the whizz-kids.'

'And you're not nervous?'

'Yes. I don't like change. I shall manage.'

'You won't be faced with terrifying decisions?'

'No more than now, I imagine. If you don't want to make decisions, of a certain and limited sort, you don't become a bank manager. I can make my mind up. Slowly. In time.' The father laughed dryly at himself and his shortcomings.

David Clark then began a long, thorough, intelligent cross-examination of his son about his prospects. They both enjoyed themselves. The old man declared that his education had been old-fashioned, but thorough. He could still remember Chaucer, clause analysis, the principal parts of irregular Latin verbs, trigonometrical formulae, chemical equations.

'Has any of it been useful?' the son asked.

'Not really. But I'm glad I learnt it. It showed me I was capable of acquiring new pieces of knowledge. Thoroughly. There are school-leavers who come to me for work now, qualified up to the nines on paper, but they can't spell, don't read anything. No, I know what you're going to say, but they're as careless with computers as with anything else.'

'What are they interested in?'

'Football, sex, television, money.'

'Personal appearance?'

'Some of 'em are so scruffy I wouldn't employ 'em emptying the dustbins.'

'Perhaps that's why they've promoted you. A bit of old-style discipline. Victorian values.'

'I doubt that. But I tell you, Tony, when I hear of your Sixth-Formers discussing Immanuel Kant in their spare time, for whatever reasons, I can't help thinking "Thank God somebody's doing his job properly." You. And others like you.'

Father Clark fairly ran the streets in excitement.

The young man had not realized before how involved the laconic bank manager was in the details of his son's career. Before today he'd dismissed David Clark's half-sentences of encouragement as a faint, peace-keeping, expected echo of his wife's sentiments.

This holiday he had discovered his parents, to his own amazement.

XVIII

Clark drove into Jennifer Hope's drive at twenty-five minutes to eight.

His gentlemanly ring on the bell went unanswered, but

194

finding the main entrance unlocked he strolled into the hall and rapped at the door to Jennifer's flat. She was not at home. Without hurry he left the house and outside in the cold found the curtains of her rooms undrawn. He stood, gently chipping at the bottom step with his right foot.

'Not before seven,' she had warned. Three-quarters of an hour later she had not arrived.

Annoyance grew. At home his father had always insisted on punctuality, had from National Service made a virtue of the instruction 'On parade five minutes before time'. The surest way to rouse the phlegmatic David Clark's anger was to keep him waiting. Now well-instructed, his son fumed.

He decided to walk round the house in the dark, but the substantial iron gate into the back area was either locked or rusted in. He peered through the bars at the same variations of blackness against blue-black sky as he saw this side. Large trees rose irregularly from the perimeter; below was a fudge of soot-grey shapes. He looked at his watch and kicked the iron gate. A quarter to. Disgruntled, he made his way back to the car out of the sharpness of wind.

He felt pleased to be in Beechnall with the new term less than a week away. The Christmas holidays had not discomposed him; he had spent time with his parents or the Lumleys without boredom. The Daniella episode now seemed unreal; the sullen girl, that unsatisfactory visit to the old woman, the ugly flat, their baffled exchanges. If he had acted properly he would have visited her today and driven up tomorrow in good time for Tuesday's funeral. He had decided not to do so; sitting at the bedside of a feverish or snuffling Daniella, exchanging stiff pleasantries with her parents, a couple he found both predict-able and disagreeable, had made his decision easy, though he knew he was ungenerously wrong. Daniella in his mind was written off; she could do little now to rouse his interest. Half-heartedly he remembered their love-making, their naked joy, the uninhibited squeals of pleasure, her fair beauty. Now in the darkness of his car the love had no more reality to him than a fiction, a romance, a pulp novel, despised for the qualities inherent in it.

Eight o'clock struck in the centre of town. He stroked his

face which bristled under his finger-tips. He felt scruffy, needed a wash, a pee, a drink, anything other than this half-hearted darkness of shrubs, bare branches. He wound his window down, heard the wind scratch at twigs; a violent gust from nowhere juddered his car. He swore, stretched his legs, clenched his fists, breathed violently.

At eleven minutes past the hour Jennifer's headlights raked the drive, flashed as she turned to park in front of him on the far side of the entrance.

She stepped out at leisure, locked her car, and swayed towards his.

'I guessed that was yours,' she said, as he began to wind down his window. 'Why didn't you go inside?'

'I did. And came out again.'

'I'm later than I expected.' The voice was unapologetic. 'Have you been here long?'

'Three-quarters of an hour.'

'I'm sorry. I didn't think you'd be anything like so early. I've been to see Susan Samson. She was Roger Clinton's secretary. Did you know her? She's never been anything like steady since he died.'

Without hurry he unlocked his boot and extracted the cases he wanted, making her wait. She showed no impatience, but led him indoors. Out in the dark garden he could not see the expression on her face.

Once inside she showed him to his room, invited him to 'scrub up' and hurried about the kitchen.

'Are you hungry?' she asked. 'Shall I cook you something?'

'No thanks.'

'A sandwich?'

'Go on, then. You've twisted my arm.'

'Don't you think it smells stuffy in here?'

'I hadn't noticed.'

To him the room shone as if it had been freshly spring-cleaned, every cushion squared, uncreased. Jennifer herself had the same neat spryness, a check open-neck shirt and denim jeans. On his way up he had wondered if the death of Hugh Pearson would have changed her. She showed signs of neither grief nor preoccupation as she bustled in and out, throwing short smiles and queries in his direction. She mentioned the recent death laconically.

When she sat down and poured tea, he found that he was hungry, and was delighted with the generous plateful of wholemeal chicken sandwiches she had put in front of him.

'Have you had a good Christmas?' he asked.

'It's not been like Christmas at all, with Hugh's death. Clarissa rang me from the hospital on Christmas Day. I was going round there for dinner. I went over to the hospital to see if I could do anything for her. I brought her back here, and she stayed the night. I took her in first thing on Boxing Day. He died a few hours later and I stayed with her. She was marvellous, really.'

'Did the children come over?'

'No. It's deadly difficult to get hold of anybody at Christmas. I thought people stayed at home, but they don't. I think Deirdre's back now, and one of the sons. But they'll be worse than useless. Or making work for her. But perhaps that's good. Clarissa's at her best when she's having something to organize.'

Jennifer spoke easily about her friend, but without much warmth, describing her parties, her good works, her interventions in social events at school, her sharp decisions.

'She'll have plenty to do?' Clark asked, after this catalogue.

'I expect so. If she stays here.'

'Isn't that likely, then?'

'Deirdre's nearly finished at school; the boys are all away. I don't suppose she thinks very highly of Beechnall. It's not exactly the centre of the universe, is it? It was only Hugh's job which kept her. They have a little house in France.'

'Will she live there?'

'I doubt it. Hugh liked to spend his summers in the Auvergne, and she was willing enough to go along with it, but not on her own.'

'She depended on him to some extent?' he asked.

'I wouldn't have said so. She didn't mind having him round. It was a curious marriage, but they had money enough to keep out of each other's way when that was necessary. They lived their own lives.'

'But they had a family?'

197

'And Clarissa brought them up. Pretty well, I'd say. For these days. Hugh gave a hand when he could, when it didn't interfere with his other concerns.'

'Such as what?'

'Oh, scholarly trips, hither and thither. He was always preparing some book. I mean, he's been on this Stendhal thing for years. And the school . . . and other matters.' She laughed, a short clatter of ironic sound. They talked for an hour, friendly enough; she had the formality of a new landlady, he thought. At ten-thirty she said she was tired, shooed him off to bed quickly, shut the house up for the night.

At seven-fifteen next morning she woke him with a cup of weak tea. Already bathed and coiffured, she moved smartly about. She left at half-past eight because, she claimed, she felt like a sharp walk to the office. She would be back at six at the latest, perhaps before; he was not to prepare an evening meal, but to feed himself during the day from the ample supplies. 'Cook or idle as you please. I'm due for a lunch that will bloat me for a week.'

As it happened, she called in about midday to change her clothes, and went off to her luncheon engagement in a taxi. He had been reading, then playing with *The Times* crossword; he had walked to buy another paper, had listened to Radio 3. Jennifer spoke brightly, instructing him to eat well, making suggestions. He asked if she would enjoy the function and she said she supposed so. She dressed in black, with a white blouse and a kind of black short necktie so that she looked not only beautiful but as if she had become a member of the clergy. When he said as much she smiled and suggested that was the idea.

He took a stroll into town, but the weather had turned colder and it began to drizzle. Soon after he returned at quarter to four Clarissa Pearson telephoned to see if Jennifer was at home; she had rung the office and the girl there had been unhelpful.

Clark outlined Jen's movements for the day, and carefully expressed his condolences. These came off his tongue more easily than he expected, perhaps because of the matter-of-fact ease that Clarissa demonstrated. He had already written to her, with difficulty, unsatisfactorily from home. She thanked him and spoke of her husband as if he'd just gone out for a meeting of the local branch of the Modern Language Association. Her judgements were not over-generous, but she seemed thankful that he had been as he was and not otherwise. She suggested that he might have been fortunate to die before he had retired.

'He was like,' she pontificated, 'a good number of you schoolmasters in that he needed his time organized. He always complained that he had too much to do, too many boring chores, but he liked to know that at 10.10 a.m. the bell would ring and his Sixth-Form prose writers would be replaced by thirty tearaways starting German. In the holidays he was lost. In fact,' her voice warmed, 'one holiday I made out a time-table for him, allocating work. I didn't know how long he ought to spend on this job or that, but I questioned him and guessed the rest. And he finished two textbooks he'd been playing about with for months.'

'And you did it only the once?' Clark asked.

'Yes. In that sort of detail. After that, if he'd found it so advantageous he could have written out his own scheme. And I always fear, myself, the law of diminishing returns. So once was enough. For me.'

Clark spoke of Hugh's kindness to him.

'Yes.' Clarissa sounded doubtful. 'Yes. I think he could be kind to those he liked, who seemed his own sort of person. He looked for allies, I'm sure.'

'Against whom?' The accusative seemed necessary, imperative even.

'Those who lowered the standards. There are some. And the Headmaster isn't altogether satisfactory. Too fond of compromise. Worm-eaten by liberalism.'

'That's T. S. Eliot.'

'Is it? He often quoted it. Out of context, he said.'

'He'll be greatly missed.' The second time. This time she did no more than murmur.

'Do you think so?'

'I'm absolutely sure.'

'He wasn't. He said to me more than once that he could fall off the face of the earth and within a couple of terms his influence in the school would be utterly obliterated.'

'I don't think that's true.'

'Don't you? It's a pity he's not here for you to tell him. Or perhaps you did.'

'I didn't think it my place . . .' Clark began. 'Or that he needed my encouragement.'

'No. He had presence; not the sort of man to take advantage of. Perhaps that's why he liked teaching.'

She offered more assessments of her husband, quite without emotion, then rang off suddenly as if she had noticed something more interesting outside her dining-room window.

Clark sat solemn-faced and pleased with himself. He had praised Hugh to his wife's face and had occupied a quarter of an hour of her time. That was what she needed: to talk to somebody who understood that her husband was dead and yet could still speak reasonably, could assure her that the world went on, minutely changed, but continuing. How he arrived at these unsupported conclusions he did not know; without deflating his good opinion of himself he admitted his ignorance.

He took himself out again in spite of the weather and drove down to see Jennifer's father. Stapleton was not at home. Annoyed to no purpose, Clark stalked round the house staring in at the windows. The inspection yielded nothing; the rooms were as tidy as usual. One could not tell whether the old man had packed up carefully and gone away to spend January and February cosily in Tenerife, or whether he had slipped out grumbling to some corner shop for a half-pound of margarine he had forgotten earlier in the day. It was almost dark, and one of his age ought not to be out on his own. Clark had asked Jennifer about her father, and she had answered dismissively that he was as usual, as right as he'd ever be. He could not remember whether Stapleton had accepted the invitation to spend Christmas with one of his sons.

Two cups stood on the draining-board, but that meant little. The young man took a second prudent prowl round the house and learnt nothing. At the end he stood for a few minutes in the rapidly darkening street, squinting both ways, but Stapleton did not appear. Clark drove back, puzzled at his disappointment. He made tea, ate biscuits, examined Jennifer's books and pictures, and found himself unable to form opinions about

200

either. A job lot? Anything from a complete Virgil, in leather with a bishop's bookplate at the front, to modern high-grade thrillers in paperback. All Dickens, Thackeray, Hardy, James, Conrad, Galsworthy. Plenty of Russians. A set of Sir Walter Scott. Some Folio Society volumes. Some history. *Oxford Books of English*, *French* and *German Verse*, the latter inscribed 'To dear Jennifer, with love from Hugh' in Pearson's writing.

At five Jennifer hammered at the door.

'I'm early,' she said, 'so I thought I'd wake you up.'

'Have you mislaid your keys?'

'No.' She jangled them in front of his face so that he wondered how much she had drunk. 'No. I like to give warning. Get the kettle on.'

She disappeared immediately to change into jeans and then the two quietly drank the tea. She talked about her luncheon and how some local accountant had tried to inveigle her to join his firm as partner. Acidly smiling, she made a joke of the offer.

'So you won't go?'

'No. Why should I transfer? He's nothing like the size of our concern. And I think he wants to begin taking things more easily. But not at my expense.'

'He's elderly?'

'Fifties. Patting my arm, though. Not too old.' Angry, snarling now.

'And do you mind?'

'It's what I expect. But I know my way round with the likes of him, in business and pleasure.' After a time she asked, 'Do you want to go out anywhere particular this evening?'

'Not really. Not unless you do?'

'You can amuse yourself? I've an hour or two's work to look over if you don't mind.'

They agreed, sat in comfortable silence, companions in warmth.

'What about tomorrow?' She sat straight.

'The funeral, you mean?'

'Yes. Have you been to one of these affairs before?'

'Yes.' Doubtfully.

'I see. We're within walking distance of the church, you know that. If it's fine we'll do it that way.'

'You're not going with the family?'

'No. Clarry asked me, but there'll be droves of relatives. They'll have the local service and then all stream off to the north of the county, Blyth, Newark, Worksop, for the committal somewhere.'

'Don't you know exactly?' he asked, puzzled.

'Of course I do. Church Hawton, where the family estate is. There's a Pearson vault.'

'Pearson's not an aristocratic name, is it?'

'Don't ask me. It's in Debrett or Burke; I looked it up once. Was Hugh a good man?'

'I think so. Clever. Decent. The sort we won't find much longer in schools. Knows his way about academically, and yet he has connections elsewhere. When he started thirty years ago there was still room for a few gentlemen to find themselves a niche in education.'

'But not now?' Jennifer asked, face solemn, hands clasped.

'No. Perhaps at one or two big public schools. But no.'

Jennifer tucked her chin back into her collar-bone, knitted her brows.

'Tell me honestly,' she began, and stopped to draw breath quietly in. 'Do I understand you to say there's no sort of career in teaching these days?'

'Not for the Hugh Pearsons.' Clark suddenly laughed. 'I don't know why he didn't try elsewhere. Temperament, I'd guess. But schoolmastering still just about offered a suitable career for the quieter specimens of his sort who had enough private money to be able to live comfortably.'

'And it's not so now?'

'No. It's been handed over to the likes of me, the lower orders. And I'm near the top of the pile.'

'You sound pessimistic.'

'It does no harm to see things as they are.'

'Yes, but you're right at the beginning of your career. Have you made the wrong choice?'

'Probably.'

'Are you going to do anything about it?'

'Probably not.'

'That's not very enterprising of you.' Her voice was flat. She did not look at him.

'There's nothing wrong with the job. If it's not done properly the country will be in trouble. But society neither regards its teachers highly nor pays them properly. You might gather from what I'm saying that I approve of the old days when the Hugh Pearsons could drop a word in the right ear and get something fixed. Or when we did well by the top five per cent and let the rest fend for themselves. Well, I can see the drawbacks, but at least something was achieved and, sadly, that system was ruined by those who wanted to do even better. The idealists.'

'But things are better, surely? Look at the numbers who pass GCSE nowadays or go on to higher education, and compare that with thirty years ago.'

'I agree and I hope you're right.'

'You're not arguing your case very strongly,' she said, almost with distaste.

'No, I'm not. Just at this minute I can't help feeling down in the mouth because this one school, admittedly a place of cut-throat competition and very uncharacteristic of the rest of the system, has lost somebody, something unique by Pearson's death. And he'll never be replaced. Not in our kind of society.'

'That might change again.'

'Pigs might fly.'

There spoke his mother, dismissing some youthful argument.

Jennifer stood up, groping about with her right hand as if to retain balance, staring into the distance, her mouth working. Finally recovering she spoke easily, without stress.

'Can you occupy yourself for a bit? Or are you hungry? I'm going to work for an hour or two, and we'll think about eating when I've done. About eight, perhaps.'

'Do you want me to start preparing. . . . ?'

'No. We'll . . . No.'

She left the room without looking back.

Clark examined his shoes. Did he believe his own arguments? He had no real evidence for his slap-dash conclusions except for bits and pieces from the quality papers or staff-room tittle-tattle. More people were offered wider opportunities, and because their subjects of study were different from his own that did not of necessity mean that these were worse.

There must always be change. He was right only when he said that Hugh Pearson's death had left a gap. That man would never again step quietly along the corridors of the school in his dusty, well-cut tweeds. Pearson was a good teacher, if slightly lazy and self-indulgent. Clark jumped to his feet. Hugh Pearson was dead. *Stop*. He wanted it otherwise. *Stop*. There was no remedy. Clark crossed the room and back, his mind blank with unreasoning regret. He did not think; he allowed sorrow to dash his spirits and galvanize his limbs so that he jerked from wall to wall, once, twice, three times. Again. Again.

He leaned now against a low bookcase.

Without aim he raised his eyes to the large modern reproduction above the mantelpiece, abstract shapes like twisted tears, multicoloured melted toffee on a black background with white accompanying, matching but annoyingly distorted shapes, blond shadows. The troubled lethargy in his head allowed him to stare at, to make nothing of the picture, hardly to realize that he was studying it.

He swore. Obscenity did not rouse him. He picked up a book. No dice. No profit. *A Diversity of Creatures*. He put it back with difficulty, eased out another. *Light on a Dark Horse*. One more. *A Group of Noble Dames*. Ugh. *The Professor's Daughter*. *One Fat Englishman*. He'd read that. Where had this job lot come from? He'd hardly heard of any of these. *As if By Magic*. He'd tried that once, and failed. He swore again, played with the jammed top line of books.

Clark straightened the tight row with difficulty, slipped on his scarf and mac, and let himself out into the night.

Wind blew scudding clouds across the moon. Twigs jostled, rustled; street lights hung small in sinister distance. Someone had switched off the lamps by the front door so that the garden stretched in blue moonlight. He remembered an anecdote of his father's.

'The evening before the Americans put a man on the moon I was taking a stroll, I think it was a Sunday, and I met Mr Davies.' A neighbour, an old grammar-school master. 'And I pointed to the moon, and said, "No man has ever put a foot there, but from tomorrow we shan't be able to say that!" '

'And what did he think?' his son asked.

'He said he'd never considered it in that way. I was taken aback. I thought he'd see more in it than I did. He was a clever old man, very well read. But no. I think he was too old to be surprised.'

Clark cleared his throat in the noisy garden. The moon pushed forwards. Sailed. Below branches thrashed. He had said to his father, 'It happens every minute. Somebody completes some action that differs, however infinitesimally, from anything ever done before, and on that account the universe is changed.' Some distance away the siren of a police car sounded. His father had answered, 'I don't know about the universe, but I'm talking about largish events.' He had gone on to argue that some processes of thought had made the atom bomb a possibility, but few had paid attention to those crucial first steps, equations, pointers. David Clark had clearly dismissed his son as dotting useless i's and crossing unproductive t's for personal pleasure, not enlightenment. Headlights clawed the sky.

Shuddering, Clark moved back towards the steps.

It was foolish to stand outside on a cold January night. For a start, he had expected more of this visit than Jennifer's argumentative welcome. He had decided she would need comfort; she did not, spending the last hours before the funeral with tax returns or balance sheets, computer print outs or green screens of statistics. Clark prodded the steps with his toe-cap for the second time this day. He had considered (odd word) that he loved her and that she was attracted to him. Evidence was now lacking. She had behaved like his landlady, kindly as long as both kept to the rules. A second Mrs Mackenzie, she who'd be spending her last night in Scotland among her relatives, a sister or an aged auntie, before she took the train early in the morning to resume her role among the Sassenachs.

When he let himself back into Jennifer's sitting room he could hear her voice, but had no idea whether she was dictating to a machine or answering the telephone.

He settled into an armchair when he had chosen a book, *A Midsummer Night's Dream*.

XIX

Jennifer and Clark rose at seven-fifteen by agreement that January morning, ate breakfast, washed dishes and divided the newspaper.

'What's the drill?' he asked, one of his father's questions.

'The service is at eleven, so we'll aim to arrive at quarter to. Geoffrey Bland will be playing the organ, and he'll do Bach Chorale Preludes and that'll be worth listening to. The forecast's good, so we'll walk. It should take twenty minutes at the outside. We'll start ten-twenty-five. Until then, your time's your own.'

'And you?'

'Half an hour's housework and then a bath. At least I'll be clean to see Hugh off.' That seemed unconvincingly cheerful.

'Is your father going?'

'Yes. Geoffrey Salmon is picking him up.'

'Does he, er, often turn out for these affairs?'

'He's been to plenty in his time. As far as one can tell, he's pleased he's the one who has managed to keep alive. I don't know. I expect he'll be glad to exchange a word with old cronies. Geoff will probably take him to the Victoria or the Reform for a drink. Lunch even.'

'And he'll like that?'

'It will make a change.'

Jennifer disappeared. Soon after ten she appeared, beautifully dressed in light grey, less formally than for the luncheon engagement of the day before. Clark congratulated her on her appearance; she claimed Clarissa had not wanted black among the women. She ordered him to make last-minute preparations, and at twenty past they stepped down the drive.

Inside the church it struck colder than the street.

Clark had stepped out smartly. His new dark overcoat covered the charcoal-grey suit, the white shirt, the black tie his mother had chosen. On the steps outside the church a man took a note of his name. Did he represent anybody? He felt proud following Jennifer into the nave.

They found a place next to the aisle on hard chairs; Jennifer made a perfunctory pretence of prayer; he closed his eyes. People addressed subdued remarks to each other. The wife of his Head of Department turned to flash a smile of recognition towards him and his companion. He recognized one or two colleagues.

Two rows of Sixth-Formers were already seated; they kept perfectly still, thick hair gleaming in place, showing decorum. The organ quietly meditated.

'"Now come Thou Saviour of the heathen",' she whispered. He realized she had named the chorale prelude.

'Very suitable,' he said.

She punched his thigh with a knuckle, laughing, all minutely.

The cold church, with its high lights and few candles like chilly stars, filled rapidly. Ushers clapped about the stone flags, reorganizing; no seats were empty. One or two late-comers had to stand, amongst them George Frensham, the man who had written the novel, looking large and sheepish, next to a very small woman in a wide-brimmed black hat. It was past eleven; the organ droned on; a further group clattered in, ready with excuses they were not allowed to offer. Clark studied an old man across the aisle wearing a black coat with a black velvet collar; his white thin hair was carefully combed round the long parting in his pink scalp. The man hoisted his glasses, lowered them, replaced them on the bridge. Clark had seen nothing of Stapleton. The air grew icier. Now all waited in anticipation, glancing at wrist-watches, uncertain of what would happen, of themselves.

A voice brayed from the west door, uncouthly loud.

'I am the resurrection and the life, saith the Lord; he that believeth in me, though he were dead, yet shall he live.'

The coffin was wheeled in by solemn men in black, followed by the family, a substantial string of relatives. The vicar's voice still rose uncontrollably noisy as if he sold cabbages from the market-stall. 'I know that my Redeemer liveth, and that he shall stand at the latter day upon the earth. And though after my skin worms destroy this body, yet in my flesh shall I see God, whom I shall see for myself, and mine eyes shall behold, and not another.'

The close mourners reached the front, were arranged in their dark, solemn rows.

'We brought nothing into this world. . . .'

The vicar was nervous, Clark decided, and shouted. His church was the nearest to the school, had but a vague connection with it. Now he was called on to take a leading rôle before this well-connected family, this Headmaster and his staff, the Master of an Oxford college, the local Vice-Chancellor, the Archdeacon, a bishop amongst the rest. Journalists noted all. His congregation sat, in relaxation, fidgeting between the dull, pointed windows.

The service was impressive, if uncoordinated, Clark decided; no one allowed haste.

A tall man, black-suited, read from the Epistle to the Corinthians marvellously well as if he were composing it, or seeing it for the first time. 'Therefore, my beloved brethren, be ye stedfast, unmoveable, always abounding in the work of the Lord, forasmuch as ye know that your labour is not in vain in the Lord.'

At the end of this he noticed that Jennifer was gently crying.

The Headmaster, without academicals, read 'Our revels now are ended' in a dry voice, and finished it with June Benn's translation of Bede's one little sparrow flying through the hall, 'coming in at one door and flying out through another' into winter night.

One of the clergymen on the staff, a mathematician, joined the vicar in prayers. The formality seemed to preclude grief though the hymns became especially poignant. Pearson would have approved of neither. The first, Bunyan's 'To be a pilgrim', went at a spanking pace which two or three times left the congregation stranded. 'The Lord's my Shepherd' (Clark turned up his nose at the banal choice) was brought to brightness by the verse, 'Yea, though I walk in Death's dark vale/Yet will I fear none ill' when Bland on the organ suddenly opened up, blazed in with brilliant reeds, so that they walked in triumph, rod and staff stiff and protective with magnificence, swallowing death up in victory.

The vicar, himself again, quietly read the final prayers, the mutes reappeared and the family filed out at length. Clarissa

208

stared serenely ahead, her face lifted and set. Deirdre had been crying. The sons looked nothing like their father. Gill Wycliffe moved stumblingly on her husband's arm as if she could barely see her way. The family, aristocratic or not, were no different from other people, tall or short, red or pale, bored or touched, steady on the feet or aged, young or ready for the grave, thirteenth baron or merest housekeeper.

While he sat waiting Clark's mind whirled, but without coherence. He neither noticed the people in the row in front beginning to stir to life, nor Jennifer on his right, nor the slight creaks of furniture, the buzz of conversation, the buttoning of coats and tying of scarves. A thousand changes ravelled themselves in his head without result; he was himself but a self that made nothing of what had gone on, flitted among tousled tracks until he no longer knew one certainty from another's vagueness. This had been a ceremony, and that proper, but it had left him unsatisfied, confused; like the polished tribute paid by Wilson Seymour, the second master, it had sounded all the virtues, the strengths, but had left the man Pearson untouched. So with this service. Now Bland strutted into a Purcell trumpet tune that punched pillars and rang brassy in the roof-vaulting; surely Clarissa had chosen that boldness. It was quite unlike her husband; his soft smile would have approved of the composer but not adopted his pomp to describe or honour himself. So. Officials and friends had chosen and read carefully and well, but Hugh Pearson and God had stood back from it all, in approbation but unconnected. Clark dragged himself towards reality. 'Curse, bless me now with your fierce tears, I pray.' No. He wanted no showmanship, merely the shadow of Pearson, the pale reflection of a pale personality, a ghost of worth, to appear, to signal with exactitude a reflection of the life. How? How?

Jennifer touched his arm.

'Are you ready?' she asked.

They slipped into the slow file, and escaped by a small north door. Outside the church was a large patio of flagstones, where the mourners congregated, and beyond that the graveyard, a wide, well-kept grassed area with cherry trees crossed by straight gravel paths and with rustic seats round the perimeter.

The sky stretched gunmetal dark, but seemed for all its cheerlessness light, lively, uplifting compared with the interior of the church.

Conversation out here was brisk. The hearse and the family limousines had already been driven off. People crossed with rapid steps to greet friends; it might well have been a wedding with jostling activity. From her group the Headmaster's wife acknowledged Jennifer and Clark with a queenly wave of a glove. Jen herself excused herself, broke away. Clark came up against George Frensham and a small woman.

'Have you sent your novel off?' he asked without preliminaries.

'Yes. But it's too melodramatic.'

'That's the last word I'd use. Have they acknowledged it?'

'Yes. A card.'

'Just the one publisher?'

'No, two. As you suggested.' He named them. Now the important business was over he introduced his wife, who shook his hand, said that Pearson's death was tragic. She was a small, sallow-faced woman with liquid brown eyes and wore a black scarf. Clark replied as she expected. She lowered her head at the encomium.

'Yes,' she answered. 'Though people didn't always get on with him. George didn't.'

'Give up, Fran,' Frensham muttered.

'And they were at the same college at Oxford. He was like that poem of Pope's about Addison. "Bear like the Turk no rival near the throne".'

That snippet of malice out of the way, she praised Pearson. Her husband listened enormous in a black overcoat, shuffling from foot to foot.

Clark shifted a yard or so to speak with his colleague, Thompson, slightly surprised to see that cynic here. They enquired about Christmas holidays, and Thompson with a long face commented unfavourably on the people around him. 'They enjoy every bloody minute' and then he grumbled, 'That verse the vicar read, "I kept silence, yea, even from good words" doesn't apply to this bloody lot, and not much to him,' presumably Pearson, 'either.' He sloped ungraciously away.

Clark's Head of Department nodded from a distance, hunched against the chill, then came across, shook hands. 'How are you? Good holiday?' He moved uncomfortably. 'Bad business, this. Could have done without it. Tragic.' He pulled the right glove off and on. 'Pearson seemed one of the fixtures. The place won't be the same.' Maddison shot out his short sentences in a low, phlegmy voice.

Quite suddenly it struck Clark that his senior was moved, hurt, but did not want to admit it, even to himself. Maddison's beautiful, tall wife approached to shake hands; she made much the same remarks as her husband, but easily, without concern. She wore a black hat, coat, stockings and shoes, but at her neck a striking pale green scarf which suited her pallor, matched her wide eyes.

Clark felt a tug at his elbow and turned. Stapleton.

They clasped hands, as befitted the occasion, and Clark wheeled to introduce the Maddisons. They had disappeared.

'How are you, then?' Stapleton's voice rang almost heartily.

Clark answered, said a word or two about his holiday, asked after the old man who grumbled about the cold wind. 'I came down to see you the other day, but you were out. Late afternoon.' They began to work out the exact time, but Stapleton could give no reasoned account of his movements. He seemed jovially pleased about this, as if he'd spent his absence in some underhand, slightly shameful occupation which he did not care to confess.

'You're staying with Jen, aren't you?'

'Until tomorrow.'

'Why's that?'

'My landlady's been home to celebrate Hogmanay.'

This threw Stapleton into gloomy reverie.

'Is Jenny looking after you?'

'Oh, yes. She's very busy. One way or another.'

'She takes her work seriously. Yes. I think we could say that.'

Stapleton had dressed suitably for the occasion in a black overcoat, white shirt, black tie, white silk scarf. His hair had been carefully cut and styled and he had shaved close. He looked what he was, a professional man, unshabby, shoes gleaming, with no signs of senility, eccentricity or helplessness about him.

211

'I don't like this weather,' he said, looking up at the grey sky. 'Catches at me.' He tapped his chest. 'Does me a power of no good.' Quite cheerfully he listed his aches and pains, his latest argument with the doctor who had written out a prescription before the patient had time to describe the symptoms. 'Hogen-mogen, I call him. High and mighty.'

Clark said he had never heard the expression. Stapleton pulled a sour face at his ignorance but offered no further explanation and began to complain about the state of the interior decoration of the church.

'Paint peeling off, plaster. Cracked windows. It's years since I've been in this place but there's no sign of trying to keep it decent. They'd do well to shut half these places down, sell 'em off for furniture repositories. No aesthetic merit about this eyesore. Big, cold, ugly barn. Built what, 1863? Nothing to be said in its favour.' He shook a finger, strongly.

A red-faced man appeared, his grey hair greased back. Introductions. Geoffrey Salmon.

'You about ready, Ernest?' he asked in a throaty voice. 'Gives me a thirst, a funeral.'

'Who's that? Over there?' Stapleton.

The crowd had begun to thin out.

'Who? That woman? Over there with her arms spread? You know her. That's the widow of your old side-kick Roger Clinton. Second wife.'

'Is it? I'd met her. Either she's changed or I'm going gaga.'

'Or both.'

The two men laughed.

'Would you like to join us for a drink?' the red-cheeked Salmon enquired.

'No, thank you.'

'He has to do as he's told,' Stapleton said. 'Our Jen has to issue a pass-out.'

Clark did not answer, and the smirks died on the faces of his companions. They shook hands, mindful of the occasion. The young man straightened his gloves, looked about for Jennifer. She stood with an animated group of women of her age, all smiling, chattering hard: Mrs Clinton, much at ease, made one of them. Bland, the music master, emerged from the church, a

212

battered case under his arm. He headed for Clark, one of the few staff members left.

'Didn't expect this,' he said. 'A bad job.' He sucked at his teeth.

'I enjoyed your Bach,' Clark answered.

'Thank you. They don't keep their organ in very good trim.'

'It sounded well. Did Mrs Pearson ask for that Purcell?'

'No, no. I thought once the coffin was out of the way, I'd liven things up. No, she'd no idea. They were both Philistines when it came to music. He was a highly educated, literate man, but music meant nothing to him.'

'Tone-deaf?'

'I don't suppose so. No interest. Came from a school with good music, too. No. Don't know.' He sighed and sighing walked away, as if he'd no idea that his companion was no longer with him. 'Don't know.'

When Jennifer came across five minutes later she introduced him to two of her companions, young married women, both attractive. They continued with their conversation as if Clark had the details at his finger-ends. He stood, pleasantly puzzled.

'You're not coming to lunch with us, then, Jen?' one asked.

'I've my living to earn,' she answered. 'On, Tony.'

They rushed out of the churchyard and along by the iron railings.

'Were these replaced after the War?' he asked.

'No idea.'

'They cut them down for munitions, usually.'

'These?'

'I don't know about these. Most. A waste of effort according to my father.'

Jennifer found no comfort; they walked together in speedy silence. Half-way up a hilly street she stopped.

'Steady now. It's not a race.'

'I'm sorry. I didn't realize. . . .'

'What did you make of that, then? The service?'

She was still standing, mouth in a thin line.

' "Suitable" is the word, isn't it? "Decorous"? The vicar was too loud for a start. The man who read St Paul was marvellous.'

'I don't know who that was.'

'I took him to be one of the family.'

'Possibly.'

Jennifer still held her ground. She was not short of breath, but paused as if she needed to ask him some important question which she stressed by her immobility. She concentrated on herself. Nothing came of it. They set off again, accelerated and paused. The flat seemed cold and dark; she had neglected to switch the heating on when they left for the church. They ate lunch in silence, and then soon after twelve, having heard the news headlines, Jennifer left for the office.

'I'll be back about five, and knock up a quick meal in the microwave. I'll do a Mrs Mackenzie for you.'

'She doesn't use a microwave.'

'You'll be back to traditional cooking tomorrow.'

She changed her clothes and drove away, giving him no instructions. Clark mooned in a chair before setting out for the woods near Blidworth where he parked and followed the forest trail, marked by blue-topped poles. The paths were moderately dry except where horses had churned the hollows and in the cold he met one other person, a cloth-capped man with a dog. Having completed the round, three or four miles, he set off a second time at a furious pace. Angry, disquieted, he pelted along, once trying to lose himself by taking an unmarked short cut between bushes, and returned red of face, pleased with himself. Back at Jennifer's flat he carried his shoes indoors, stood them on old newspaper, but could find neither brushes nor cleaning material in the place. He sat, scoured *The Times*, making himself read an article on archaeology in which he had no interest, and a women's page piece on abortion. Outside it was now dark, the heating was comfortingly on, and he drew the curtains. Jennifer did not return as promised at five, so he made himself a pot of tea and settled to a book he had never heard of, a novel about an eccentric schoolmaster, 'Mr Olim'. At five minutes past six Jennifer returned, offering a dull apology for her lateness, saying that her underlings needed more help and encouragement than she did at their age, and made for the kitchen, refusing all offers of aid.

She was noisy about her cooking, but did not countenance assistance. When the meal arrived, soup, a huge plate of cod, potatoes, vegetables, parsley sauce, followed by chocolate cake, he ate heartily. His walk had made him hungry, while she barely touched the fish.

'This isn't very interesting,' she murmured. He spattered his potatoes with vinegar.

'Fills a long-felt need.' He enquired about her afternoon's activity, but she could barely rouse herself to answer.

'I earned my money today,' she grumbled.

They washed the dishes with little attempt at conversation. She received his account of the winter woods with boredom. In the living room she poured two large waterless whiskies, lifted her cut-glass tumbler to him, muttered 'Your health' and subsided into frowns. She had not changed her clothes, but the neat working uniform hung creased and untidy; she had kicked off her shoes.

'Are you all right?' he asked.

'Yes. Tired. I'll recover in a bit.' She pointed to reviving whisky.

'I thought the funeral might have upset you.'

'Did it worry you?' Sharp, unpleasant.

'Yes. I didn't think Hugh Pearson would die. And yet people paraded there, dressed up, pleased with themselves, bothered about their own concerns.'

'What else would you expect?'

'Probably I gave the same impression. I don't know. I couldn't help telling myself that he ought to have been with us, that it would have been a hundred times better if he had just been, oh, present. That's silly, I realize. If he were alive there wouldn't have been any reason for. . . .' He broke off. 'Hugh Pearson was a somebody,' he added lamely.

'We're all somebodies.'

'You know what I mean. Somebody out of the ordinary.'

'Do you think so? I found him pretty indecisive, really.'

'You think he didn't make the most of himself?'

'He could be charming. I suppose from what they tell me he did well by his pupils. But. Oh, what does it matter now?' She sipped. 'He's dead.'

'Mrs Clinton was there.'

'Why do you say that? Do you know her?'

'No, I don't. But her husband's death seemed to throw everybody. It caught Hugh Pearson out.'

'They weren't particularly close,' she demurred.

'Well, it was Hugh his wife sent for. I was up at the Pearsons' house at the time.' Jennifer made no comment. 'Did they ever find out why Clinton committed suicide? Nobody seemed sure.'

'Roger,' she said, 'Roger was a strange man. He was a tremendous worker. Drove himself. And he had some strokes of luck, in the property world, which made certain that his slaving was properly rewarded. I used to ask him if he believed he was worth all the money he was making.'

'And?'

'He didn't want to know. He wasn't either educated or ruminative.' She smiled acidly at her own word. 'The profits were there for the taking, and he grabbed. That's all there was to it, in his eyes. He did, he thought, what anybody else in his right mind would have done.' She sat still. 'Tony, be an angel, go and fetch us some water from the kitchen before we drink ourselves silly.' She issued precise instructions about which jug he was to choose, how many ice-cubes to put into it. When he returned, every order punctiliously followed, she had not moved and her glass was untouched. Quickly she straightened herself, poured whisky, reached for the jug.

'More water for me, please,' he asked.

'Coward.' She smiled, pleasantly for the first time that evening. 'I don't know. Perhaps Roger was like Alexander, sighing for other worlds to conquer. I doubt it. The property market hasn't been quite so lucrative for a year or so, but it's picked up lately. Liz, his wife, thought it might have been some very minor setback that caught him off balance. He was volatile. But disappointed as he might have been over some obstacle, he'd enough sense to understand that, by and large, he was still doing well. He liked his own way, and would go to any lengths to get it.'

'I see.'

Jennifer drew in her breath, lifted her tumbler, stared at it, and held it to the light before returning it to waist level.

'I had an affair with him. Did you know that? Though it was

216

nothing. It lasted for a few weeks. I was in a mess with Edwin at the time, and didn't know half I was about.'

'Was he married?'

'Yes. To his present wife. They were married soon after we were. But he liked to try his hand, if that's the expression, elsewhere, and he saw I was, well, receptive.'

A curt shudder raked Clark's back; cold closed in on him. Jennifer, for all the difference it made to her expression or posture, might just have announced that she had once been Clinton's accountant. Clark was shocked, knew it to be so, could not deceive himself.

Jennifer now took a token sip before setting the tumbler down.

'It meant nothing,' she said. 'We weren't alike. He was at a temporary loose end, and I would have done anything to get at Edwin. It was never going to come to much. I knew it, and to give him credit, so did he. He had his priorities sorted out. Work first, I realized that. Work, work, work. But why he killed himself. . . . If I had to guess it would be that he'd set about something, building something, buying something, and it hadn't come off to his liking. He'd be blazing furious with himself, but I shouldn't have thought suicidal. And yet, from what we can make out, he chose his train and drove out to walk under it. To do that I'd have thought at least part of his mind must have been thoroughly divided and disturbed. Look at the ghastly mess. And the innocent engine-driver. Not that Roger had much imagination.'

'He wasn't playing "dare"? Like children?'

'I doubt it. He wrote letters, he'd worked it out. He must have meant it. But there are easier ways of killing yourself.'

'Perhaps he didn't want it easy?'

'What do you mean?' She snapped, grabbing at her glass.

'He perhaps had to do the heroic thing.'

'He could think big, but. . . . It's years since I had anything to do with him. I met him at my father's once or twice, and the firm has dealt with some of his accounts. No. I don't know. His wife doesn't either. He left her well provided for.'

They sat in uneasy stillness.

Suddenly Jennifer jerked herself straight again, as if she

217

couldn't control the abundant latent energy in her body. Her eyes were wide, wet, shadowed.

'You don't think I should confess we had an affair, do you?'

The sentence hit Clark a heavy blow. She had searched him out.

'It's up to you,' he answered, weakly.

'I asked about you.'

' "Kiss and not tell" is better,' he said, recovering.

'I don't tell everybody.'

'I didn't suppose for a minute that you did.'

'I wanted you to know. So that *you*, not anybody else, would see me as I was.'

'I guessed,' Clark said, dryly as he could, 'that you would have had lovers.'

'Why?'

'You're an up-to-date woman. You know your mind. You can stand up for yourself. You can claim your pleasure, or look out for it.'

She paused again, fiddled with her glass, turning it in complete circles rapidly with her finger-ends. He had gabbled to cover his embarrassment.

'Claim pleasure?' Voice low, musing. 'That's a curious expression.' It was indeed; it did nothing to express his meaning, merely to emphasize his agitation, lack of balance, his unspoken plea for clemency, for soothing untruth. He stared at his feet, out of his depth. He fought a powerful opponent, beyond his class.

'I had an affair with Hugh, at much the same time.'

She had spoken, startling him, in a low flat voice. At first he could not bring himself to answer; there seemed nothing to say; his confidence had rotted on him. He clutched at his knees, lolled about.

'God!' Had he spoken? He had no idea. If he had the strength he'd have forced himself up to his feet, and left the room. 'And he's dead.'

'Yes. There was one more, but he's still alive. You don't know him. He lives in London now.'

'Jennifer, why are you telling me this?' He'd attack her.

'First of all, so that you'd know how I feel. Today. At the

funeral.' She sipped, temperately. 'Not that I'm claiming much for this affair, either. We were both too buttoned up. We both felt guilty about Clarissa, who's a fool in some ways, but we both felt an obligation to her. It lasted for only three or four months, before we let it go.'

'And the third?'

'That was more serious. What we might call of long standing.' She pulled a sour mouth. 'It finished twelve months back, almost to a day, when he moved to London.'

'Was he married?' He had not heard a whisper from anybody.

'Yes. To a Catholic who wouldn't divorce him. We had no thought of marriage, I can honestly say that, in the two and a half years it lasted.'

'Do you hear from him?'

'No. Well, I had a Christmas card, which is more than I sent him.'

'Why, for God's sake?'

'We'd both had enough when he was offered this promotion. He was glad to go; I was glad he went. It had been good in many ways, but we both. . . . He was a home-bird, and I needed change. I was really upset though, when I knew he was leaving. Raving. Beating my pillow. Shouting, biting the head off everybody. He was deserting me. And then after a week of it, I suddenly thought, "This is what you want. If he hadn't moved away, you'd have thrown him over in the next six months." It was as easy as that.'

'Are you sure?'

'Of what? What do you mean?' Slight animation in her face.

'I never know my mind as clearly as that,' he said. 'I'd be up one day, and down the next.'

'So was I. But the basic knowledge was there: I'd had about sufficient of him.'

'It wasn't just a way of comforting yourself?' he pressed.

'Oh, motive. Motive. Who am I to lay down the law why I do this and not that? But if it was, it was exceedingly convenient. I'm speaking honestly when I say we'd had enough. We may not have admitted it at the time; we were both sore, felt rejected, let down. That's why I say I'm short-breathed, need change. Neither my marriage nor this affair lasted long. Yet in both cases it was love, great physical attraction, sexual compatibility, interests in common, a real wish, on my part at least, to serve, to please, to share, put it as you like. And in both cases it came to grief.'

She sipped gently.

Clark stirred. The woman spoke quietly, but with strength. What she had said had impressed rather than her manner. She seemed neither moved nor flustered. Clarity was the aim, to make him understand.

'So you see,' she continued, 'this morning made an end.' She hesitated on the word, unwilling to exaggerate, to waste a cliché. 'Let's not overstate the case. I saw a fair amount of Hugh after it was over. I visited the house. He and Clarry came here. Clar and I went to a WEA class on music together. What I'm trying to tell you is that we could be in one another's company without embarrassment. When the affair finished I'd guess Hugh was relieved. He felt quite the man taking on an extramarital commitment, but he was glad when it was done, the danger and the small deceits finished. And we could remain friends. We weren't ever in love in any deep sense. I'm not saying there was nothing in it; Hugh could be a charmer. But I didn't like his timidity. I suppose at school now he didn't show this, but with me he was looking over his shoulder the whole time. It didn't suit.' She laughed, in genuine amusement, and took a small temperate sip at her whisky and water. 'But now this man, this friend is dead. And we made some sort of admission of it to ourselves at this morning's service. We shan't see him again. The bit of difference to the world that was Hugh Pearson has been taken away.'

'I hate that,' Clark said. 'I grudge it.'

'That's it,' said Jennifer.

'Did he drink when you knew him?' he asked out of the blue.

'To some extent. I don't know how serious his problem was, or if it was a problem at all. That shows how little I knew him. We sat here, as you and I are doing, and drank whisky, but he didn't seem any more affected than you are. I guess he'd had rather a lot when he fell down the stairs, but there were just the two of them, no children, no guests, just a blank with the telly

220

screen full of the sort of rubbish he detested. Then they'd both take to the bottle. Neither of them had much idea of how to occupy spare time. Hugh was fine with a school timetable with its ordered choppings and changings and books to mark or, less so, an edition to prepare. And Clarry getting the place all set up for a dinner party when she could cook and bake and organize for days on end. But they didn't know how to rest.'

'Couldn't they talk to each other?'

'In public, yes. In private, no. They'd said it all hundreds of times over.' She glanced at him. 'Isn't that what all marriages are like? Even my short one to Edwin. There comes a time when there's no renewal, when there's nothing left to exchange.'

'In every case?'

'Yes. But some are lucky or haven't got very high expectations, and come to terms with it. Or because of religious or ethical beliefs hang on, and so find something or are prepared to put up with the aridity. It's sad. In our case it was worse. We began to hate each other.'

They sat in blank silence, not touching their drink.

Clark, stunned, afraid, pulled himself together.

'Jennifer, I like you. Very much.'

'What's that mean?' Amusement flickered in her eyes.

'I am fond of you.' The words stumbled out, one by one.

'And what I've just said is disappointing, is it?'

'I don't know about that.' He recovered spirits. 'It sounded particularly honest, but I can't tell even if it's true. We . . . I . . . often say things in the mood of the moment.' Now he struggled. 'I hate to think of you involved in these affairs. But it doesn't alter my opinion, no, wrong, my feelings for you.'

'And should it?' She had whisky in hand, mocked him.

'Should, should.' He shrugged. 'I love you.'

'One moment, young man.' She laughed out loud. Alcohol or native resilience reasserted itself. 'Are you sure?'

He stood up.

'No,' she commanded. 'No physical contact. You can't wrestle yourself into love.'

Clark sat down; she had repulsed him as Daniella had. He had obeyed her order; he ought to have persisted. Should, should. Now it was too late.

221

'Today I feel dry, withered, physically,' she said. 'But I have thought seriously about you. I'm attracted to you. At the school they speak well of you, so I was a bit shaken when you talked so pessimistically of teaching. Not that it matters. You'll make something of it, and if you want to change you'll be able to do so. We'll take you on to train as an accountant, if you wish.' She giggled at the offer, but without looking up. 'But I'm eight years older than you, Tony. That could be a drawback.' She shrugged. 'And I earn rather a lot more than you do at present. So it's not altogether straightforward.'

'Nothing is,' he said, helping her.

'Oh, I don't know.' Cheerfulness there. 'But not tonight. I feel so wretched. No, that's wrong, so weary. At work I could barely drag myself up and down from my desk, never mind explaining anything. I think I love you, Tony. Really. That sounds, to use your word, grudging, and it is. On the whole I'm optimistic; I bounce back. But let's leave it. I tell you what: we'll meet again, here, on Saturday afternoon. Will that do? Thanks. Thank you.'

Jennifer shook her head, finished her whisky.

'Any more?' she asked, lifting the bottle.

'No, thank you.'

She made sure the screw-top was tight, and stood.

'Bed now for me. It's early. I'll take a couple of sleeping tablets.'

They kissed; she walked out with bottle and glasses, but returned almost at once.

'I saw my father. Yesterday. I just called in for ten minutes.'

Clark looked up, puzzled. She straightened the table. 'He seemed sensible for once. Just as he dressed himself properly for the funeral. He can do it if he wants.'

'You think it upset him? Hugh's death?'

'It might just have stimulated him. I don't know. But he talked to me in a way that was out of the ordinary. He's never been one to speak seriously to me. About anything. He was over forty when I arrived . . . and I was a girl. Not that he didn't appreciate women in their restricted place. He did. But. . . . He wouldn't want to give too much of himself away to a daughter.'

222

'Why not.'

'His generation. He was born just before the First War, and served in the Second. It was a man's world.' There was no trace of tiredness now in Jennifer's voice.

She swivelled quickly, like a dancer, hands fluttering in one quickly beautiful gesture.

'Anyway, there we sat. He wasn't grumbling nearly as much as usual. About other flat-dwellers being noisy, or the neighbours' riotous parties, nobody doing a stroke for you. Or the boys hadn't written. Again. There wasn't any of that. He picked his cup off the table, and looked at it, and said, "At my time of life you begin to wonder what it's all about." I wasn't very affable, and said, "What's that mean?" He just rubbed his face. "Why are we here?" he asked. "When something like this Pearson thing crops up you think, 'Why him, not me? Or what have I made of my turn? Or what's all this amount to?'" It wasn't very enlightening, but at least he was trying to express himself to me. I feel a bit touched by it now. I wasn't very helpful to him then. I just said I'd no hope of an after-life, and he said he hadn't, either; it wasn't that. Anyway, he didn't like the idea of a second go.'

'But you were pleased with him?'

'Not then so much. But I am now. I feel sorry that I wasn't more forthcoming. It's typical of me, but it's the first time he's ever come out with anything like that. And that was only a little bit. Unconnected with me and my sympathetic face.' Her right hand clenched. 'Something forced it out of him, and I just happened to be around. That's all.'

'What about when Clinton died?'

'No. No. Usual grouses. Didn't understand it. No need. Not like him. Stuff of that sort. But Hugh's death had knocked Father Ernest about for some reason. As it had me. Perhaps his age was telling on him.'

'Did you speak to him this morning?'

'Yes. He was back to normal. Complaining. Crotchety.'

'What did he say?'

'Oh, good turn-out; mothballs made him cough; look at that woman's hat. All these people he hadn't seen for years crawling out from under the stones. He was very cheerful for him. He'd

223

recovered from whatever it was, and was looking forward to lunch with his cronies.'

'Why are you telling me this, Jennifer?'

'I was just thinking about running the bath when I knew I had to. It's a compliment to you. In a way. You had to be kept informed.' She smiled. 'I owed you an explanation.' Again the smile, in benison. 'I've earned my bath and bed now; I've said my prayers.' It was beyond him, out of her character.

She held her arms out, and they embraced, gently. When he grasped her more tightly and she felt his excitement against her she detached herself and he allowed it.

Two days later, two miles away at midnight, Ernest Stapleton collapsed in the hall of his house.

He had clambered out of bed, and one of the students upstairs, coming in late, had found him by the downstairs lavatory. The young men called 999, then Jennifer on the father's brave instruction. She had driven over, arriving as the ambulance left.

'He was conscious, yes, but in pain. He'd taken some tablets, kept them in his pyjama jacket, he showed me, but they brought no improvement.' The student spoke carefully; he smelt of beer. 'He told me what to do, ambulance. Then you. He said it was his heart.'

'Was he in much pain?'

'Yes. He was half kneeling by a chair. I couldn't tell whether he was trying to sit down on it, or lie on the carpet or what. The ambulance was fairly quick, and they did things for him. Oxygen. Injection, I think. They seemed to be ultra-efficient. Treated him and had him away.'

'Did he say anything?'

'He kept drawing his breath in as if hurt. "Oh, my bloody chest," he said once. And when they had put him on this stretcher he said, "Tell Jen which hospital." You came soon after.'

'He was alive?'

'Oh, yes. Quite conscious.'

The daughter had set off for the hospital, found her way to the right place, was instructed where to wait. An hour later the duty registrar walked out to inform her that her father was dead. The doctor spoke carefully. All they could do, they had done. He answered questions, explained the circumstances in which there'd have to be an inquest, told her how to proceed. He seemed genuinely sorry. He led her to the body, offered further instruction. A nurse provided a cup of tea. Jennifer drove home, sat down, drew up a list of things to be done first in the morning. It was now three o'clock. She bundled herself to bed, slept fitfully until six. By seven she had contacted her three brothers, had spoken to an undertaker, had cried a few exhausted tears. At eight-fifteen she telephoned Clark at Mrs Mackenzie's; he was preparing for his first morning back at school, had no idea what to say. She in weary amazement felt superior, pitied the man.

'Shall I call round in the lunch hour?' he asked.

'I don't know where I shall be.' Unhelpful.

'This evening then?'

'All right. About eight.' Reluctant, flat, inhuman.

'Let me know,' he said, 'if there's anything I can do.'

'I don't think there is. Come and talk. There might be other people here.'

He remembered the death fitfully as he rushed about in school, glad he was busy, had pupils breathing down his neck. When he returned home Mrs Mackenzie waited behind with a prepared pot of tea and serious face.

'Have you heard any more? About Mr Stapleton?'

He had not.

'When you told me this morning you looked so white and drawn, I was worried. You said it was his heart. There's nothing in the paper amongst the deaths. It's too early, perhaps. Tomorrow.'

Clark told her what little he knew; he could not remember what he had said after the 'phone call; his landlady received it all as new. She did not know Mr Stapleton herself, though his firm were her friend Miss Stafford's lawyers.

'Have you any idea how old he was?'

'Seventies.'

'That's not old these days.' Mr Mackenzie had died in his fifties; his relict must be nearing sixty. 'It's a good way to go, but a shock to those left. Is . . . was his daughter upset? She would be.'

225

'She's sensible. Stapleton was the first real stranger I met here. Unconnected with the school.'

'Yes. You've been very unlucky. With Mr Pearson dying. Both within the fortnight. That's most unusual. In your very first school holiday.'

He nodded, drank his tea, while she related sadness. At this time of the day, while she was preparing dinner, one rarely saw her. Clark appreciated her effort, said so. She skipped over the tears of things, included the death of her husband, poured a second strong cup. He felt stiff, both physically and emotionally, incapable of fluency, frozen. She dismissed him upstairs so that she could see to dinner. The schoolteachers came in, were not offered tea; they disappeared chattering, already in the rut by this their third day.

The landlady treated him with special consideration over the evening meal. She had obviously announced the news to the schoolma'ams who expressed embarrassed condolences; they had no idea who Stapleton was or his relationship with Clark. Twice after the meal, the young women, who were going out, refused coffee. Mrs Mackenzie used the same sentence.

'It's bad. On the first day of term. And so soon after the other.'

She had invited him into her small breakfast room, a private place of photographs, two Vermeer tablecloths and a television set, a place he had never seen before, to serve coffee in her best china. She made the effort; the starched white cloth on the tray, the coffee grounds not instant, the milk jug guarded by a small cover with a beaded margin. The room was not well lit, not very warm. As soon as he left she'd slip back to her kitchen, the clearing up, the preparation for breakfast, conscious of duty. She repeated her lament.

'It's terrible for you. On your first day back. And so hard on the heels. . . .' The Scottish r's rolled. It was as if she thought that Clark's academic advancement and the reputation of her adopted town had been spoilt by untimely dying. Her lodger laughed to himself at her awkwardness, was grateful to her for the effort, but was glad to escape upstairs pursued by offers of help. 'Anything I can do, anything, Mr Clark. You've only to mention it.' When he crept down to drive to Jennifer's the

226

landlady was waiting for the creak on the stair, appeared with suitable face, wiping her hands.

'Please convey my sympathy to Mrs Hope, if you will be so good.'

The woman lacked all social grace, but knew her duty. An hour later he would be describing her, her writhings, her cobbled sentences to Jennifer, as they shrugged and smiled.

Jennifer seemed preoccupied.

She had been at work for an hour or two 'to pass the time'. She had chased about all the morning. She had established that there was no need for an inquest. The funeral would be in a week's time, ten days after Hugh's.

Jennifer fidgeted, could not sit still, and though her eyes were wet, shadowed, she made no great show of emotion. She talked about her father at length without much affection but willingly. He was a successful man, self-made. It was perhaps as well that he had died when he did before his wits went astray, before he was carted off to doze all day, to slobber mindlessly, reeking of urine. 'He hated that. He always said he'd kill himself, if he had enough nous left to know what was going on.'

When Stapleton had retired, she recalled, he had joked about writing his memoirs.

'Did anything come of it?'

'I shouldn't think so. We'll find out when we go through his papers.'

'Who'll do that?'

'I shall, I expect. My brothers will leave acts of filial piety to me.' Her sharp, old-fashioned phraseology jolted him. 'He had a title all ready.'

'What was it, then?'

' "The man who shot his wife." '

Clark said Stapleton had mentioned the incident to him; Jennifer gave an account of a comparatively minor accident in the garden with a shotgun. She, a schoolgirl, had been staying the weekend with a friend, knew nothing until she returned when both parents were to all appearances exactly as she had left them.

'Pure accident,' she said, 'if pure's the word. And yet he liked to make out that he meant it. Used to joke about it. To comparative strangers.'

227

'What did your mother say?'

'Nothing. Typically. Except once when she slightly lost her temper and snapped at him. "You must have been aiming at something else to hit me. You're a worse shot than I am." '

'Did they practise shooting?'

'Not to the best of my knowledge. I couldn't make anything of it. It was silly and twisted in my opinion. I guess he was embarrassed, perhaps, by his clumsiness with his gun.'

'They got on well?'

'Yes. We-e-ell. Yes. My mother stayed at home, and he chased about making money. That suited them both, as far as I could see. I never thought about it when I was young, to tell you the truth. Mummy was there, taking the decisions. He was "at the office". That was the expression.'

'Unfair?'

'I'm not saying that. It suited my mother. She had her own way in many respects. And he was genuinely lost when she died. I was in the Sixth Form then. It all happened rather suddenly. She'd been ailing, or off-colour for some time. She died within a fortnight of going into hospital. What amazes me now, when I think about it, is why they married. She'd have been pretty, and he'd have been the rough diamond. Odd.'

A long silence.

'I want to marry you, Jennifer,' Clark said.

'Oh, yes.' Thin, acidulous. She watched the floor.

'I know this is not the time to be saying anything, but I'm serious.'

'I expect you are. But I'm in no position to give you an answer.' She paused, held out a hand, the left, index finger pointing upward, to prevent further speech from him. 'Not because of my father. I didn't care much for him. Hugh's death affected me more, and God knows he meant little enough. No, but he's disappeared. My father, I mean. Before I always knew he was there, even if I didn't much like what he was up to. Now he's gone there's a gap. I hate change of that sort.'

'Even for the better?'

'You know what I mean. He was there. Now for the first time in my life there's no such entity as Ernest Stapleton.'

'What about when your mother died?'

'I was seventeen, and at sixes and sevens with everybody and everything. At that age you have a fit if you can't find your tennis-racket or the skirt you want. But you recover. I loved her when I quarrelled with her, and there was plenty of that going on. I was resilient. Now, I'm middle-aged. It's hateful. You don't understand what I'm saying, do you?'

'I think so.'

Clark never found out what she meant by her question, or if she meant anything at all, as she fell into abstraction. But he had said the right words. These deaths had conjured real speech out of people.

He continued to think so. He put in a note to the Headmaster asking for time off to attend the Stapleton funeral. To his surprise Short sent for him, sat him down, expressed conventional sorrow. Sentence followed proper sentence over fingertips held together perhaps nine inches from the mouth; the eyes, brown and unwavering, stared at nothing. Suddenly Short coughed.

'It must seem bad to you,' speech had quickened, 'two deaths like this at the beginning of your second term. You're not superstitious, are you?'

'Not really.'

'It has the appearance of too much of a bad thing.' Mrs Mac's point. 'You don't feel it reflects on the school or the town. They aren't unlucky?' Clark considered the Headmaster's naïvety. 'That's not what you think, is it?'

'No.' Clark shook his head with vatic solemnity.

'I am a mathematician, and I therefore, I suppose, look for patterns. As in this case. Though it would be ridiculous to expect two deaths at the start of every term here.' Short twisted his mouth; a bleak joke. 'Literary texts will also have their own kinds of patterns, won't they? And their strength and weakness will depend to some extent on these?'

'Yes,' said Clark.

'I suppose, too, that like mathematics there has to be some kind of background of understanding against which the patterns will be seen to take their shape. I am no sort of mathematician now, but in my twenties while I had a research fellowship and could hold my own with some really bright young men and knew my way about, I have seen mathematics which made no sense whatsoever to me. I suppose I did not know the language. You think I'm a fool, don't you, Clark?'

'No, sir.'

'Chuntering on about patterns. And mathematics.' The Headmaster looked at his junior colleague, his brown eyes in wrinkled skin, not unfriendly. 'All I'm trying to say is that we are pleased with the way you've settled in, and we don't, I and your Head of Department and Seymour, a shrewd judge, don't want you put off by these unfortunate coincidences. You think it unlikely? Good, good. But I will tell you this, and I speak from experience, I have seen people discouraged by very much less. They start off on the wrong foot through no fault of their own, and they never recover. I intervene here with you, and that is why. I do not want you to be side-tracked or distracted. You have done a good term here, Clark, and I want you to know it. Of course, it's what happens after twelve years not twelve weeks that really counts, but I want you to have a word of encouragement.'

'Thank you.'

'Not at all. That's it, then.' The Headmaster was on his feet; he was expert at clearing his study of litter of any kind. 'Glad to talk to you. You might think about this business of literary patterns, or those in life, and give me your views some time. Perhaps on paper. Yes. That would give me time to think about an unfamiliar topic. We mathematicians tend to force them on to life.'

Clark found himself on the corridor, outside a closed door.

The old man had not shaken hands, but he had shown friendliness, demonstrated his confidence in his young colleague, and flailing about for something interesting, as in morning assembly or Sixth-Form studies, had beached with this talk of patterns. A line hummed in Clark's head:

'Thou cunning'st pattern of excelling nature.' The man who killed his wife. The man who shot. Clark made for the common room.

People searched for right words.

He remembered this incident when he visited Jennifer in the next few days before the funeral. She gave the appearance of

230

normality; she drove every morning to work, seemed capable of talking about her father's affairs, made arrangements for the entertainment of her brothers and wives, fed the mourners. She said little; too little, in Clark's view. She seemed smaller, less human, more of a high-class servant. One did not know what she thought and when he tried to talk her back to life, she was as likely to turn away as to tell him to shut his mouth. He called in each night, rarely found her alone, took her once, at the weekend, into Derbyshire where they walked under cold limestone in dull light and bitter wind.

He proposed marriage once more from the driving seat of her car. In a lay-by. She dropped her head.

'I'm in no state to think about an answer, never mind give one.'

'You've allowed me to drive your car,' he argued.

'And is that the equivalent?' Her voice betrayed a whisper of warmth. 'I don't think much of your scale of values, Mr Clark.'

'I can be pretty determined.' He fought on. It did not seem so to him.

'We'd have to have all these brothers and wives here. You haven't really met them yet.'

'I don't mind what you say,' he continued, 'as long as you talk. It's when you're quiet and tucked away I begin to worry. But, if I may say so, that's a pretty trivial argument you've just raised.'

'No doubt, but that's what I keep telling you, though you won't listen. I'm in no state to consider your proposal. I don't know how I stand. All the items on the balance sheet don't seem to be there.' She raised her hands. 'No, Tony, it's the truth. I'm glad you're here at this moment. But this funeral and the other have left me so uncertain that I can't even make up my mind when or where I'm going for my summer holiday.' Now she laid a hand on his arm; the fingers were smooth, almost plump, and healthy; the pinkish nails elegantly almond-shaped. 'I'm in no-man's land.'

'When do you come out?'

'That's the worry. I seem stuck, static. I've no will to move. Perhaps once we've had the funeral, and I can give my whole mind to people's wealth or lack of it for a week or two then I'll be all right. At present it doesn't seem important.'

'Compared with death, you mean?' He'd put it to her bluntly.

'No. Not in the way I think you mean. Nothing's worth anything; nothing's worth doing or bothering about. Or I haven't the energy to bother. Or the sense of direction. I feel old and addled and weary.'

'But I love you.'

'So you say.'

'Does it,' he began slowly, edging his way along his own question, 'make it worse when I keep on at you?'

'Why should it?'

'Well.' Clark stopped, as he paused in his classroom to make sure the scholars were listening before he began his explanation. Jennifer stared, the verb carries too much energy, ahead. 'When I feel down or disappointed then any sort of little drawback that I could dismiss in the ordinary way without a qualm just proves too much.' He foresaw her answer. 'Not that I'm saying my proposal is insignificant. It may be to you even if you think you're not judging matters properly, but not to me.'

'Yes,' she answered. 'But sometimes you have good news which cheers you.'

'Does this lift you?'

'No. You know it doesn't. I can't help it.'

She laid her head on his shoulder. The movement was deliberate; she had had to move her position, unfasten her seat-belt. He took her hand. She seemed for the moment in his care. They sat silent for perhaps ten minutes before she said she was getting cold, and wanted to go home. They kissed warmly. As he buckled up he said, 'I wouldn't be surprised if D. H. Lawrence had walked this road as a young man.'

She sat upright, touching her hair.

'That's no recommendation to me.' But without rancour.

Stapleton's death had left his daughter very well-to-do, though the complicated estate would need a great deal of time and money spent on it. She explained her position in detail a fortnight after the funeral and then proposed marriage to him, almost offhand.

232

'What do you say?' she asked, schoolma'amish.

'Yes, please.' He giggled at his own childishness.

'Is that all?'

' "Reader, I married her." '

He explained his joy in silliness, too shocked for understanding. They clung to each other, kissed, began to learn. To his surprise he realized that his landlady, the straight-corseted Mrs Mackenzie, once he'd given her his good news expected him to move in at once with his fiancée. 'No,' he said, 'I'll serve the rest of my sentence here until July. I'm very comfortable. And old-fashioned.'

Their friends, expressing felicitations, were cagey, wary, unsure. When he said as much to Jennifer, she punched him, waved her new engagement ring at him and asked him what he expected. 'They're very conventional for all their fancy talk. They don't like cradle-snatching.'

'Patterns?' he queried.

She pulled a comical face of incomprehension.

July weather became brilliant for the day. The two short speeches dazzled. On the very morning the happy pair received a small inexpensive present from Daniella delivered by the disapproving Clark parents. Patterns. The registrar spoke parsonically, the Headmaster was absent, Gill and Ambrose both wept. Clarissa had a summer cold. Edwin, conveniently abroad, sent a small Henry Moore drawing. The three brothers, wives and children acted memorably in character. Nobody forgot. Anything.

'Against the dark and time's consuming rage.'